WHERE ARE YOU?
Part 1
10 MINUTES

"Uncertainty is the cruellest tormentor, and the mother of all uncertainties is the unknown whereabouts of a loved one.
People go missing every day. Children disappear.
Wives and husbands walk out and never return home.
All would agree with one fact – it's easier to handle the worst truth than to live without it.
To suffer the relentless, unanswered questions.
Like falling from a cliff without ever reaching the bottom.
Impossible to start to heal because the injuries are still unknown.
Did they choose to leave? Are they captive? In peril?
Then the biggest question of all – are they still alive?

Then, in desperation, when all avenues are exhausted, when there is nothing more to be done, with no end in sight, a person will throw out their hands to the universe and scream into the vast unknown – WHERE ARE YOU?"

**Cover design
By KO Productions**

Also by Leigh Oakley

3 part thriller series – A Love to Die For:-

Part 1 – Troubled Minds
Part 2 – Tortured Hearts
Part 3- Restless Souls

2 Part thriller series – Precious Stones:-

Part 1 Diamonds in the Rough
Part 2 – Jewells of the Manor

Murder Mystery

No Doubt She did it

Sci Fi

These are NOT my shoes!

Where are you? - Ten Minutes

Chapter 1

Amelia was not a pretty girl.

This fact had been cruelly and abruptly revealed to her at the tender age of eight years. Unleashed like some ferocious animal, it rampaged through her world, devouring her blissfully ignorant happiness and changing her life forever.

Nothing more than a single breath emitted from gently smiling lips. A breath moulded into three words had dissolved her self-esteem as quickly and completely as sugar in hot tea.

It was the day her happiness evaporated.

Perhaps it was rather simplistic to blame the speaker of those words for everything that happened afterwards but there was no doubt that it had been the catalyst of what was to come. It had been the planting of a seed that would grow silently inside her soul. Its creeping vines rampaging through her world of sorrow and self-hatred until she despised the existence of physical beauty. Rejecting completely the value of physical loveliness and seeking advantage and validation beyond the carnal. Digging, searching, and reaching far beyond normal boundaries.

Far into the unknown.

She could still remember the exact moment her vibrant world turned to grey. A single comment from a thoughtless shop assistant was all it took. The joyous contentment of childhood ripped from her by a seemingly unremarkable moment on an equally unremarkable Saturday morning.

It had been in the last throws of the school summer holidays in 1966. England had won the world cup and football frenzy had consumed most of those cheery weeks with hoards of boys re-enacting the goals of Geoff Hurst out on the littered streets while the girls, driven into the safety of the small gardens with their skipping ropes, retaliated with name-calling and occasional bombardments of grass sods.

It had been a summer of high spirits, national pride and joyous contentment.

It had been on one such day that Amelia and her younger sister had protested at being dragged from that lively sun kissed street to take the bus into town for new school shoes.

Brenda had resigned herself more quietly to her mother's demands, but Amelia remained steadfast on the pavement, desperately pleading her case. It was sunny and she was in the middle of a game of sticks. Her friends needed her to make up the number and shopping was for rainy days.

Celia already had Brenda by the hand, guiding her into the house when she fired a parting warning at her obstinate elder daughter.

"If you are not in the house in two minutes Amelia, woe betide you!"

Amelia knew when she'd lost the argument and threw the ball to another child.

She smiled at her mother's threat. She didn't even know what those words meant but she knew it was an empty threat because Celia Simpson was the softest mother in that street. Most of her chastisements were in jest and her parenting rested wholly on a precious and respectful understanding between her and her daughters. It was that special understanding that caused Amelia to give in and follow them down the path.

Celia brushed their hair in turn, slipped on their summer jackets to cover the soiled dresses and herded them out of the door.

There would be a time when Amelia would suspect that some sixth sense had caused her to protest so rigidly that day and when Celia would wish she could turn back the clock and allow her children to remain in play.

But the bus arrived on time and eight-year-old Amelia and six-year-old Brenda ran to claim the front seat without a hint of resentment. Celia sat compliantly in the seat behind after flashing an apologetic smile to an elderly gentleman for the unruly behaviour of her daughters.

That journey into town had been indelibly etched in Amelia's memory as the last moments of her happy, carefree life. Of the last moments she'd spend in joyous laughter with her adorable little sister who was also her best friend.

They had been singing for the entire journey. The hit 'These boots are made for walking' had reached the No 1 spot and they were stomping back and forth across the front window with a made-up dance routine as they sang between gasps and tears of laughter. Celia tried to hush her daughters, but the other passengers were applauding so she eventually gave up with a reluctant but somewhat smug smile.

In reality, Celia would have loved to join in the dancing with her daughters and, had they not been on a public bus, she would have done so. Celia, like her husband, was passionate about dance. They were the first couple on the dancefloor at the local social club and later on, when the rock and roll music started, everyone would stand back to watch them. Tom would be wearing his drainpipe trousers with red winkle pickers and Celia would be twirled around in her rockabilly full skirted dress with the net underskirt. Her beehive lacquered to perfection.

Before they settled down to start a family, Tom and Celia had been the couple to beat at all the local jive contests. They practised regularly at home after pushing back the furniture and regularly sending the needle abruptly across the record with a hefty bump into the radiogram as Tom failed to capture the outstretched hand of his spinning wife.

"That's another scratch!" Celia would snap breathlessly.

"You know what I'm going to say to that!" Tom would laugh.

"Yes." Celia would sigh. "The jive is an 'all or nothing' thing. Not for the faint-hearted."

Scratched records or not, Celia enjoyed Tom's attitude and she loved the rewards of his unbridled, reckless enthusiasm. She loved to win.

Even after the children came along, she loved being labelled the party family. She revelled in the envy of other mothers when their husbands referred to her as sexy, fun and energetic.

Celia was everything a man could want in a wife and the icing on the cake arrived when she became the local Avon representative.

Celia Thompson seemed to have it all and, unlike most mothers who couldn't wait to get the kids back into school, Celia approached the new term with a heavy heart.

She listened to the wives on their street as they relished the re-opening of the school gates and how, on Sundays they would encourage their husbands to go to the local club and their children to Sunday school so they could put their feet up with a magazine or get together for a natter. Celia was not in that camp. Celia relished the company of Tom, Amelia and

Brenda. It seemed nothing short of a miracle that the sisters played so amicably together, and she felt blessed for every bit of the harmony and playfulness of her life.

"The washing can wait!" she would say with a smile if there was the chance to go out blackberry picking or making up a dance performance for Tom when he arrived home from work.

"How old are you?" Tom would laugh as his wife greeted him in a net curtain cloak to announce the start of the show in the living room.

Childhood was important to Celia, and she intended to make sure her children would look back on these days with fond nostalgia and remember her as a devoted and fun-loving mother.

Without realising it at the time, those were the days Amelia was truly happy. The only days.

The bus pulled into the layby in the town centre, and she took a hand of each of her daughters to help them down the high step onto the pavement.

Once inside the shoe shop they'd been teasing each other and making fun of the short-sighted shop owner. They were barely paying attention to the conversation when the missile struck.

A young female assistant was approaching them with an open shoe box and one black shoe in hand when she called to the manageress.

"Which girl is to try on these size nines?"

"The pretty one." Came the reply.

The girl handed the shoe directly to Brenda with a smile.

Perhaps the comment might have gone unnoticed had it not been for Celia's over-protective outrage. What happened next had been so shocking that it caused everyone to immediately backtrack on what their ears had heard. Words that were still retrievable from the silence they'd hung in.

"The pretty one!" Celia bellowed into the woman's face. "How dare you! Both of my daughters are pretty! Why would you say such a thing!"

The woman turned red but didn't reply.

The young assistant looked down at the box she was carrying and remained silent.

The silence spoke. It spoke more loudly than Celia's outburst. More clearly than the red-faced woman's mumbled words.

Amelia was not the pretty one.

And in that small window of silence, by definition, Amelia had been labelled the ugly sister.

The next memory Amelia had from this day of devastation was being dragged bodily from the shop with Brenda hopping on one foot and holding her old shoe akimbo. Amelia could see that her sister was already crying as their mother continued to hurl abuse at the entire establishment and vow never to return to this vile place with its insulant, rude and evil assistant.

Amelia was in shock. Obviously, something devastatingly terrible had just happened and she was at the centre of it. It felt serious and frightening, brutal and catastrophic. She was shaking with fear as they climbed onto the homebound bus.

Looking back from her teenage years, Amelia could see that her mother had compounded the impact with her violent outburst. Blowing the incident into some huge revelation that had thus far been fiercely protected. A secret she was never meant to hear. Now the bubble had been popped and she stood naked in the undeniable truth.

Even the popping of the mythical Santa bubble two years later, paled into insignificance against the revelation that she was not a pretty girl.

Brenda took the news almost as badly as her sister. Up until that day she was also unaware that their differences in appearance had a name. A rating. A winner and a loser.

That Brenda's golden blonde waves were the winner over Amelia's mousey, dry straggles. That Brenda's olive complexion deemed Amelia's sickly grey and blotchy face a clear loser. There wasn't a single feature on which Amelia came out on top. Brenda's plump nose turned up at the end, but Amelia's was straight, thin and severe. Benda's lips were full and dark in pigmentation giving the appearance of plum-coloured lipstick, but Amelia had been dealt a pair of pale thin lips that seemed almost invisible against the background of her mottled face. Above all, Brenda's vivid green, almond shaped eyes could not compare to Amelia's which were bluish grey and set deeply in reddish, mottled sockets.

Brenda felt equally devastated.

The brutal sword of truth had fallen between the sisters and created a divide that could never be repaired. For the first time in her life, she was powerless to restore the relationship with her beloved sister. No apology nor act of kindness was going to fix this. She had nothing to bargain with because the issue was nothing other than her own appearance.

Despair turned to resentment but surprisingly the resentment was aimed at her own beauty and not at the plainness of Amelia.

Being the pretty one had ruined everything.

The effect on Celia had been equally devastating.

Up until that moment she had loved her children equally and treated them in accordance but now she had lost the equilibrium. She found herself favouring Amelia, praising her without cause and then feeling the guilt of it. This was not Brenda's fault either! She would then try to make amends and the whole situation became a confusing mess.

"You need to stop this, Celia!" Tom bellowed at her after both girls had retreated in tears again. "You've blown this out of all proportion."

"But we are their parents, Tom. This is all our fault. It's our genetics that caused this."

"Don't be ridiculous. It's just the luck of the draw. If you want to blame anyone blame mother nature but stop taking it out on our kids. They don't know what the hell you're doing with all this see-sawing between them. You're acting like a mad woman!"

Celia knew he was right, but it didn't prevent her from the barrage of self-retribution or of continually striving to rebalance the self-esteem of her children.

In the quiet of the night, she could see her folly so clearly. If she had simply smiled politely, paid for the shoes, bought the kids a milkshake and allowed them to sing on the front of the bus on the way back, the comment would have been forgotten. The words dispersed and diluted by her own refusal to pay them any attention, give them any credibility or to allow them to nest in the minds of her impressionable children.

Sometimes Tom tried a different approach in dealing with his increasingly obsessive wife.

"You need to let this go, Celia! It's not like Amelia is an ugly child. She isn't!"

Celia frowned.

"She isn't!" He repeated. "You're just making her feel that way because you're obsessing over one stupid comment from one stupid woman.

She was still silently frowning when Tom picked up a school photo of the two girls together and placed a hand over the image of Brenda.

"Look! Look at our daughter. Look at Amelia. Yes, she doesn't have the same heart-shaped face as Brenda, but she is still a lovely looking girl."

He pushed the image up to her face.

"Look again Celia! She had an oval face, a strong jaw, a beautiful wide smile and a straight, perfectly proportioned nose. Amelia has her own type of beauty. The only person making her feel ugly, is you! Her mother!"

Celia looked at Amelia. Grinning beside her sister. She tried to see what he saw but under his hand she could see the button nose of Brenda against the sharpness of Amelia's. In some ways, Tom was right. All things are relative, and Amelia had just been unfortunate to have such a pretty, little sister.

She sighed and removed Tom's hand from Brenda's image. Her girls were equally beautiful to her, but she knew that the rest of the world would see it differently.

Her task changed that day but not necessarily for the better. Her new task was to correct mother nature's mistake and to restore the equilibrium.

From that day on, Celia did everything in her power to show Amelia her own beauty, but it was too late.

Both her daughters rebelled against pretty clothes, ribbons and curls for different reasons.

Amelia didn't want her appearance to feature in her life at all and Brenda just wanted to be plain, and she wanted it badly.

The first day back to school arrived and Celia got up early to make the fire and put the uniforms to warm before padding upstairs barefooted to wake the girls.

As she entered the room and walked towards Brenda's bed, she felt something soft and slippery under her feet. In the half-light from the hallway, she saw a mass of shiny blonde trusses lying on the floor beside the kitchen scissors! She looked to the pillow to see a head of hideous tufts and patches of baldness.

Celia fell to her knees holding the soft curls to her lips and cried silently for several moments before she woke her daughters to face the start of another awful day.

"I just want Mealy to love me again. The way she did before!" Brenda sobbed as her mother tried to trim the mess she'd made of her head.

"Amelia does love you! Tell her Amelia! Tell your sister that you still love her!"

Amelia didn't speak. It was bad enough that Brenda had been the pretty one. Now she'd made it even worse. Now she would be blamed for Brenda's hair! Now she was both ugly and mean and it was all Brenda's fault!

Amelia was sent to school with a note that Brenda had the flu, but the note was never delivered. She walked into the small wood beside the school and sat on the wet grass in a small clearing where she ripped up the note and flung it to the wind.

She then lay on her back and looked up into the sky between the waving trees, through the drifting rain clouds and beyond. She felt close to something there. Something or someone she could never describe or explain but the comfort of it was so utterly consoling. Up there, way up there, was something beyond physical looks or bitter words and she breathed it in, soaked it up and revelled in it for hours. Thankful that there was a place beyond this one, a peaceful place where mother's didn't scream and cry and sisters didn't hack off their hair.

Brenda spent the day crying. Wishing that Amelia would turn beautiful. Wishing that her own face would turn ugly. Wishing she was dead.

Celia spent the day nursing inconsolable regret. Knowing now, without any doubt, that her outrage on that Saturday morning had been the cause of it all. The careless comment from a thoughtless woman that could have been batted away like a small insect.

But she hadn't done that. She hadn't responded with a silly joke or filled the silence with frivolity and moved on.

Instead, she'd validated the comment with a rage born of a painful truth. She'd given it wings. Wings that flew it headlong into their lives and wedged itself between her daughters like a malignant tumour that would continue to grow over the years. Pushing them further and further apart.

Amelia and Brenda would never be best friends again and it had all been her fault.

Weeks turned to months but the more effort she made to repair the damage, the more it seemed to grow.

Celia stopped paying attention to her own appearance in some unconscious act of solidarity, or perhaps a subliminal protest against the relevance of beauty.

Her desperation to undo the undoable served only to nurture and feed it, to revive and exalt it and the harder she tried the worse it seemed to get.

Celia was barely eating or sleeping during this period of obsession. Home cooking had given way to oven chips and frozen burgers.

Their homelife was accelerating on a downward trajectory.

"Please stop this now darling." Tom sighed after yet another of Celia's futile attempt to balance the scales.

She'd bought dresses for the school Christmas party for her girls and the larger was very obviously so much nicer than the smaller one.

She emerged proudly with the two dresses and held them up as the sisters were finishing their tea.

"I should have bought them earlier," she said apologetically. "There wasn't much left in your size Brenda, I'm sorry."

"It's alright mummy." Brenda replied as she took the green checked dress with the red belt. "It does look Christmassy."

Amelia stared at the larger dress her mother was holding. A full skirted cream velvet dress adorned with sequins and a pink satin bow.

"Well?" Celia asked with a smile. "What do you think?"

Amelia sighed.

"I think you should save it for Brenda to grow into. I'll wear the one I already have."

She started to walk away when Celia jumped into her path.

"I bought it for *you* Amelia. You'll look lovely in it. What's wrong?"

"What's wrong is that you're trying to disguise my ugliness with a pretty dress but that only makes it worse! I don't want to be noticed! I want to be invisible! Are you stupid?"

"Don't speak to your mother that way!! Her father's voice boomed suddenly from the kitchen. "Your mother spent every penny she had on that dress and because of it, she has nothing new to wear for herself!"

Amelia stood her ground.

"Well she can take it back and use the money to buy herself something nice for Christmas.!

Suddenly her father's face was in the doorway.

"No, she can't because she spent the entire night altering it for you! It was too big, but she wanted so badly for you to have it that she didn't come to bed last night. She took the whole thing apart and put it back together again. She was so excited to give it to you and you've just thrown it back in her face!"

Amelia pushed by him and stormed out of the door into the cold air. After a few minutes Brenda followed.

Amelia headed straight for her happy place at a speed her little sister could never match. She fled down the street and turned onto the muddy tree-lined path pushing nettles aside as she hurtled round the twists and turns she knew by heart, until the familiar light of the clearing came into view. She lay down between those tall trees and peered into the dusky sky. The winter wind was blowing fiercely through the trees. The ferns around her whipped her cheeks and the roar of the wind deafened her ears yet still, she felt the welcome calm of solitude. The treetops danced their angry, threatening dance but all she could feel was the thrill of it. She closed her eyes and drank it in as though quenching some raging thirst.

As she opened her eyes again and stared into that vastness above her. She knew in her bones that there was something wonderful out there. Something majestic, powerful and unyielding and it both comforted and terrified her. This was the place she longed to be. This was home.

In the distance she could vaguely hear her sister's voice.

"Mealy! Mealy!"

For a while she ignored it. Brenda was capable of making her own way home, but as the cries persisted, she felt an ache.

None of this was Brenda's fault. None of it was her mother's fault or even her own.

She stood up reluctantly and left her sanctuary.

"Over here!"

Immediately she heard her sister's footsteps hurtling towards her.

"Come here you." She called affectionately.

Brenda rushed into her arms and hugged her tight.

"I don't want you to hate me Mealy. I don't want to be pretty!" She stammered between sobs.

"It's alright Brenda. I've just been silly that's all. You should enjoy being a pretty girl and I should enjoy having a pretty sister. That's how its going to be from now on."

"But…."

"No buts. I know now that there's more to life than how we look. Hearts and minds are what matters."

Brenda frowned as they silently, hand in hand, back towards the road.

Amelia was recalling one of her mother's attempts to make amends for producing a plain and drab offspring – "A pretty face will soon fade Amelia, but the mind does the exact opposite. It blooms and grows. You have a good strong mind and that's what people will admire you for, if you work at it. Time can never steal that away from you."

Brenda was lagging behind as they stumbled along that dark path with the wind howling around them.

"I don't know what you mean, Mealy." She called against the gusts that snatched her words and whisked them away. "Are we friends again?"

Amelia stopped abruptly, bobbed down and took her little sister by the shoulders. "Let's just say that you have your pretty face and I have my exceptional mind." She laughed. "Yes we are friends again. We will always be friends."

She kissed the little girl firmly on the forehead.

Brenda grinned from ear to ear.

"Do you want to sing on the way back?" Amelia asked as she recaptured the freezing hand of her little sister.

"Can we sing the one about the boots again?"

"That's a good choice," Amelia smiled as she tugged Brenda along the dark path in the knowledge that, although her baby sister was terrified, she trusted Amelia completely.

"Come on, slow coach. Your turn to start the song."

The darkness became as irrelevant as the stinging nettles and scratching brambles as they stomped and sang along that path.

The rift between the sisters had been healed.

As they continued to stomp, Amelia realised how much she had missed Brenda. She felt whole again. Whole and somehow taller. Brave and honourable. Peaceful and proud.

Tomorrow she would show her mother that she was a better person, a better daughter, and a girl worthy of the love she'd been lavishing on her.

Tomorrow they would be a happy family again.

But tomorrow would be too late.

Chapter 2

Back at the house Celia was numbly listening to another bout of her husband's criticism.

"When are you going to start treating them the same again!" He rebuked. "This would all be in the past by now if it wasn't for your selfish obsession to vindicate yourself! Stop feeding it. Stop making it the headline of every bloody day!"

"I just want to fix it!"

"You can't. Sooner or later, they would have realised that one of them was a bit prettier than the other and they would each have dealt with it privately. They'd have accepted it and moved on. I can't remember the last time I saw you laugh or play with the kids. You've been nothing but a zombie since this stupidity started!"

"You think I've blown this out of proportion, don't you?"

"Er… just a bit! You're obsessed Celia! It's the reason behind everything you do. The kids wouldn't care so much if you didn't!"

"You think I'm a bad mother?"

Her voice was breaking with emotion.

"No, I don't. I think you had a perfect little life and now there's a blip and you can't bloody deal with it! You were so used to being the envy of every woman on the estate and you can't bear even the slightest flaw! Look around us! Look at the parents with kids who have real problems, but they don't collapse in a heap do they? Look at the White's for instance. They have Lucy. How do you think she copes, knowing she took the thalidomide tablets because she didn't want to throw up? Wake up Celia!"

Celia's eyes were welling up. "You're right. I know you are." She said softly. "It's just that the girls are not the same anymore. They've become enemies."

"No. They've become rivals and that's down to us."

"To *me* you mean."

He pulled her gently towards him without replying.

"This futile mission to undo what's already done is sucking the joy out of every bloody day. You might as well start every day with the announcement that Amelia is not a pretty girl. There's no wonder the rift between them keeps on growing! You are a wonderful mother Celia but lets get some of that family joy back shall we?"

She replied by curling her arm gratefully around his neck, causing him to stroke her hand.

"Look at you. You're all skin and bone." He whispered as his hand circled her bony wrist. "This has to stop Celia. We have to make it stop."

He felt her nod against his chest and kissed the top of her head, feeling the crispness of the hair lacquer against his lips. Celia still took pride in her appearance and her 'Cilla Black' bouffant was impeccably styled and dyed a subtle shade of amber despite her neglected diet and dark circled eyes.

That night Celia took a good look in the mirror after taking a shower and removing her heavy make-up. The image before her was debilitating. She no longer filled the cups of her nightdress and her ribs protruded through the flimsy fabric. Her eyes were dark hollows against the lard-like flesh of her bare face and her combed-out hair stuck out in a dry, crisp, amber wedge.

She quickly pinned it up with a hair slide and wrapped her thick dressing gown around the emaciated form that had once been her curvy, firm figure.

As she warmed the milk for Ovaltine and buttered the scones she had been so consumed by that image that she hardly noticed the change in her children. She failed to absorb the return of the happy bedtime chatter in the next room, or the way Amelia waited for Brenda at the foot of the stairs to help her climb with the remainder of her hot drink.

Tomorrow she would go to the chemist and get something to build her up.

She lay in bed that night with the determination to restore harmony and happiness to her family. Optimistic that tomorrow would be the start of an upward turn.

She had no idea how wrong she was!

The following morning, she waived the girls off to school and made her way to the chemist to buy the items on her list.

She was barely listening to the girl behind the counter rambling on about sudden weight loss as she browsed the shelves behind her for Complan, Minidex and a large jar of Horlicks.

When she looked back to the girl to ask for them, there was no-one there.

After a few seconds Mr Chapman, the pharmacist, appeared with a smile.

"Morning Mrs Simpson. My assistant tells me you've lost considerable weight recently?"

"She had no need to bother you." Celia smiled back. "I just want a few things to build me back up to my previous curvy self."

"Well. That will probably do the trick, but I would be a lot more comfortable if you were checked out next door first."

"The doctor? I don't need a doctor. I've just been a bit anxious recently and not been eating properly."

Mr Chapman smiled again but kept his distance from the counter.

"The thing is Mrs Simpson; my assistant has noticed that you seem to have a bit of a lump on the side of your neck. It's probably nothing, but you should really get the doctor to take a look at it."

Celia glared accusingly at the young girl who'd betrayed her by raising some alarm.

"I'm sorry," the girl whispered apologetically, "but we've been told to watch out for this sort of thing."

"What sort of thing?" Celia snapped as she quickly felt around her neck.

Under her left jaw, there was a large oval swelling.

"Oh, that's just a swollen gland. I get them all the time." She lied.

Neither replied for a moment but she noticed they were both standing back from the counter.

"Listen." Mr Chapman comforted. "I'll give the doctor a ring right now and you can pop round and then come back for your shopping."

Celia nodded but she could feel her legs weakening beneath her. It was obvious that they both suspected she had something serious. Serious and infectious.

She listened to the whispering of Mr Chapman on the phone before he re-emerged from the back room.

"The doctor can see you right away but he needs you to use the back door if you could please."

The memory of that short walk from the chemist to the surgery on weak, shaking legs was to be indelibly etched on Celia's memory for the rest of her life. Just as the minute detail of that morning at home would be relived over and over as the last day of normality.

The normality of sitting at the breakfast table with Amelia and Brenda feeling positive about facilitating the renewed friendship between them. Hugging them both so close, as she pulled on their bobble hats and wrapped them in matching scarves before standing in the cold on the doorstep in her thin cardigan waving until they were totally out of sight. She was sure that her renewed attitude was already rubbing off on them as they walked shoulder to shoulder down the street.

That was the day she had a small window in which hope had returned and a small promise of happiness had seeped back into her life. She held onto that feeling so tightly. Drinking it in over and over in her weeks of isolation on the Tuberculosis ward. She refused to accept that the pulling on of the bobble hats would be her last physical contact with her daughters. The last hug or the last image of them walking to school.

So venomously she'd protested as the ambulance arrived outside the chemist and took her to the isolation wing for tests. Only the reassurance of her doctor caused her to comply.

"I'm sure everything will be fine, and you'll be home for lunch Celia." He said, shaking his head as though she was being silly about it all. "As soon as they know what it is you can come back for your shopping, and we'll get you back to your old self."

She noticed that he was still standing back. She noticed that the ambulance men were wearing masks. She noticed the look in the eyes of everyone she met that morning.

"I'll call the school and the factory, so everyone knows where you are." The doctor called as she stepped into the ambulance.

Every second of that morning was branded on her brain. Every moment of fear, terror, hope, and heartbreak as each took turns to consume her.

Then came the self-preserving notion that she was stupidly over-reacting, would deliver a few seconds of respite, before another bombardment of possibilities struck.

Six weeks later, as she lay alone in her hospital bed surrounded by masked and gowned nurses, she recalled that 'bobble hat hug' over and over again.

"I'm going to get better!" She called through the glass window to her daughters as they stood outside on the grass.

Tom had an arm around each of them. Supporting them bodily as though it was already over.

"Why are you sad? I'm going to be fine." She called breathlessly. "I'm not done, do you hear me? I'll be home for Christmas!"

Amelia nodded and put her hand up to the glass against the outline of her mother's skeletal fingers and Brenda tried to smile but they had never seen her like this before. Her hair matted with dark roots. Red ends protruding like a porcupine's spikes. Her face almost skull-like.

Amelia jumped back as her mother struck the glass with her fist and screamed. The image was terrifying. This monster-like form banging frantically on the glass in some sort of insane rage couldn't be their mother!

She buried her face in her father's coat as Brenda started to cry and the sound of the banging became louder and louder.

Tom watched as Celia eventually slid down the glass and out of sight. He pulled his children close, closed his eyes and swallowed hard before taking each of them by the hand and quietly guiding them back to the bus stop.

Inside, Celia flopped back onto the bed and pulled the oxygen mask over her face.

This was a fight she was going to win. This was not how it was going to end. She was going to hug her girls again. Kiss her husband again. Make breakfast again.

The desolate faces of Tom, Amelia and Brenda were whisking up a rage within her. She had to fix their misery, dry their tears, heal their wounds and restore their happiness.

She was a fighter, and she would win this battle.

She had to live.

"I have to live!" She screamed at the universe. "I have to live!"

The tears trickled down the sides of her face onto the pillow as she repeated those words over and over between gulps of oxygen.

Tom sat on the bus with a hand of each child in his, knowing that this was no ordinary bus ride. This was the start of the journey to a new and different life.

He knew it with the same certainty Celia had felt in knowing that the short walk from chemist to doctor's surgery had been her walk to the gallows.

Chapter 3

Tom had no recollection of who arranged the funeral or who paid for it.

Those days were a blur to him just as they were to Amelia and Brenda. People came and went. Food came in Tupperware containers and schoolteachers visited without any real purpose.

The only memory the girls had of their mother's funeral started with the adults returning to the house after leaving them alone with a woman they'd never seen before.

Their father opened the door in his full Teddy-boy regalia and went straight upstairs after ruffling each of their heads in turn.

They sat silently on the bottom step as the congregation filed by them and into the living room. A few they recognised but most they didn't.

They heard their dad's footsteps behind them and parted to allow him to pass but he no longer looked like their father. He wore loose brown flannel trousers with a taupe woollen jumper and his notorious quiff had vanished leaving behind the stubble of an army regulation crew cut.

The barely recognisable man walked between them carrying the carefully folded jacket and drainpipe trousers topped with his carefully balanced, shiny winklepickers. He walked out of the front door and they heard the sound of the metal dustbin lid being removed and replaced.

Their old father had disappeared as completely as their Rockabilly mother and, in his place a new father returned.

Brenda and Amelia exchanged a glance of sombre acknowledgement. The fun and laughter, the essence of the house they knew was gone now.

They remained on the bottom step and listened to the chatter in the other room. People they didn't know telling each other what a wonderful woman Celia had been. Justifying their presence at the wake of a woman they had barely acknowledged.

Then, among this meaningless, empty babble, one voice very close to the doorway, caught Amelia's attention. The words were clear and loud enough to reach her ears, pierce her heart and crush her already battered soul.

"I wonder how she got it?" came a woman's voice.

The voice that answered was one that Amelia knew well. It was the voice of the doctor's receptionist who'd seen fit to turn up even though she hardly knew their family.

"TB can lay dormant for years with no symptoms at all. Chances are that she was exposed to it a long time ago, but something triggered it. Activated it."

Her voice had a tone of eager gossip about it. She spoke excitedly. Clearly enjoying the opportunity to parade her knowledge.

"I didn't know that. Like what?" Came an unknown voice.

"Lots of things but it usually flares up when the immune system becomes weak. Stress or poor diet for instance."

Amelia dropped the cheese sandwich she'd been attempting to nibble at and stared in Brenda's direction, expecting to share the terrible truth, but the conversation had gone over her sister's head as she tried to poke the prawn out of her vol-au-vent.

Leigh Oakley

The awful truth was hers alone. Her terrible secret. The burden she would carry alone. The fact that she, the ugly sister, had killed her own mother. That the stress and sleepless nights her mother had endured due to her tantrums had awoken the monster that had taken their mother's life.

She put down her plate and clicked open the front door. She walked a few steps and then ran. She ran and ran. Down the street, through the park and into the wood. Her wood.

As she reached the clearing, she threw herself to the ground among the bracken and stinging nettles and sobbed. She sobbed until her throat and ribs ached and her eyes became bruised and dry. Cold and exhausted she then turned onto her back and peered up to the sky.

Today the sky was neither menacing nor exciting. Today it was still and silent. Grey and cloudless. As empty and colourless as her world. Her mother was gone now and would never come back.

The mother who had fought like a tigress for her, adorned her with kindness and worried herself into the grave, was lost forever. She was too numb to cry any more, too desolate to scream. She could only stare into the grey vastness above her and whisper.

"I'm sorry mum. I love you. Where are you?"

The sky didn't react. The silence remained. The vastness kept it's secret and the grey cloak of nothingness stood its ground.

She held the sky's stubborn stare until she could no longer feel her numb fingers. Her hair clung to the blades of grass, cemented by ice and her feet had no feeling but she no longer cared.

She closed her eyes in her special place and wished to die.

The burden was too heavy to bear. The regret too painful and the sorrow too deep. Her only solace would be to throw herself into her mother's arms and beg for forgiveness.

She stared up into the grey sky until the shapes of the trees were no longer visible against the fading light. She smiled as the black of night engulfed her in its comforting cloak. The cloak that would carry her safely back into the arms of the mother she had so cruelly betrayed.

She closed her eyes again and prayed.

Her next recollection was of being jiggled through the icy air in the dark. Her father's voice was just audible in the distance and then the banging of running feet.

Her head flopped forward against her father's chest as he ran into the house and dropped her onto the sofa.

Warm blankets were thrown over her as people jabbered frantically around her. She slowly opened her eyes to the sea of faces peering at her. Faces white against the blackness of funeral coats. Someone held her head and tipped warm soup into her mouth. Through the open curtains she could see it was dark outside. As dark as the day itself. She closed her eyes again, to sleep or to die. It didn't matter. She needed to rest.

Awakening brought with it a new brand of heartache.

The distraught face of her father. The tears of her sister. The love and kindness of friends and neighbours. The compassion she didn't deserve. Another burden to bear.

"You're a very lucky girl." A voice scolded.

She studied the man with the stethoscope as he held her wrist and checked his watch.

"If it hadn't been for your sister, you would most probably have been dead by now."

She hadn't even questioned how she'd been found but now she was visualising Brenda raising the alarm and trying to find her way down the track. Her six-year-old sister had saved her life and suddenly she was grateful for it. The word 'dead' had suddenly terrified her and it seemed incredible that she'd ever felt differently.

A valuable lesson had been learned that day. Amelia recognised that each, and every one of us, has immediate access to a self-destruct button. That it takes strength to live through each and every day of life's challenges, but it takes just one second of weakness to push that button.

She resolved to face up to her wrongdoing.

Quietly she crept upstairs and opened her wardrobe to face the Christmas dress that would never be worn. She gently brushed the cream velvet against her cheek and stroked the hand-stitched rows of tiny needle threads. Each one felt like an arrow through her heart. Each one a testimony of a mother's love and desperation to heal her injured daughter. Today Amelia wanted to feel every morsel of the pain she deserved. She wanted to absorb it and accept it without excuse or validation.

This ritual of examining every stitch, of knowing every push of the needle her mother had made throughout that sleepless night would feature heavily in Amelia's life for years to come. The dress that would never be worn but would be worshipped as the ungrateful daughter's punishment and an aid to the atonement she would never feel. Self-hatred and dogged regret would be her constant companions, but they would be hers alone. Her remorse and guilt were not for sharing.

She would never repeat the words of condemnation she'd heard at the funeral. She knew that she deserved to be blamed but the shame was too terrible to imagine, so she kept her crime a secret. A secret between her and God. She would confess only to her mother when they met again. But for now, she needed to make sure she didn't inflict further pain on her father or Brenda, so the cross was hers and hers alone to bear.

Christmas day came and went with nothing other than a cheese sandwich and the queen's speech. No-one wanted to celebrate without mum. No-one wanted to decorate the tree, wrap gifts or smell a roasting turkey. Nothing was worth any effort without the woman who had been at the heart of it all.

On boxing day, Tom's father made an unexpected visit. Apart from the exception of the funeral, the fat old man who walked with a stick had been restricted to visiting only at birthdays and Christmas.

Widowed several years earlier, the bad-tempered heavy drinker lived in the adjoining village and filled his pensioners bungalow with pipe smoke and foul language.

Although the girls referred to him as Grandpa, Celia's disapproval of his lifestyle and abrupt, abusive manner had kept the relationship politely distant.

"Decisions have to be made Tom." He said sternly as the girls sat eve's-dropping from the stairs again.

Their father didn't reply.

"Do you hear me, Tom?"

"Yes, I hear you."

"So?"

"So?"

"You need to make a plan Tom. Either Celia's parents need to move over from Ireland, you need to move there, or you need to give up your job and take care of the kids."

"None of that's an option." He replied sternly, surprised at his father's concern for either him or his daughters. "They would never move here and I'm not going there either. I can't stand the sight of them."

"Well, I hope you're not looking in my direction. If you can't pack in work, there's only one solution. You'll have to put them into care."

Amelia grabbed Brenda's hand and squeezed it tightly.

Now there was silence.

Brenda's tears were rolling down the side of her nose but Amelia immediately wiped them as she pulled her sister close.

"They are not going into care!" Tom bellowed. "Get out of my house! I can't believe you'd even suggest it!"

"Well what big plan do you have then eh?" The old man screamed back. "That's the thanks I get for paying for the bloody funeral and wiping your arse for weeks! What's your plan then?"

"My plan is to throw you out of my fuckin' house. Put them into care? Just get out! Get out!"

Amelia was hugging Brenda reassuringly.

"It's going to be alright Brenda. Dad will have to stop working but we can help out. I'll get a paper round and we can grow spuds down by the shed. We'll be alright."

Brenda rubbed her eyes and then frowned.

"Is that true then?" she asked

"Is what true?"

"That Grandpa has been wiping dad's arse?"

Amelia laughed out loud and hugged her again.

Tom overheard the chuckle and smiled.

He smiled at the resilience of his daughters, but he also smiled at the irony that Celia's wish had been granted. The rift had been healed between Amelia and Brenda. She would have found some comfort that her death had not been in vain.

He had no idea that the rift had already been healed by the daughter who'd found her peace in the solace of the empty sky and gusting wind several weeks ago. A friendship with solitude that would one day lead her into unimaginable horror.

As his father stormed out, Tom took a deep breath and stole himself for the challenge ahead.

He was no stranger to death or to hardship. As a child he'd suffered the fear and deprivation of rationing and bombing. As a boy, he'd witnessed his grandparent's resilience after the tragic news of their teenage son killed in action at Normandy. Grief was a part of life back then. Too much of it, too often, to be able to devote years of mourning to each new tragedy.

"Life is too short for wallowing in things that can't be changed." His Grandma would say as she dusted and kissed the photograph of her teenage son who'd failed to return from war.

She didn't want to know the ordeal he'd faced or how he met his end. It would be too painful and totally irrelevant now. She'd loved him and now he was gone. That was as much as she could deal with. Life had to move on.

Her other son had escaped enlistment due to a hearing impairment which miraculously developed just after war broke out. There were rumours that Gerald had pierced his own eardrum but whatever the reason for his impairment, it seemed to improve considerably after VE day.

The words were never spoken but they were always just a whisper away. The coward, the deserter, the selfish, yellow-bellied bastard. The same selfish bastard who'd just slammed Tom's front door.

Tom was determined to be the opposite of his father. To be the brave one, the hero, like his uncle Jack, like his grandma.

He blew out the air he'd just inhaled and wrote a letter to his manager at the asbestos plant. He then sealed it into an envelope and took it in person to the factory he hadn't walked to since the day Celia walked to the chemist.

He clutched the letter and tried to dismiss the memory of the last time he trod this path. It had been the day he'd left Celia and the kids in bed to start his shift. He'd been feeling happy that day after his chat with her the night before. There had been a spring in his stride but today his stride was one of dogged determination.

He got what he wanted that day. Reduced hours, a regular day shift and no weekend overtime. It was more than he'd hoped for but the plight of a widower with two children created its own brand of undisputed empathy despite the size of the company.

The plant had been the sole reason that his own ancestors had migrated to Rochdale when it opened in 1871 and the name of Simpson therefore carried some weight.

It was, however, somewhat of a hollow victory. His reduced hours meant reduced pay, and running a home was so much harder than he'd imagined. The Avon money had bridged a bigger gap than he'd realised, and life became almost unbearable.

School clothes were never clean, toiletries became unaffordable luxuries, and most of his cooking was inedible.

He had to do something and he had to do it fast.

As a logical man he decided that the broken part was the part to fix. The part to replace.

He needed a woman.

Chapter 4

The replacement part came in the form of Sheila from the corner shop. A spinster, (still in her thirties but deemed to be firmly on the shelf), was an easy target.

Sheila was a little on the plump side with brown wiry hair usually hidden under a silk scarf tied at the nape of her neck, giving her the look of a fortune teller. Her blouses were colourful and her skirts mostly calf-length with frills or tassels. Their late mother often referred to her affectionately as Gypsy-Rose-Lee.

"I'm in a bit of a pickle you see," he told her. "Two girls to raise and I can't cook or iron. I can't work out the bloody washing machine and I need to get back onto my old shift pattern to make a good wage."

Sheila stared aghast at the unprompted bombardment of personal information.

"I don't see what that has to do with me?"

Tom realised he'd blurted it all out without any preamble and took a breath before starting again.

"I'm a practical man Sheila. I can offer you a room and board for free if you'll look after my house and kids. You could rent out your cottage for a bit and still do a few shifts in the shop if you like. That money would be all yours and the rent money from your cottage could be put away for a pension. What do you think?"

"You seem to have a lot worked out for a visit to the corner shop!"

"But what do you think?"

"I think you've a damn cheek Tom Simpson." She scowled. But then her scowl gave way to a grin. "Let me think on it."

Sheila didn't think on it for very long. She'd spent years longing to be a mother with a real family. Something she'd recently given up on. Something Tom knew far too well!

The gossip surrounding the history of the lady in the corner shop had once been feasted on for several years. Fabricated and exaggerated by the bored housewives who frequented Paddy's on a Saturday night in their catalogue frocks, as they handed round sausage rolls from Tupperware boxes.

"She's a wrong 'un that Sheila! Just like her mother."

Leaning forward to whisper their loudest about the illegitimate girl who'd run away to escape the debauched lifestyle of her harlot mother. The stories, like all stories, collected further embellishment from every tongue they touched as they were repeated, coloured, and bulked out like a perpetually rolling snowball.

The truth, as with all truths, was extremely less disturbing.

Sheila was indeed a teenage runaway but her departure had nothing to do with her mother's lifestyle which, although unusual for the time, was as mundane as any other. The bulk of the rumours had been fabricated in the desperate quest to uncover the identity of Sheila's father. Partly because unmarried mother's were a rarity in the sixties but mainly because she had acquired a quaint little house at the edge of the village to which she held the deeds.

"She's a kept woman, that one! And to someone with money!" The gossipers would tell each other over and over in the hope that one of them might hit on the identity of her wealthy, illicit lover.

Sheila had left the village abruptly. That was a fact. She'd climbed into a camper van one Saturday morning and disappeared with a group of hippies a few weeks before the end of the school term.

"You must be so worried about her?"

This was the favourite opening gambit of many busy bodies who would throw it out at the village harlot in the hope of catching her at a moment when she might just spill the whole, terrible story.

"Not at all." She would smile, "She's just having a bit of teenage freedom. Spreading her wings before life pulls her into its drudgery. Something that might have done us all a bit of good."

It was a reprimand disguised with a condescending smile and it was never well received. The harlot had somehow managed to make a very upstanding wife and mother feel small and narrow minded.

The harlot remained a mystery throughout her daughter's absence and particularly in relation to her own frequent absences in which the house remained unoccupied for a week or maybe two at a time.

"She's gone off with her fancy man again!"

The mutterings continued.

"I bet his wife's wondering where he is!"

"Yes, I'd like to whisper a few things in *her* ear if I knew who she was!"

But no-one knew who she was.

There was no ear to whisper the poison into and no new gossip to share.

Well not until six years later when the runaway daughter suddenly reappeared in all her glory.

A beautiful hippie girl who had finally come home.

The village was suddenly alive with renewed speculation but none of it came near to the terrible truth that Sheila had returned to nurse her mother through her final days. That the woman's weeks away had been hospital stays and that the cottage had been left to her by her fiancé who'd been killed in a farming accident after taking out insurance prior to their wedding.

It took a while for the gossipers to eat and digest their own words. Time to adequately vindicate themselves for believing the tale-telling fabrications of persons unknown.

The finger-pointing and accusations as to who invented the unjust tales, were as loud and lively as the stories themselves and it wasn't until the funeral, that the villagers packed away their hostility, and took pity on the warm-hearted, hippie girl who was now alone in the world.

Sheila accepted their warmth, oblivious to their recent animosity towards her mother, and remained in her childhood home among the community she'd grown up in.

For the two years that followed, she'd led a quiet life in her inherited house with the little garden. She'd worked in the local shop and become a quirky, well-liked personality, known for her big heart and her passion for meditation and yoga. The tools with which she was able to quieten her secrets and soothe her broken heart.

But today that peaceful existence had been challenged with the plea from Tom Simpson to become a substitute mother to his children.

Her heart had been tossed into the air.

This could be a huge mistake or a colossal and wonderful opportunity. Her heart came down on the side of opportunity.

She moved in a week later and Tom returned to his shift pattern at the asbestos plant.

For Amelia and Brenda, the arrival of Sheila felt like the appearance of the fairy god mother in a tragic pantomime scene and in the weeks that followed, it almost felt like things had returned to some state of normality after a long, arduous battle. The struggle of surviving every new day.

To say that Sheila was eccentric was a huge under-statement, but she was kind and pleasant and a wonderful, imaginative cook.

They all rubbed along together quite nicely with periods of something almost bordering on happiness, punctuated by moments of extreme sadness.

They were riding the waves of grief and heartbreak, but they were doing so together, as a group of people who cared about each other, as a family.

Sheila had infused their home with a gentle understanding and an unassuming manner as they negated the stony, unsteady road of healing. The bumps became smaller and less frequent, and the colours slowly became more vibrant, but the empty space that Celia had occupied, would never be filled.

Amelia found herself frequently pondering her mother's words about developing her mind. She tried hard at school and was already the top of her class, but she suspected her mother expected more from her. Something else. Something different.

She turned to the woman who might have the answer.

She turned to Sheila.

In the privacy of her room, Sheila burned incense and meditated. The girls would make fun of the humming and although Amelia laughed as enthusiastically as her sister, behind the laughter hung a deep curiosity she couldn't ignore.

One night she tapped on Sheila's door and was welcomed with a smile.

"What is it?" Sheila asked mildly.

"Have you ever contacted anyone?"

Sheila's face turned pale. She knew exactly where this was heading.

"I'm meditating not raising the dead!" She laughed.

She could see Amelia's embarrassment.

"You *were* talking about the dead I assume?"

Amelia nodded.

Sheila immediately swept Amelia's thin straggles back from her shoulders affectionately and pulled her close.

"You mean your mother?"

Amelia didn't reply.

"I can understand your longing to contact your mum love but that's just not possible."

"Why not?"

"The mind is very powerful, and it can be trained to push all kinds of boundaries but in my experience, the wall between this world and the next is not one that can be broken through."

"But some people do it all the time!"

"Do they? Are you sure about that?" She frowned as she gently pushed Amelia back to look at her.

She felt the skinny shoulders shrug beneath her hands.

"Mum said I should develop my mind because that's what people would admire me for. She said that humans only use a very tiny part of their brain."

"Yes, I think that's true." Sheila smiled, "but I don't think she was talking about setting up a telephone line from earth to heaven!"

Amelia giggled and then frowned again.

"What then?"

"I don't know but I've been studying a man who claims to be able to bend objects just by looking at them."

Amelia's eyes widened.

"His name is Uri Geller, she nodded towards the small table where a row of spoons had been arranged.

"You've been trying to do it?"

"I have, and I think that's the kind of mind power your mother wanted to explore. Go on now. Back to bed." She said softly as she guided Amelia back towards the door.

Amelia hardly slept that night as she tried to make sense of her mother's prompt to further the ability of her mind. A thought that also consumed her throughout the next day.

"Have you actually bent anything?" She asked as the family sat down to eat that evening, deliberately playing with her spoon.

Tom hid a smile behind his forkful of chips.

Sheila peered at Amelia from beneath her wiry fringe and grinned widely.

"We don't get anything without perseverance in this world young lady. If you want to develop the untapped talents of your mind there are three requirements. Concentration, peacefulness, and perseverance."

Tom stuffed the chips in his mouth, Brenda giggled behind her hand and Amelia simply nodded and replaced her dessert spoon.

This was the path she was going to explore. She had long-since given up on paying any attention to her appearance. If her mind had the capacity to bloom, that's where she was going to focus her attention. Her mother had told her as much and now she was certain that her mother had sent Sheila into her life for that very purpose.

Not once did it occur to Amelia that her mother had simply been encouraging her to study hard and to get a profession.

The following day she joined the village library and ordered three books – Meditation, Clairvoyance and Bats! If her mother was right that humans use only a fraction of the brain they've been given, she was going to tap into that sleeping section of grey matter and awaken it with a bang!

Tom frowned at the array of books strewn across the kitchen table but was happy to trust his eldest daughter's whims to the guidance of his housekeeper and friend. Consequently, he paid little attention to their exploits.

The only exception being his intervention when Amelia became dotted with bruises around her body.

"Enough is enough!" He scolded when she emerged in her short-sleeved nightdress looking like an abused child. "I think you need to leave the sonar to the bats and go back to bending spoons!"

Amelia huffed her resignation with minimal protest. Her success with sonar had been another disappointment. She'd read of blind children who'd developed it, but her own success had failed to progress beyond the ability to sense when another person was standing behind her. Whatever sonar waves were bouncing back at her were barely detectable to the brain she was trying to train.

Her numerous experiments over the next two years all ended in frustrated disappointment but her home life, at least, had regained a little of the 'light and air' she'd once remembered.

It would be wrong to say that the former joy had been re-established, but the presence of routine and stability had created its own brand of second-class happiness.

Sheila and Tom continued to rub along nicely and sometimes they would sit together in the garden drinking wine and chatting for hours.

"Have you thought about getting married?" Amelia blurted to Sheila after one such evening.

"To your dad!" Sheila laughed "No! Of course not!"

"But you get on really well and you're both single?"

Sheila froze for a moment. Then, without speaking, she slowly raised her eyes to meet Amelia's. Amelia looked directly into that intense stare and immediately she understood. She knew exactly what Sheila was about to say.

"My dad isn't single. Is he?"

"No. He isn't, and he never will be."

"You think he's still in love with mum?"

"I know he is, and I know that he is raising you girls in the belief that she's watching his every move. He believes that one day, he'll be reunited with her and when that happens, he wants her to love him for everything he's doing right now."

Amelia suddenly felt guilty for betraying her mother so easily. She'd never spoken to her parents about religion, but she'd heard her father singing hymns at weddings and always noticed how proudly he bellowed the words.

"I take it that you don't share your father's beliefs then?"

Amelia frowned. "Do you?"

"If I'm honest, my beliefs sway back and forth in the wind depending on my last experience, but I do know that it would be a holy show if your dad turned up at the pearly gates with a daft old bat like me on his arm! She'd likely slap me in the face with her harp!"

Amelia laughed out loud at the vision of it.

"Now," she added, taking a swig of her gin and tonic, "If they were divorced then that would be a different story!"

Amelia was still laughing.

"You fancy my dad?"

"You bet your boots I do. He's a real looker, your dad. I'd have jumped on his bones in a heartbeat!"

Amelia held her aching stomach as she tried to breathe. She hadn't laughed like that for the longest time.

"Seriously though. He's a good man, your dad."

Amelia stopped laughing and turned her face upwards into the loving expression of the woman who'd become her sanctuary.

"And you are a good woman, Sheila." She said gratefully.

Sheila smiled and patted her hand. "Time for bed."

That few minutes with Sheila had opened Amelia's eyes to so many things she hadn't known. Her father's religion, Sheila's huge and righteous heart but, above all, she remembered the moment of eye contact with Sheila. The moment in which she could feel what Sheila was about to say, what Sheila didn't need to say out loud.

She lay in bed thinking about it over, and over again.

"I'm going to give up on the bat sonar." She told Brenda who'd been laying silently in the other bed.

"I was just thinking about that!" Brenda gushed, "you must have read my mind!"

Amelia didn't reply for several seconds. Had she really read Brenda's mind as well as Sheila's or had she sent her own thoughts to Brenda? She was certain that it was one or the other. The silence continued.

"Mealy?"

"Think of a colour Brenda."

"Not that again! I'm going to sleep." Brenda yawned. "You can mind-read my dreams if you like."

Amelia turned onto her side and tried to recall everything she'd read about mind-reading.

Chapter 5

By the start of secondary school, she was losing faith in any of it. The coincidences continued at the same rate. Too many to ignore, too few to analyse. The whole thing had become her Achilles heel. Teasing her with its random and infrequent appearances. Forbidding her the chance to master it, forbidding her the freedom to ignore it.

Her unkept appearance, strange solitary behaviour and lust for disappearing alone into the wood soon earned her the nickname of The Witch, and sometimes prefixed by the adjective she already related to. Ugly Witch.

With Brenda still at primary school she had no friends at all so she immersed herself in her studies, hoping that her mother's speculation might result in the discovery of something spectacular.

She spent most of the school holidays with her younger sister or alone in that clearing in the woods - her happy place, where she would wile-away the hours, lying on her back and gazing into the sky. Gazing into the unknown. Peering through the gaps in the clouds. Still searching. Searching for her mother, for the life to come, for something bigger than herself. Concentrating, being peaceful and persevering.

In termtime she sat at the back of the class where no eyes could judge her. Where no-one could stare at her matted hair, dirty nails or blotchy face with the sharp witchy nose.

Sometimes she would hear the whispers but never did another soul confront her. Instead, they avoided her. No-one wanted to light the blue touch paper of Amelia Simpson, the witch girl and although she had all the academic answers no-one approached her. No-one dared to ask the school weirdo.

She would remember those first years at secondary school as another phase of darkness.

As a family they had worked their way through the healing process with lightened hearts but on reaching the end of it there seemed to be nothing. Nothing at all.

Amelia didn't care or even notice.

She did, however, notice her father's progressive withdrawal as he spent more time alone in his bedroom and less time sipping wine with Sheila.

Slowly but surely, he was passing the parenting over as though preparing her for full-time motherhood.

On one occasion she passed by his door and heard him whispering. She put her ear to the door and tried to make out the words. The words were not as recognizable as the rhythm. Her father was praying but not to God. He was praying to the wife he'd last seen with her face against that windowpane.

She listened as his voice became more desperate, more urgent and more terrifying.

"My God, Celia. It's been six fuckin' years! Not a word, not a sign but I know you're out there somewhere. I can feel it. I know you are! For Christ's sake speak to me! Give me a sign! Anything. Jesus Celia! Where are you!"

Amelia jumped back from the door in terror. It sounded like he was planning a reunion!

She ran straight to Sheila.

"Look Amelia. I've done a lot of poking around in the unknown, as you well know and the only time that I've ever been convinced that a deceased person has been contacted has been while they were in some sort of transient state."

"Like what?"

Sheila sighed. She felt she had already said too much for a young mind to deal with.

"Like what?" Amelia persisted.

"Like a person who hasn't really grasped that they've passed. A soul somehow stuck between worlds but eventually they move on."

"You think my mum has moved on?"

"Yes Amelia. I'm certain that she has."

It was Amelia's turn to sigh.

"I do think though," Sheila said more cheerily, "that maybe in that transient state, your mum sent your dad to find me."

"Really?"

"Yes, I do. You said she wanted you to develop your mind and who better than me to help you with that?"

"I guess so." Amelia agreed feeling suddenly comforted at the thought that Sheila had been chosen by their mother as she left this world. Almost like handing them over to a trusted child-minder.

"Goodnight Sheila." She smiled as she kissed the newly exalted child-minder on the cheek.

She felt Sheila's hand stroke her hair and knew that they would be safe in her care, but she wasn't about to allow her father to check out!

For his next birthday, she saved her pocket money and presented him with an iron crucifix.

The shock on his face was startling as he stared into the small plastic box.

"What you got him that for?" Brenda laughed as she handed him the large parcel which failed to disguise the box of chocolates within.

"I just thought he might like it." She shrugged.

She felt her father's hand touch hers.

"It's perfect, Amelia. Thank you."

Sheila nodded her approval to Amelia as Brenda frowned.

Nothing more was ever said about the crucifix, but Amelia noticed that she never saw her dad again without the cross hanging around his neck.

She was in no doubt that he believed in heaven and that meant he believed that their mother wasn't just watching over him but waiting for him.

She hoped that cross would remind him that suicide was a sin against God. She needed confirmation.

"Do you think mum's watching over us?"

"I'd like to think so. Except when I neglect her vegetable patch!" He grinned.

"Dad?"

"Yep."

"You're not planning to leave us, are you?"

"Leave you? Where would I go?"

"I mean, you might leave us for heaven?"

"What makes you say that?" He replied uncomfortably. His face flushing a strange shade of purple.

"I don't know. I just think about it a lot and it scares me."

"I will be here with you, for as long as you need me." He smiled weakly. It felt like a trick answer.

"We'll always need you dad. We will need you forever."

"Forever it is then."

"You promise?"

"I promise."

This time there was no smile, only a sigh of disappointed resignation.

There would be a day when Amelia would recall this moment with a heavy heart. When she would realise that those tortuous years her father was to face, would be her fault.

But for now, she heaved a sigh of relief and hugged his neck.

She wished she knew what he was thinking. She was still sure it was possible to tune in to another person's mind but her efforts to pursue that particular talent had waned away amidst frustrated tears from her little sister.

The anger of finally admitting defeat lay in the dogged belief that Brenda was not trying hard enough, not concentrating long enough or not staying focussed. They had experienced occasional but incredible moments of undeniable success but these were short-lived, unpredictable, impossible to prove, and extremely rare.

She'd read about a pair of twins who claimed to communicate fluently without speaking but the sibling connection was not the reason that Brenda had been bullied into her gruelling experiments.

The sole reason that Brenda had been her only subject was simply that Brenda was her only friend.

She was convinced that there were so many worthier candidates all around her, committed and talented individuals with minds she could easily train but such individuals lay hidden among the masses. The unapproachable, mean, malicious masses and without the confidence or skills to approach such people, they were totally beyond her reach.

Well, that was, until the arrival of Frank.

Not until half-way through fifth form did any classmate even register on her radar until the day when she arrived at her chemistry class to find that her seat had already been taken.

At the back of the classroom a tall boy with a mop of dark, shining, floppy hair was arranging his books on her desk.

The whole class fell silent and watched as she entered.

The young man continued to empty the contents of his satchel onto the desk, oblivious to the tension around him.

She could feel the eyes of the entire room on her. Waiting for her reaction. Hoping she would provide some entertainment by demanding him to move or dragging him bodily from her seat. Cursing him with some incantation from the bowls of hell.

Amelia did neither.

She smiled warmly at the boy and took the seat in front causing the immediate resumption of classroom babbling. Exchanges of disappointment at the absence of an anticipated confrontation.

She sat calmly, but uncomfortably, in front of him for forty minutes. Feeling his eyes burning into her. Judging her. Squirming at every morsel of her repulsive existence until the bell rang and she could escape into the throng of the masses as they flooded into the corridor.

"You were writing the symbols without even looking them up!" Came a voice from behind.

"Pardon?" She replied as she turned towards the unfamiliar voice.

"I said you seem to know the periodic table by heart! I was watching you write the formulas as though you were writing a letter!"

"Perhaps you should concentrate on your own work instead of mine?" She said firmly to the figure that now towered above her, oozing confidence, with satchel on shoulder and one hand in his pocket.

"Frank Porter." He smiled, extending his free hand.

"Amelia Simpson." She replied without reciprocating - keeping her dirty, broken fingernails firmly out of sight.

"Well, Amelia Simpson, you seem to be the kind of friend I could do with. I'm useless at Chemistry. Perhaps you could teach me?"

"Isn't that what the teachers are for?" she snapped sarcastically noticing his southern accent which sounded superior to her broad Yorkshire twang.

"Really? I can't say that I'd noticed."

She gave in to a smile.

"Could you walk me to the next class?"

"I could ...but I won't." She called as she started to walk away.

He immediately laughed and ran to catch up.

She entered the maths lesson in front of that dark-haired boy with the heavy fringe and took her usual seat at the back. He followed closely and claimed the desk beside her.

"Why are you hounding me?"

"I'm just a sucker for an open book." He smiled.

She had no idea what he was talking about but she wasn't going to take the bait.

As the lesson started, her focus switched instantly to the equation on the board. This was her moment. This was the time she always shone. Frantically scribbling down columns of figures in her race to be the first to arrive at the answer.

She didn't notice that Frank was paying no attention at all to the blackboard or the old man standing beside it with his monotone voice and curt manner.

Frank was amusing himself flicking through the pages of that open book.

Amelia felt something that caused her to pause midway through her calculation. Some sort of abrupt interruption to her train of thought. Slowly she turned her head to the right. The boy was staring directly at her, only inches away, his bushy monobrow menacingly framing piercing dark eyes.

She gave a small gasp as a sudden chill shuddered through her body and looked quickly away.

She could hear other students already shouting out their answers but losing the race was not her main focus today.

Something terrifying, unsettling and inexplicably exciting was happening right beside her!

Too nervous to confront it and too sceptical to acknowledge it, she decided to simply ignore it. To feign disregard. To taunt and provoke it into making a second appearance.

She carefully copied the new question from the blackboard, repeating the formula in her head number by number slowly and meticulously. "Minus b, plus or minus b squared, L, O, O," She was no longer in control of the symbols her mind was listing! The symbols that her hand was repeating. Her eyes widened as she watched the involuntary movement of her own hand following the dictation she could hear in her head.

"K, A, T, M, E,"

Her hand relaxed and became hers again but she was sweating with fear. On the sheet of paper, were the words. "LOOK AT ME"

She stared at those words for several seconds as the chatter around her faded away to a distant noise.

Her heart was beating against her chest as she forced her head to turn again in the direction of the suspected perpetrator.

Nervously, she turned her head again. Fearfully, inch by inch as her heart continued to thump against her chest. She gasped! Her heart held its breath, and she did the same. Frank's face was only inches away!

The class continued with its task. Whispering, scribbling and huffing. Totally oblivious to her peril. Unaware of the terror that was taking place at the back of the class.

She quickly covered the words she'd written as though hiding her weakness, might somehow protect her from further attack.

She glanced again in his direction to check if he'd noticed and he relaxed his face, smiled, and nodded back towards the blackboard as though chastising her for not paying attention.

Eventually the bell rang for lunch, but Frank remained seated. She waited until the chairs had stopped screeching and the babbling had migrated onto the corridor before standing up to confront the boy who, she suspected, was trying to intimidate her.

"Why were you staring at me throughout the whole lesson?"

"I wasn't!" he protested, "I looked at you twice. Just twice."

"Well, it seems strange that you were looking every time I looked over?"

He didn't reply.

His silence caused her to stop collecting her books and look in his direction again. Frank was smiling.

"Have you considered that you might have been the one to look up as soon as I started to watch you?"

"You were trying to get my attention?"

"It's just a little trick I do sometimes."

"A trick?"

"Yes, it doesn't work with everyone, but I could feel it was going to work with you. I try it out on people when I'm bored. And that lesson was beyond boring!"

"You actually think I felt you staring?"

"I don't know. Did you?"

She fastened the toggles on her satchel and flung it over her shoulder.

"You're weird Frank Porter."

"I prefer to call it interesting."

"If you were interesting, I'd be interested, now wouldn't I?" she snapped with a confidence she was definitely not feeling. This boy hadn't merely caught her attention. He'd put words into her mind that had flowed out onto her page without any help from her!

"I think you *are* interested actually." He grinned. "Maybe not right now because you're still getting over the weird staring thing but tonight, you'll think about me. Probably for hours. Then tomorrow you'll be desperate to see me again."

"What subjects have you got this afternoon?"

Frank took out his timetable and frowned.

"Metalwork and History."

"Good. I've got Biology and Geology, so it looks like this is the end of a wonderful friendship. What a shame."

Frank stood and watched as she flounced off and a smile broke instantly on his face.

Amelia spent the final lesson of the day reliving that terrifying maths lesson. She studied the three disturbing words scrawled haphazardly on the page. Disturbingly, it didn't even look like her own handwriting.

That evening Amelia was determined not to spend any of her valuable time thinking about the floppy-fringed boy with the conceited belief that he could command her attention whenever he pleased. She opened her geology homework and tried to concentrate on the difference between igneous and conglomerate rocks but there was a distinct mental block. A mental block called Frank Porter!

Eventually she made the conscious decision to give him some airtime, if only to clear her head for a moment so she could get on with her homework.

It was difficult to separate the boy from the event. Something was holding her attention, preventing her from moving on from it, and that something was a blend of fear and excitement.

She'd spent years chasing a theory. Years of wondering why no-one ever questions those frequent moments when a person suddenly blurts: -

"You must have read my mind!"

- It happens to everyone. But, tonight, because of this boy, she was suddenly asking herself why *does* it happen to everyone, and how normal is it? Why does everyone just laugh it off? Accepting that its just another unexplained phenomenon.

Perhaps it was just what people do. Accept the unexplained with a shrug in the same way they used to accept the appearance of a rainbow. A coincidence that appeared when sun and rain combined. No-one bothering to join the dots!

She, on the other hand, had been trying to join many dots for many years and yet now that those dots were lined up and within reach she was backing away and she didn't know why.

She scrawled a hurried explanation for the damned difference between the rock types, stuffed her geology book back in her bag and lay for a moment before Sheila called her down for tea.

She knew exactly why she was backing away. The simple fact was that she was terrified. The idea of telepathy had danced before her eyes like the sugarplum fairy. Magical, enticing, and comfortingly unreal.

Except that now, it wasn't.

Her fear of Frank Porter had just been thwarted by a more powerful emotion. He was just a teenager like her. He'd simply stumbled on an unusual ability, and he didn't seem at all disturbed by it. On the contrary, he seemed content to regard it as nothing more than a trick he could play on his friends.

The new boy at school was an idiot. Maybe a genius.

Whatever he was, he was no longer intimidating.

He was incredibly exciting!

She walked to the window and looked out at the night sky into the vast unknown. The place her mother resided. The place devoid of secrets and assumptions. The place of answers, understanding and peace.

This annoying boy had caused her to feel the closest she'd ever felt to something truly remarkable.

She recalled again, the moment she'd seen her own hand scrawling those words over the page. She shuddered.

This prankster, this class clown, seemed to have stumbled into an incredible discovery.

It didn't occur to her that he might be an accidental and incompetent carrier of something immeasurably dangerous.

Tomorrow, she intended to seek him out.

Just as he'd predicted.

Chapter 6

"I want to learn!" She blurted out, making a grab for Frank's elbow as he passed in the opposite direction.

"And good morning to you too!" He snapped irritably.

"I'm sorry!" She called after him as he continued to walk briskly by.

She stood and watched him march haughtily for a few strides, then his rhythm slowed until he came to a standstill, turned and smiled.

"It's not something I can teach you! I don't even know how it happens myself!"

"But you can make it happen?"

"Sometimes."

"I want you to show me. Tell me what I'm thinking right now!"

He laughed.

"What's funny?"

"You are! Believing that I can just read your mind in the corridor. Turn it on like a tap!"

"Can't you?"

"No! It's definitely not a precise science. Meet me at the gate after school and I'll divulge the extent of my magnificent talents." He winked.

"I'm only interested in one of them."

"Maybe…. For now, anyway!" He grinned.

She didn't respond. Irritation and disappointment had caused her to turn and walk away. His flippant manner and persistent negativity held no promise of the kind of commitment she'd been hoping for. Contentedly bewildered by his own random ability, fleetingly amused by the pranks it created, and arrogantly absorbed in his own libido, he was going to make a derisory accomplice.

But as the afternoon crawled by, she made the decision to use his weaknesses to her advantage. Using his inflated ego as the key, she would squeeze out every drop of information before tossing him aside.

She waited at the gate as arranged but it seemed he was in no hurry to keep their appointment. If he was playing the power game, she'd already waited too long. She was about to leave when he finally appeared looking dishevelled and slightly damp.

"Sorry," he mumbled casually. "Football went on a bit and there was a queue for the showers."

She could smell the soap from his skin. His tie was hanging from his gym bag and his shirt unbuttoned. He was obviously telling the truth and consequently he was instantly forgiven. The coldness she'd been feeling towards him in the last ten minutes had suddenly warmed to an inner glow. A glow that seemed to be flushing her cheeks as she noticed the black curly chest hairs protruding from the open neck of his school shirt.

He caught her staring and immediately fastened the lowest button.

This feigned modesty triggered her feigned indignance.

A dangerous game had already begun.

"So, explain why this thing can't be turned on like a tap." She said sharply.

He smiled smugly at her over-compensated curtness.

"Well." he said, starting to walk homeward without asking if she was heading in the same direction, "it's a bit like going to sleep."

She followed without complaining. It was her way home anyway.

"What? I don't understand?"

"You know that moment when you decide to go to bed but sometimes you fall straight to sleep and sometimes you stay awake for hours?"

"Yes."

"Well, it either happens or it doesn't. You have no control over it do you?"

"Guess not."

"Well, it's exactly like that. You do everything you can to encourage sleep but sometimes it just doesn't happen does it? You turn off the lights, pump up the pillows, have a warm drink yet you're still wide-awake waiting for your brain to behave."

"I suppose that makes sense but surely there's some sort of common denominator for when it works and when it doesn't?"

"There you go, trying to apply science to it. Believe me, if I knew how and why, I'd be shouting it from the rooftops but as it is, it's pointless to mention it to anyone. No-one wants to be the school weirdo do they. Present company excepted."

"You think I'm the school weirdo?"

"So they tell me."

"Is that why you tried your little trick on me? To see if I was weird enough to tune in?"

"Maybe."

"I don't know if I should be insulted or flattered!"

"You shouldn't be either. I felt something from you the moment I got physically close."

"You called me 'an open book."

"I did. That's exactly how it felt and I couldn't resist giving it a shot."

"Look Frank. I don't like playing games so I'm just going to say this as it is."

She glanced at the stupid face he was pulling and ignored it.

"I know the names they call me here and I'm under no illusions that I'm a rather unattractive person. You, on the other hand are obviously the polar opposite so let's not pretend otherwise. There's going to be a lot of fallout for you if we spend any time together, but I really do want to know more about this."

"What are you asking?"

"I'm asking if you would give me a bit of your time to explore this. Tell me what you know and if the teasing gets too much then I'll understand. There will be a lot of teasing!"

"Yeah, but I'm a big boy you know!" He winked and nodded back towards his recently buttoned shirt.

She felt her chest tighten slightly. This boy, with a single comment and a nod of the head had enlightened her to the fact that he was way past puberty, that he was no longer a boy but a man. And with the smile that followed he'd triggered a feeling she'd never felt before.

For the first time in her short life, she'd been made to feel like a girl. A girl with a boy. A young woman with a young man. A boy had winked in her direction!

She was still daydreaming when Frank continued.

"So, how do you intend to explore this because it seems the school corridor isn't much of an option. Somewhere quiet where we won't keep getting interrupted."

"I know just the place." Amelia grinned. "Follow me."

It was early October, but the evenings were still warm and the nights still light until after 6pm.

She marched proudly and purposefully in the direction of her special place and Frank obediently followed.

Until that day, she'd never noticed the distance, the darkness, or the difficult terrain of the familiar route to her private sanctuary. She skilfully negotiated the brambles and nettles, navigated around the waterlogged ditches and rabbit holes, knowing every inch by heart, but Frank was wincing and stumbling. Cursing and tripping his way along and constantly falling behind.

"Are you insane!" He bellowed as he peeled another blackberry tentacle from the sleeve of his blazer between finger and thumb.

"Almost there now." She encouraged as the patch of light through the trees came into view.

Triumphantly she stood in the clearing to announce the arrival at her special place.

"Well, it's private. I'll give you that. Not very relaxing though."

Even in the clearing it felt like late evening rather than late afternoon and the familiar eeriness Amelia loved was already descending.

Quickly she foraged under a bush and pulled out a folded plastic sheet which she spread out over the grassy patch and turned to Frank for approval.

He shook his head slowly from side to side in disbelief before sitting down on the makeshift blanket and tending his many wounds.

Amelia dropped down beside him and lay face upwards to view the opening of sky that she called home.

After a few minutes and several ouches, he lay down beside her and peered up in the direction of her stare.

"It does work better, the closer you are to someone." He said as he shuffled up to her.

"Isn't it beautiful?" She asked.

"It's certainly something." He replied sarcastically.

"So tell me what we need to do."

"I have no idea."

She sat up abruptly. "What do you mean?"

"I mean that all we can do is to wait, I suppose."

"You suppose?"

"Look, I've never tried this with anyone before so I think we should just lay here together quietly and see if anything passes between us."

"Alright. Let's try it."

After several minutes of silence, Frank sat up and huffed.

"This is never going to work because I think we're both absorbed in making it work. We're just trying too hard."

"Perhaps this place was just a bad idea?" She replied without moving.

"It's a nice place though. I mean to be private and to enjoy the silence." He replied.

"Shall we just do that then? Just enjoy my place together before we go home."

She hoped he wasn't thinking she had romance in mind!

Frank lay back down in agreement and closed his eyes.

"No flirting!" He said suddenly.

She didn't reply.

"Open book. Just like I said."

She smiled. They had made a start!

Amelia continued to peer up into the fading sky and breathed deeply at the pure joy of it. She then looked over at Frank. His face looked peaceful and vulnerable. She followed the contours of his body down to his soft but strong hand.

Almost unconsciously she slipped her hand into his.

He didn't react. He just allowed it to rest in his open hand for a few moments. She held her breath. Eventually he curled his finger gently around hers and they continued to lay together in silence until the light was almost gone.

"We'd better be heading home?" She whispered.

"I suppose so. Are you cold?"

"No but I think I should be."

He was the first to stand and brush himself down before helping her to her feet.

"You'd better lead the way."

She nodded obediently and stuffed the sheet back under it's bush before turning to the path.

Above them, the crows screamed their nightly exchanges as they circled above. Swooping and soaring. But the screeching of this ritualistic roosting dance seemed only a whisper compared to the deafening silence between them as they walked mutely back to civilisation.

As they reached the road Frank heaved a sigh of relief and then turned towards her.

"You're not, you know."

"I'm not what?"

"You're not as unattractive as you think and there's nothing wrong with your legs."

"Why would you say such a thing!" The words had left her mouth defensively before she'd had the chance to pick them more carefully. She knew exactly why he'd said it because that's exactly what she'd been thinking when she dared to reach for his hand.

"Oh God!" She gushed. "We were doing it!"

"Well, I was." He corrected. "You're a bit of a one-way communicator I think."

"See you tomorrow then?" She smiled.

He answered with a wave of the hand.

"Oh," she called after him, "You weren't singing Crocodile Rock in your head by any chance, were you?"

Frank turned and stared.

"You heard that?"

She waved cockily and left.

Frank remained in the same spot. Amelia had tuned into him and heard his repetition of the song he'd used to block her out!

It had been a battle. A real battle. He'd listened to her and then suddenly he'd felt her thoughts go blank and knew she was concentrating on him.

He had to stop this.

Exciting as it was, he couldn't risk it.

He no longer trusted his ability to block her out nor did he trust his own mind not to wander into the things she must never know.

That night he couldn't sleep.

He tried to analyse what had happened between them.

In only a few short hours this strange outcast of a girl had got under his skin.

He'd been playing with her for amusement just because he could. He'd felt that familiar presence of a door left ajar, a mind wide open to intruders like himself and he'd marched through it without knocking.

It was an unusual but harmless prank and it typically ended in silly girls running away from him in a buzz of excited alarm but with Amelia things had quickly taken an unforeseen turn.

No-one had taken him seriously before. Teachers had chastised him for inciting distress with his nonsense and victims had adopted a careful distance, but none had ever turned the tables on him before.

But Amelia was not just another silly girl. She hadn't run away but stood and faced him. Now she was taking steps towards him intent on wheedling out the truth and he already knew why. She had the same unsettling gift.

He turned over in his bed and tried to think it through.

He'd only ever known one other person who could do the same thing and she was long gone, but he still recalled the thrill of it and the temptation to engage with Amelia was tempting.

He had to stop.

Things were different now. His head was no longer full of harmless frivolities they could experiment with. It held truths and realities he couldn't share but still, he found himself searching for rationalisation to pursue this.

He slammed himself onto his back again and opened his eyes.

The terrible truth was that, in only a few short hours, he could feel himself falling for the plain, irritable, shabby girl who had reached for his hand and inadvertently touched his heart.

His whole body had tingled at the touch of her soft fingers and his heart had ached as he caught those awful thoughts in her mind. Her abysmal opinion of herself.

Perhaps he was being too hasty? Perhaps he was more than capable of blocking her out when he needed to. He'd done it before. Perhaps he could pursue this safely.

But perhaps his heart was ruling his head.

He made a bargain with himself.

He would stay in contact with Amelia, but he would ease off on the experimental telepathy and block her when necessary. He'd explore the potential of a romantic relationship from a safe distance and for that, he needed a stooge. Someone who would innocently and unwittingly obstruct their alone time. He needed a big fat green gooseberry!

Suddenly, Frank obtained a questionable new best friend. Brian was neither fat nor green, but he was a sickly shade of yellow. A tall gangly limbed, studious boy who'd been inflicted with a slight stoop and a heavy dose of acne!

Brian became his ardent companion. The poor boy, rapidly exalted into this bizarre friendship, wore a perpetually bewildered expression somewhat resembling shellshock. His sandy coloured wire hair, a stark contrast to Franks black glossy mane. He would loiter in the background like a subservient yet grateful slave with his protruding teeth poking through the lips of his over-crowded mouth. It was an unlikely friendship, and no-one seemed more bemused by it than the boy himself.

Despite the knowledge that Brian's father owned the local garage, none of the boys from school had previously taken any interest in befriending him. It seemed that, even the chance to sit behind the wheel of the cars on the forecourt and the opportunity to learn about mechanics could never compensate for the undeniable fact that Brian was, an out and out girl repellent. A repellent of the only desire more compelling to a teenage boy than fast cars.

Brian was elated to be welcomed into this new dynamic, but Amelia was irritated by the sudden intrusion into their cosy liaisons.

For Frank this arrangement was buying him time to assess the situation and quantify the danger. His head was telling him to walk away from this girl, but his heart was constantly reminding him of the way he felt when her hand reached for his. There was something so pure and absolute about it. A feeling so undeniable that he couldn't shake it and didn't want to. Instead, he relived it repeatedly. Those few seconds that he would always remember as a moment in the soul.

Brian's presence was seriously restricting their opportunities for alone time. Something that suited Frank but served only to dishearten his girlfriend.

Amelia was becoming sulky and irritable. It was very clear that she suspected he was making excuses to avoid any closeness.

"I'm not feeling anything from you today!" She huffed, pulling her hand away from his, during one, highly infrequent evenings of lying beneath the trees.

"I was blocking you." He laughed.

"You think you can do that?"

"Not sure," he lied.

"You've done this before haven't you?" She said accusingly.

"It's easy," he smiled, "all you have to do is to tighten your mind against the other person. Make it tight like a fist."

"Who with?"

"What?"

"Who have you done this with before?"

She frowned as Frank stood up without answering.

"I have to go, it's getting dark and I'm cold. We won't be able to do this after school for much longer."

He reached out a hand to pull her to her feet.

She remained on the ground.

"Why don't you answer Frank? What aren't you telling me?"

He crashed his way through the bushes and called harshly over his shoulder.

"My sister! Ok? I used to do it with my sister!"

Amelia jumped to her feet and hurtled after him without stashing the sheet.

"Frank! Frank wait. Please wait!"

Frank stopped in his tracks without turning round.

She caught him by the arm and turned him towards her. His eyes were tightly shut and his bottom lip was quivering.

Instinctively she folded him into her arms.

"What is it Frank? I'm so sorry. Please tell me."

Frank gave himself a moment to think of a plausible explanation. An explanation that didn't give anything away but as near to the truth as he could get.

"My sister was a couple of years younger than me and we did this all the time."

"Was?"

"Yes. She's no longer with us." His lip was quivering again.

"Oh I'm so sorry Frank."

Amelia didn't urge him or even ask how his sister had died. All she did was to hold him close and allow him to sob into her arms until he recovered. This moment, as she held him so tenderly, triggered an emotion deep inside. He knew that this girl, this compassion, was a rare and welcome find. He'd unearthed the softer side of Amelia Simpson.

This was a woman he could trust. A woman who goes all in. A woman he could love.

"I owe you an explanation" He sniffed as he wiped his nose on his sleeve. "I don't want to shut you out."

"You don't owe me anything." She replied softly. "I just want you to be alright."

Frank took in a huge breath to compose himself and then blew it out loudly and smiled.

He felt suddenly stupid. He needed to defensively lighten the moment.

"Maybe I was practising. There might come a time when I don't want you to know I've got another woman on the side."

"On the side?" She laughed. "On the side of what?"

"Of whatever this is." He grinned, allowing his eyebrow to dance comically.

"Are you asking me to be your girlfriend Frank Porter?"

"That depends."

"On what?"

"On if you'll accept. I'm not going to ask unless you're going to say yes. I don't take rejection very well."

It was her turn to feel stupid and defensive.

"If you need a girlfriend, there are lots of pretty girls out there. You can take your pick."

"There's a pretty girl right here."

"Stop being a dick, Frank. It's not funny."

"I mean it. I think you're very attractive Amelia Simpson.

"Sod off!" She snapped again as she brushed herself down.

Frank caught her by the wrist and pulled her close.

"Look at you. You're quite lovely when you're not growling at me."

She was still writhing her wrist in his when he leant forward and looked into her eyes. She held his gaze for a second and watched his eyes close as the grip on her wrist relaxed.

She remained perfectly still as the warmth of his breath caressed her cheek.

She held her breath, paralysed by fear and anticipation. His lips brushed against hers with the delicacy of a butterfly's wings as he hovered for several excruciating seconds on the brink of touching. She felt every molecule of her body tingle. Her legs started to shake as her heart drummed the beat of some petrifying awakening deep inside. She felt the gentle pull of his hand in the small of her back as his lips brushed hers and then settled in the delivery of a tender kiss. She remained motionless as he waited a second and then returned his lips to hers. This time, she returned the kiss and their lips moulded together, moving in tiny circles of thrilling pleasure.

She could feel his body reacting against her, but it was neither alarming nor unwelcome because her own body was already doing exactly the same thing.

Then the kiss ended, and his hand fell away from her back as he released her.

He smiled mischievously, squeezed her hand affectionately then turned to leave.

"I'll see you tomorrow then." He called, without looking back.

Amelia stood numbly and watched him go.

She didn't dare to protest but she desperately wanted him to turn back. She needed him to turn back because something had changed. Everything had changed.

She would be going straight home now but she knew it wouldn't be the same for him.

She knew exactly where he'd be going. Straight to the youth club where Brenda and all the other normal girls would be. Then he'd be calling in at Paddy's working men's club with those same dolled-up 13-year-olds in tow, hoping to scrounge an illicit Babycham from the older boys with their shameful flirting and teasing smiles.

Older boys like Brian......or like Frank!

She watched him disappear through the trees and felt her stomach tighten. Twisted, by the fist of something she didn't recognise. Something terrifyingly urgent and sickeningly painful.

Nothing was the same anymore. She didn't feel the way she had a few moments ago. That kiss had changed everything!

Suddenly everything Frank did mattered. Everywhere he went and everyone he met mattered.

One small kiss had ignited the flame of something that was now burning out of control and his every move had a colossal effect on her.

The kiss that lit the flame had also sealed a deal. A silent promise had been made and any attention he gave to any other girl would now be a derogatory and demeaning insult.

It would also hurt like hell.

Frank was hers now.

This was a whole new level of enlightenment and the urge to run after him raged inside. This was jealousy in its rawest form. The compulsion to burst into the club and confront him over that kiss. She needed to know where she stood, and she needed to know right now!

As she strode menacingly from the wood a figure stepped out into her path.

"Brian! You gave me a fright. What are you doing here?"

"I saw Frank heading out alone, so I thought I'd check you were OK."

Amelia grinned. He'd obviously been stalking them. Feeling left out as usual.

"That was a fortunate coincidence then?" She teased.

"Shall I walk you home, then?"

"Just to the end of my street if you like."

Brian smiled his gratitude.

"I'll see you later then?" He said casually as they reached the corner.

"Yep. See you later."

As Brian turned to leave, she grinned again.

His jumper was covered in grass at bits of bramble! He had obviously been spying on them again! It wasn't the first time she's suspected it but she's never mentioned it to Frank because she felt sorry for Brian. Maybe he was hoping to catch them sharing a kiss, but she suspected he just wanted to be included in their mind reading experiments. She imagined him laying somewhere close by and trying to tune in.

The encounter with Brian had broken her train of thought and thankfully interrupted her rampage of certain humiliation and saved her from herself.

She headed for home with a sigh of gratitude, shuddering at the vision of the pathetic scene she'd been about to create.

Back at home she rescued her tea from the oven where it had been warming since Brenda got home. Brenda's plate was already in the sink where she would have tossed it in her rush to get changed and curl her hair.

"It'll be ruined by now!" Sheila called from the living room.

"It's fine thanks" Amelia called back cheerily as she prodded the crust of a previously delicious chicken stew.

She shovelled it in and then went to run a bath with her thoughts still on the imagined scene at Paddy's.

This Friday was no different to any other but she'd never before wondered what Frank might be doing, or even cared but tonight she could think of nothing else. Of the girls that would be throwing themselves in his direction. Attractive, curvy girls who were more than capable of creating that same stir in his body that she'd inexplicably managed to rouse.

As she bathed, she looked at her own body. Skinny and boyish. She wrapped a towel around her and used the edge of it to clear the steam from the mirror.

The face that frowned back at her was not a pretty one, but it wasn't as ugly as she'd perceived it. A plain but acceptable face. Her eyes were deeply set and a little too close together, but it did give her an aura of intensity. She quite liked it. Her nose was straight and sharp, adding a touch of harshness and a hint of 'don't mess with me" and her lips, although thin, were wide and inviting. Suddenly she smiled at that image and as she did so, her wide smile lit up that face.

She was not the pretty one, but she was the interesting one. She could see, for the first time, exactly what her father saw.

She was a handsome girl.

She got into bed and set about the weekend's homework.

She was still working when Brenda crashed into the bedroom and flopped face down on the bed.

"A good night then?" She asked with a smile.

"Carol's dad bought us both two brandy and Babychams!" she slurred as she tried to pull the blanket over her fully dressed body.

"Did you see Brian and Frank at the youth club?"

"Yeah. They were playing pool in the other room though. They didn't come into the dance room …oh! I'm going to be sick."

"Did they go to the club after?"

She heard Brenda wretch and the puke hit the bowl.

"Brenda?"

She heard another wretch and less puke.

The chain flushed and Brenda appeared, green and sweating at the bedroom door.

She smiled a silly grin. Her lipstick smeared to her ear where she'd attempted to wipe her mouth. Mascara pooling under her watering eyes and several strands of golden hair, now straightened and dulled by puke, plastered across her cheek.

"No. He didn't go with us. He went straight home. That mate of his with the yellow headed boils joked about him having a new girlfriend so it looks like you've missed the boat Mealy! You need to tart yourself up a bit!"

As Brenda ran back to the bathroom to deliver another heave of vomit into the bowl, Amelia put down her finished homework and pulled the sheet over her head with an excited and satisfied grin.

Chapter 7

Amelia and Frank had embarked on a unique journey together. Unique and complicated.

What started out as a joint venture of discovery had suddenly been infused with romance and its associated emotions. The relationship was far from a level playing field as Amelia strived for complete immersion while Frank teetered around the edge of it with his secrets and fear of discovery.

There was however, a new and supportive bond between them since the emotional moment of Frank confiding about the death of his sister. An undeniable compassion had grown between them. The teasing and smart remarks had evaporated in the warmth of an affectionate and committed alliance.

Frank knew that if it wasn't for his own trepidation there was no doubt that they would have made exceptional progress because, despite his own reluctance, the connection between them was still gathering momentum.

Amelia was desperate to throw caution to the wind, but her lack of self-esteem combined with her perception that Frank was holding back was causing her to falter.

Brian had become the third amigo. His presence often resented, often welcomed, alternatively by one or the other of the lovebirds depending on their state of mind as they swayed back and forth between the desire for privacy or company.

Such was the relationship between them. A seesaw of contradiction which tipped back and forth between hunger for the unknown and the fear it carried.

But despite this divide, there was no denying the fact that a great love was growing between them.

Mostly they met up with great anticipation and excitement at the prospect of reinforcing and developing their discovery but there were also times when they met silently, walked to the spot without speaking and lay down in the clearing together with only the outreached hands to acknowledge each other's presence.

It was on one such silent encounter that everything changed. Amelia felt his hand in hers and closed her eyes to appreciate the warmth of it. Today her hand almost tingled at his touch, causing her to hold it a little more tightly. She opened her eyes momentarily to gaze up into the grey lifeless sky and then closed them again to focus on Frank. The vast unknown above them had nothing to offer today.

She felt weightless, almost floating on unusually warm air. The sensation that she was being turned caused her stomach to surge as though left behind on a roller coaster ride. She was no longer on her back put upright. Upright and standing. Her eyes were still closed but she could feel that her feet were bare and cold. She wriggled her toes into the damp sand beneath her and listened to the waves. In the distance, gulls were squawking, and the sun was warming her face.

Slowly she opened her eyes without fear. The experience was too intoxicating and gentle to incite any fear as she peered along the golden beach towards a small group of people crouching over a blanket.

She knew these people and her hand was now waving in their direction as they continued to pack up their belongings. Shaking the sand from the blanket and stuffing everything into two large bags.

She closed her eyes for a moment against the sun's glare and when she opened them again she was looking at rows of tiny houses. Her feet were still damp but now inside gritty brown shoes.

Children chattered around her. Children she couldn't see but who were excited by the tiny people and tiny houses of what seemed to be a scaled model village.

"Get a move on or we'll never get round it all!" A familiar voice called to her. She liked the voice and new it well. It was her mother's voice!

She held her breath and kept her eyes fixed on the miniature bridge under which a small trickle of water ran.

"Did you hear me?" The voice called again, "Come on Grahame, get a move on!"

"What?" She blurted abruptly.

Suddenly she felt the grip tighten on her hand and someone gently tapping her face.

"Amelia?"

She opened her eyes to see Frank's face only inches from hers.

"Are you alright?"

"I don't know. I think so. I don't know."

"What happened? Did you fall asleep?"

"I don't think so."

"So?"

"I thought I was on the beach somewhere and then at a model village."

Frank grinned.

"What is it?" She frowned. Suddenly irritated by his smugness.

"My God Amelia. This is incredible!"

"What is! Spit it out!"

"I was remembering a day from years ago and you saw it. You did, didn't you?"

Amelia felt the blood drain from her face. Sharing feelings silently was one thing but this? This was frightening.

"We have to stop this, Frank. It's beyond weird now! You just recalled a memory."

"Yes, what's wrong with that?"

"What's wrong with it, is that I was bloody there! I mean I was there! Not thinking of it but actually standing in a fuckin model village with a stupid little bridge and wooden kids paddling in it!"

"You did see it!"

"Yes I did and I'm going home now. We're not doing this anymore!"

Frank caught her by the hand and pulled her towards him.

"Amelia. You didn't go anywhere. You just felt my memory. That day was probably the happiest day of my life, so I recalled every little detail of it. That's why it looked real to you."

He felt her relax a little.

"That was the only day I went to the seaside in my entire childhood. We lived in the middle of London and we didn't have a car but that year we rented a caravan in Devon. It was amazing!"

"It scared me Frank."

"I'm sure it was a bit of a fright but it wasn't real."

He could feel her shaking.

"I don't think I was just tuning in to you Frank. It was more than that."

He pulled her close again to let her know he was listening.

"I heard a woman call and it was my mother's voice."

"Are you sure?"

"I recognised it as my mother's voice and there's only two reasons that could be. The first is that my own mother visited me tonight or the other is that I recognised it as my mother because..."

"Because what?"

"Because I'd *become* you!"

"You don't believe that?" He laughed.

"It's a very special feeling, hearing your mother call you. I should know because I haven't heard it for many years but what I heard today? Well, that was it. I think she was your mother, but I was you! Except she called me Grahame!"

Frank's heartbeat quickened.

"Sometimes things get a bit muddled I suppose but you got most of it right!" He tried to sound reassuring "It's not so scary when you think about it. I mean, I was just sharing a memory, that's all. Please don't give up on this. You must see how special we are? How special this thing between us is?"

"Of course I do and tomorrow I might get it all in perspective but for now I just want to go home and feel safe."

"Yes. Ok I get it. Come on."

He pulled her to her feet and wondered if he'd spoiled everything by trying to push the boundaries. He needed to ease off a bit and give her time to recover but he'd never reached this point before. Not even with his sister, and what had just happened had ignited a new flame inside him. This was incredible and he knew, without doubt that this was the woman he wanted to spend his life with.

He couldn't lose Amelia and he couldn't hold back anymore. He was considering telling her everything.

Any doubts he had about trusting her had fallen away. This thing between them was not just special, but unique. He knew it and he knew that she did too, and now it was on its own trajectory and the thrill of it had him in its grip.

He was falling in love with her. With her remarkable intelligence, her outspoken manner, her sensitivity and her kindness but, above all, her ability to enter his mind and, in time, for him to enter hers.

One day, he was sure, he would be able to give her the freedom of his every thought.

"What are you thinking?" He asked as she walked in silence.

"You tell me!" she snapped sarcastically, "you're the one in charge of this supernatural shit!"

"It's not supernatural!" He laughed. "We were probably just born before our time."

"You think we're freaks of evolution now!" She scoffed.

"Yes, if you want to put it that way. Scientists have proved that telepathy is possible. You do know that don't you?"

"No, I didn't."

"Well, they have. There's nothing scary about this Amelia, we are just communicating in the way everyone probably will in a hundred years' time."

"You are so full of shit, Frank Porter."

"It's the truth. How do you think pictures fly through the air and land up in your tv? It's all part of the same thing. Air waves carrying pictures, voices, and ideas through the air. The only difference is that the human brain hasn't adapted yet to be able to trigger that process but believe me, it will!"

"So, you're saying that we are more science fiction than spooks?"

"Not science fiction. Just science. One day we won't need to be standing at the end of a wire in a phone box or a draughty hallway. You'll see!"

"But I won't see will I? A hundred years from now we'll both be dead so you can never say 'I told you so' can you?"

He laughed out loud and gave her a shove.

"Oh, I'll say it! I'll shout it across from my cloud to yours when we are sat playing our harps."

She giggled and then frowned.

"That's a weird thought though, isn't it?" Her tone became mellow. "Does it frighten you? Being dead, I mean."

"Of course, it frightens me. The harp looks like an impossible instrument to master!" He laughed again and she grinned.

He felt the relief. He'd managed to lighten the mood.

As they kissed goodbye, Amelia's trepidation had already started to subside. As often happens, a once vivid horror starts to fade and with it, fades the terror it incited.

Within days, she was ready to explore again but with a more wary and tentative agenda.

Frank had learned his lesson and pulled the mind-games back a notch. At the same time he pushed the romance up a notch and the result was delightful.

He began to realise that his hunger for the unknown need not be satisfied in an uncontrolled frenzy but could be taken at a pace contusive with a long-term relationship.

This connection was something they could spend a lifetime exploring if fate was to allow them to make a life together.

Suddenly Frank was making plans and visualising his future with Amelia by his side and children who would go to the beach whenever they wanted to.

As soon as she reached sixteen, he intended to propose!

They had already become inseparable, and Amelia slowly began to embrace her femininity aided by the discovery of her mother's old Avon box.

In those weeks of consumption with one another, Amelia had taken her eye of the ball without even noticing. She'd been pre-occupied with her forthcoming sixteenth birthday which rendered a physical relationship with a boy legal. Not that she was a prude but Frank, who was already sixteen, had been worried about the committal of such a crime.

They'd talked about it and agreed to wait.

She had become so pre-occupied as the days counted down that she had failed to notice Sheila's frequent absences. She was going out more in the evenings and staying out much later when she did go out.

Only when she arrived home from school one Friday night, still glowing with the memory of Frank's parting kiss to find Sheila pacing the kitchen and Brenda already seated at the table, did she suspect something was wrong.

"Sit down Amelia, I need to talk to you both."

"Where's dad?" Sheila could hear the panic in Amelia's voice.

"Your dad is fine. He's gone for a drink at the club for an hour."

"Dad? At the club! He never goes to the club!"

Sheila's face drained of colour. She stopped pacing and sat at the table with Brenda.

"Please sit down for a while."

"I'd rather stand, if you don't mind." Amelia said curtly.

She didn't want to sit down because she didn't want to hear whatever was coming. She could sense it was something bad and standing seemed the best way to fight it. To circumvent whatever was about to descend.

"Alright." Sheila sighed, instantly recognising Amelia's tack.

"The thing is girls, that I've met someone."

"Someone?" Brenda frowned.

"A man. I've met a man and I've been seeing him for a while."

"Does dad know? Is that why he's gone to the club?" Amelia snapped. "Have you broken his heart?"

Amelia knew she was being unfair even before her words fell but she didn't want this. None of it! Sheila was their mum now and she couldn't just meet another man! It wasn't right! It wasn't fair!

"I've not broken your dad's heart Amelia." She said softly. "Your father's heart was already broken, you know that."

"But you've broken it again!"

"Oh Amelia, darling," Sheila reached for her hand. but she pulled it back out of reach.

"Come on, Mealy." Brenda comforted. "Sheila has looked after us, all of us, for years. We can't expect her to sacrifice her whole life just because we want looking after. She's right. There's no room in dad's heart for her as a wife. She deserves to have someone to love her. We all deserve that."

Amelia stood silently. Purple faced with fists clenched for several seconds.

"Look how you feel about Frank Mealy! Would you give him up to look after the kids of some other guy who's never going to love you!"

Amelia didn't speak.

She looked from one to the other. The two faces of reason but to her they were the two faces of conspiracy. Of treachery and betrayal. Not just of her father, but of the whole family and of her mother who had supposedly sent her to look after them.

She ran out of the room into the hallway and took the stairs two at a time as she raced to the sanctuary of their bedroom where she threw herself on the bed and sobbed.

Only when the tears would no longer flow, when her chest ached from heaving and her eyes were puffed and sore did she quieten and try to think.

Downstairs, she could hear voices talking quietly. Her father's voice was among them and even though she couldn't make out the words, he seemed calm, causing a new wave of anger to crash over her! This time the anger was toward herself!

Downstairs, three people were discussing a situation, sensibly, compassionately rationally. Three adults, including her little sister! She, however, was having a tantrum like a five-year-old!

She went into the bathroom and splashed cold water onto her face to sooth her puffy eyes.

It wasn't Sheila's fault any more than it was her dad's. She loved him but he couldn't love her back and that was the measure of it.

As she stood staring in the mirror at her infantile self, there was a gentle tapping on the bathroom door.

She opened it and fell into Sheila's arms.

"I'm so sorry Amelia. I wish things were different.

"I know you do. You deserve this. I know that."

She felt Sheila's familiar hands cradle her head and turn her face towards her.

"Will we still see you?" Amelia blubbed.

"Oh love! I'm not going anywhere until after Christmas and I'm literally going to be living two streets away, You'll see me all the time."

Amelia sighed her relief and nodded.

"It's your birthday in a few days, so let's think about that shall we?"

Amelia smiled for a second and then frowned.

"Can I ask you something?"

"Anything."

"How are you going to live with this man when you love my dad. I know you do. I can see it."

Sheila pulled her close again to hide the emotion on her face as she tried to find a way to reply.

"I was alone before I came here Amelia and it wasn't nice but your father and you girls have filled my life with so much joy but soon you will be getting lives of your own. Getting married and moving out. My job here is done and I can't see a future for me living here alone with your dad, can you?"

"I suppose not." She sniffed. "But you do love him?"

"Yes, I do. With all my heart but that's never going to change his heart and I don't ever want to disrespect the memory of your mum. How could I?"

She felt Amelia tighten her embrace in appreciation.

"So, what about this other man then?"

"He loves me. He loves me like I love your dad and I do like him."

"And that's enough?"

"You're still very young love, and sooner or later you'll realise that happiness comes at a price. Sometimes a sacrifice but mostly, a compromise. I've learned that its far better to like someone who loves you than to love someone who like you. Do you understand that?"

Not only did Amelia understand it but she committed it to memory. Embracing the wisdom of it and recognising it as the recipe for a drama-free, pain-free marriage.

"Isn't it still better to love someone who loves you back though?"

Sheila raised her eyebrows.

"Are you talking about the boy you can't seem to be separated from?"

"You know about Frank?"

"Of course I know. I have eyes and ears!"

She pushed Amelia back a little to look at her face before continuing.

"Finding a love like that is rarer than people would have you believe. Lots of people think they have it but when you really have it, you're in no doubt."

"I have it." Amelia grinned. "Frank and I have something so special. I can't imagine it ever fading away. It just gets stronger and stronger. You might not believe me but we can read each other's thoughts sometimes."

"Oh, I believe you." Sheila said thoughtfully. "It happens more often than folk realise."

Amelia just nodded. Suddenly she had no desire to invite Sheila into her private world with Frank. She'd spoken as if the connection between them was normal and wanted to leave it there.

She could have told Sheila how they'd taken to saying goodnight in houses that were half a mile apart. That she'd started to feel his presence as he approached her house. That she could feel his love reach out to her in the dead of night and warm her to the core.

This connection, this love was terrifying in its manifestation, mesmerising in its beauty and was relentlessly thrilling her beyond all reason.

She forced a smile and returned to the kitchen to eat with Brenda who squeezed her hand as though affirming that they would be alright without Sheila.

As she ate, she began to accept that things do change in life and Sheila was entitled to embark on a new adventure. Just like her own new adventure in the arms of Frank, but that didn't quieten the dread of impending loss that was gripping her chest or the raging fear of losing yet another mother.

Chapter 8

By Saturday morning, she was pacing as she waited for the hands of the clock to crawl round that wretched face. Hands that would finally grant her permission to leave the house and meet up with Frank without resulting in a tortuous wait in the freezing fog at the edge of the wood.

Brenda was still sleeping even though it was past ten but that wasn't unusual. She would often rise around lunchtime and then head off into town with friends after spending at least an hour on hair, makeup and customising her outfit with pins, belts, scarves and whatever else might transform the image into a three ring circus.

Amelia had no such appetite for any of that. Her energy and focus feasted on deeper entities. Those far removed from the world of fashion or transient friendships but today she had found herself longing for validation and security on a more physical level.

Suddenly, in the wake of Sheila's announcement and the ensuing breakdown of her contented family life, she craved to be wanted, valued and desired in a more tangible way.

The mental connection, the fond words and spoken promises no longer satisfied her need to certainty. She needed more and she needed it right now.

She arrived a few minutes early and stood alone in the icy wind on that winter morning with only one aim in mind. She wanted to claim Frank as her own and she intended to do that in the only way men seemed to understand. Sex.

She shifted her weight from foot to foot to try to keep the circulation moving in her toes which were precariously stuffed into Brenda's high heels. Her hands were stuffed in her coat pockets, partly for warmth but mostly to enable her to prevent the bottom half from blowing open and revealing the mini skirt and seamed stockings. The latter of which she had sneaked from Sheila's drawer the previous night. Her hair, washed, conditioned, and curled was now gusting around her face like a frenzied flag – whipping her painted eyes, tangling itself in knots and repeatedly sticking itself to her lip gloss.

She checked her watch again. He was late. She tried to stay positive. If she allowed her annoyance to spoil the mood then everything had been for nothing. This was her chance to gain some peace of mind. Her chance to gain some commitment. To feel safe.

Eventually she spotted him as he rounded the corner, battling against the wind.

"I didn't expect you to turn up!" He called into the gusts that snatched away his words instantly. "It's freezing. We can't go in there today."

She knew he was right, but her disappointment was as visible as his look of disbelief that she'd worn high heels.

"Perhaps we should leave it for today?" He smiled comfortingly but instantly detecting she was feeling rejected.

He checked his pockets. He didn't have enough for the café.

"Look. I've got an idea. Brian is working the petrol pump this morning at his dad's garage. There's a bit of an office with a fire and a couple of chairs. We could go round there for a chat or something?"

It wasn't what she had in mind at all but he had a point about the wood. What girl would want to lose her virginity in freezing mud with teeth chattering?

She nodded and took his hand.

"What the hell have you got on your feet!" He laughed as she started to totter alongside him.

She didn't reply. There were no words to vindicate any of her stupidity that morning.

Eventually they arrived at the garage where they entered the small office without knocking. Brian was sitting on a moth-eaten chair stuffing a Mars bar into his mouth.

"Can we get warm for a bit, mate?"

Frank didn't wait for a reply before pulling the other chair close to the small electric fire and nodding for Amelia to sit down.

"There's a kettle over there and a bottle of milk somewhere if you want a cuppa." Brain smiled, obviously excited to have company for a change.

Amelia sat down and removed a shoe to rub her foot in the warmth of the glowing coil.

"Looks like you've got a customer." Frank added as a car pulled onto the forecourt.

"Bloody hell! Why can't people stay at home when it's like this!" Brian cursed as he stuffed the last third of the Mars bar into his mouth and headed for the door.

Amelia was still rubbing her foot when she noticed Frank staring.

Her coat had dropped open and her stocking tops were suddenly on display. She quickly put her foot back down and pulled the coat shut before speaking.

"A cuppa would be nice, don't you think?"

"An explanation would be nicer." He replied with his eyes still fixed in the direction of the revelation.

"It's nothing," she babbled, "I just misread the weather today."

"I think you misread quite a lot of things today!" He sneered. "You look like you're on the game!"

She jumped up and headed for the door but he hurled himself in her path.

"Look. I'm sorry. I didn't mean that but what's going on here?"

"I just wanted to surprise you." She stammered.

"Well, you've shocked the fuckin' hell out of me so I think you can consider that box ticked!"

"I thought we could…you know. It's my birthday on Monday."

"You're bloody insane! I'm not going to be bulldozed into freezing my nuts off in that fuckin' swamp with thistles on my bollocks and nettles up my arse just because it's your birthday!"

"I know." She sighed. "I don't know what I was thinking. Let's just forget it. I'd rather walk back on my own."

"Sit back down woman." He smiled. "I'm just saying that it's not the most romantic idea I've heard of, but that doesn't mean it's not the most romantic thing anyone's ever done for me."

She was still standing when Brian burst back in rubbing his hands.

"What's up with you two? Do you want a cuppa then?"

"Yes we'd love one wouldn't we Amelia?"

She shrugged and sat back down while Brian chattered about his twenty pence tip and broken tyre inflator as Frank sat silently in the other chair.

She glanced over and caught him looking at her. He grinned. She grinned.

"I mean, what use is twenty fuckin, pence? Did I miss anything?" Brian called from the sink area.

Instantly there was a blare of spontaneous combined laughter.

"I know." Brian smiled. "I should be on stage. I'm a funny guy, me."

The laughter roared again, causing Brian to beam at the two of them.

Another car drew up and as Brian disappeared again, so did the laughter.

"I'm sorry. It was a nice thought." Frank said with sincerity, "and when I think about the amount of pain you went through. I mean with those heels…" his voice was wavering again, "and that bloody draughty coat!" He couldn't finish.

She was laughing uncontrollably. Wiping the tears from her face and the snot from her nose.

"Stop it!" She pleaded, "I can't take any more."

The door opened and Brian ambled back inside.

"This is such fun!" He giggled. "I'll make the tea."

The three of them finally managed a degree of composure and drank the tea before Brian got another customer.

"We've got a capri in for service in the garage," he called on his way out, "Go take a look if you like. Twin exhausts and cams. It's the dog's bollocks!"

Frank looked at Amelia in a way he never had before. She didn't recognise or understand it, but it gave her a shiver down her spine.

The power of that look caused her to avert her eyes without knowing why. Something felt dangerous. Challenging. Resolute. Inevitable.

Gently she took the hand that was now dangling before her and followed where it led.

Through the garage door, round a dirty pit, and over to a gold coloured Capri. He ran his hand along the shining body and tried the handle of the passenger door. It opened. Without a word she slid into the car, he closed it, walked round to the driver's side and slid in beside her.

He gave her that look again but this time she held his eyes with hers and closed her door. Without breaking eye contact he reached behind him and quietly clicked shut the door on the world outside.

Chapter 9

The total time they spent in that car didn't amount to more than fifteen minutes, but Amelia would one day, consider it to be the most important time of her entire life.

Every single second was to be indelibly etched into her soul, allowing her to recall every touch, every kiss and every breath of it.

She would remember the first gentle kiss and the way her hand trembled in his. The way she held her breath as he unbuttoned her blouse and the bodily shaking which no longer seemed to be attributed to the cold.

She remembered hoping that he knew how all this was supposed to work because she had no idea but the worry of that lasted only a few seconds. Seconds in which he'd allowed his hand to rest lazily between her knees as he licked her naked breasts. Suddenly, the questions and worries had left her mind. Pushed aside by a burning desire to be touched and touched everywhere. As his hand started to move up her skirt she was silently praying for him not to stop. Praying that they wouldn't be interrupted. Praying for him to give her the pleasure she was anticipating. Instinct had taken over and she knew that there were no rules to be obeyed and no recipe to be followed.

She remembered hearing his zip go down and the fever she was already in the grip of was suddenly raging. She wanted this more than she'd wanted anything before and her hand reached down without any hesitation as she curled her fingers around the physical proof of his desire for her.

There, on the grubby seats of a second-hand car they created something truly wonderful. She felt herself melt into him, silently allowing herself to be absorbed by him until she seemed to no longer exist as a separate person. They were one person because he was inside her physically, mentally and spiritually and in those moments momentous things happened.

As he thrust into her, the waves of pleasure ripped through her entire body, she heard the silent promises she longed to hear, felt the pledge of his heart as it pounded with hers, felt the touch of his soul and the burning of being branded as his. Forever.

This is the way she would remember those fifteen minutes. Forever.

As he grunted and collapsed into the footwell she was too disorientated to even notice. Not until her heartbeat had started to quieten, did she recover her faculties enough to return to her surroundings.

The grappling for clothes, wiping of brows, straightening of hair and recovery of shoes happened in a daze and before her mind had caught up, she was being pulled back towards the small office by his clammy hand as he smiled and tugged her close.

"I love you." He whispered as he opened the door to find Brian seated and staring out onto the forecourt.

"It's a great Capri." Frank said confidently but Frank offered a half smile and continued to stare out of the window.

"Your tea's cold." He said curtly.

"Yeah, sorry about that."

Amelia could see that Brian was not happy and she had some sympathy for him. He'd been so excited that a couple of friends had dropped in and now he was probably feeling used.

She tried to think of something to mitigate their behaviour but there was nothing to be said. Brian was right and the best thing to do now was to try to give him some attention.

"Do you work for your dad every Saturday then?"

Brian looked at her suspiciously before replying.

"Not always. It's not like I'm planning to be a grease monkey. I've got bigger plans…and cleaner ones."

"Oh! What is it you want to be then?" She smiled as she studied the pitiful face before her. A face no longer jovial or beaming but deflated and sad. A thin, spotty, sickly face that was unlikely to ever attract a girl.

"I'm going to study Astro physics." He announced proudly. "Then I'm moving to the states. I'm going to work for NASA."

"Well," Frank smiled, "No-one can say it's not rocket science!"

She gave Frank a disapproving dig in the ribs and his smile vanished.

"That's very ambitious Brian but I've got a feeling you're determined enough to make it happen."

"Thank you."

As she looked at Brian's face she noticed his eyes were watering and she felt instantly ashamed.

She placed her hand over his and gave it a squeeze, but his eyes were now on her laddered stockings.

"We'll see you on Monday then." Frank called as he tugged her towards the door.

"Monday, yeah." Brian nodded as they left.

"I feel terrible Frank. We really upset him today."

"No! You upset him!" Frank laughed.

"Me? What have I done?"

"You've just made love to another boy right under the nose of the boy who's idolised you for years!"

"Don't be ridiculous!"

"It's true!"

"He told you that?"

"He didn't have to. I didn't know until today but it's written all over his face!"

As she pulled her coat together and stumbled along beside Frank she started to recall small incidents of kindness from Brian. Things she'd put down to pity for the unpopular girl but now she was wondering if she'd just inadvertently broken the boy's heart.

"Now I feel even worse."

"We'll make it up to him. I don't want you feeling bad. Not today."

She immediately realised what he meant.

"Oh no! How could I feel bad today. I didn't mean…"

He silenced her with a kiss.

"Good. Because this is just the beginning. I hope you know that."

"Yes, I think I do." She replied as she put her hand up to his face to prevent him from pulling out of the kiss. "I love you too."

"Well that's alright then," he grinned, "because I intend to spend many years basking in that love and many more years bringing up our children in the sheer joy of it."

"Children?" She blurted, "I think you're getting a bit ahead of yourself!"

"Ah yeah. The proposal's supposed to come first I suppose. I'll work on that first."

As they got to the end of street where they would go separate ways he turned her to face him again.

"Happy birthday for tomorrow."

"Thank you. I'm afraid I won't be able to see you as my dad is taking us all out for the day. Think it will be the pictures and then the Wimpey bar but at least it'll be warm."

"It's fine." He replied. "I got you this."

He pulled a small box from his pocket.

"Don't get excited. I stole the box from my mum's drawer and it wasn't expensive but it's the thought that counts, isn't it?"

She took the box and opened it.

"Its not solid gold, its plated and that's not a diamond by the way." He added quickly as she opened the lid and looked down on a dainty gold band with a sparkly clear gem.

"It's beautiful, and at least it doesn't have an opening at the back so you can bend it to fit!"

"Only the best for my girl."

She took the ring and placed it on her middle finger.

He frowned.

"Wrong finger?"

"Wrong ring." He corrected. "It's a promise of intent until I can afford the right ring for the right finger."

"I have never loved anything more and I probably never will." She smiled as the tears started to well up.

"Oh yes you will. You'll love me more. You'll see."

"You really think that we'll get married!"

"Oh, I'm certain of it," Frank smiled as he pulled her towards him, "and don't ever forget it."

"I won't." She said playfully.

Suddenly, she felt his body stiffen against her. He held her by the shoulders firmly and pushed her back to arm's length.

"I mean it Amelia," he said harshly, "no matter what happens, remember that this is real. This is it. Don't ever doubt that and don't ever, ever give up on us."

"I won't!" She laughed.

"Promise?"

"Promise."

That evening, as she arrived home, she felt different. Everything felt different. It was the moment her world had returned to colour.

She'd left that house a timid, insecure girl and returned as a confident young woman.

In the evening she went to bed before Brenda to give herself the privacy to concentrate on Frank without interruption. Immediately she could feel his presence. He must have been waiting for her - the connection was instantaneous tonight.

It wasn't as if she ever heard his voice but nor did she hear her own voice speaking the words that came into her head. The words had no narrator. No accent and no gender. Just words as voiceless as words written on a page yet equally as capable of painting a picture.

Sometimes she'd tried to compare these words that popped into her head to the ones that came from her own thoughts, but she could never quite separate one type from the other. Neither were spoken in her own voice as far as she could tell. She wondered if it was the same for everyone.

The words would often transmute into images, concepts, ideas and feelings and today she didn't care who was speaking or suggesting because today they purged her body with love. With plans of a future that was now written in the stars and couldn't be altered. She loved the words she was hearing. Loved the images she was seeing and the joy she was feeling. Her life was finally worth living again. Restored at last to the life before the fateful trip to town for the infamous shoes!

On the Sunday she opened her gifts. A new watch from her dad, a radio from Brenda and a makeup set from Sheila.

"Oh, and I have another surprise for both of you!" Tom beamed. "Take a look outside."

A small but smart-looking Austin sat outside their gate.

"You passed your test?" Brenda squealed.

"I did." He replied proudly.

Amelia hugged him and held down the ache in her heart. Her mother had dreamed of owning their own car one day. The longing for a family car is what started the Avon job.

But she wasn't going to allow anything to spoil this moment because her mother would be smiling down on them.

In the afternoon she sat through the Battle for the Planet of the Apes but could hardly concentrate on the plot. Her mind was reliving the afternoon before, causing her to keep glancing left and right to check that no-one had noticed her flushed cheeks. Twice she caught Sheila smiling in her direction.

She tried a couple of times to connect to Frank but the noise of the film and the distraction of her family made it all impossible.

At the Wimpey bar she had her usual sausage circle with chips and beans with a banana milk shake.

It had been the perfect day, the perfect birthday and the first one in which she had managed to push down the longing for her mother and allow herself to enjoy the company of the living again.

Christmas was almost upon them again but this year things would be different. They would make Sheila's last Christmas in the house a happy one. Probably the first really happy one since their mother had woken them on Christmas morning.

As her dad paid the waitress and wrapped his arms around each of them, she knew that they were going to be alright. Sheila will become a neighbour and a good friend after she leaves. Her dad will be looked after by herself and Brenda. They'll become stronger than ever as a family and when the time comes he'll become the adoring grandad to their children and father to their husbands.

It was the first time Amelia had ever considered that she might one day have a husband and children of her own.

As they walked back to the car she looked up at the sky and quietly whispered her love to her mum.

That night, as she lay in bed, she felt truly blessed. Blessed and exhausted. Within minutes of hitting the pillow she was sound asleep.

Chapter 10

The rattle of the alarm announced the arrival of Monday morning and Amelia's feet were on the bedside rug in an instant.

"Have you shit the bed or what!" Brenda called from the sanctuary of her bedspread face tent, forged to protect her eyes from the light that was about to be switched on.

"It's eight o'clock!" Amelia objected.

"It's still blinking dark and it's freezing. I think I'll pull a sicky today."

"Come on. I'll bring you a cuppa up if you're out of bed by the time I get back up."

"You're acting all weird Mealy Simpson. Have you finally been possessed by one of your ghouls?"

"You've got five minutes Brenda. Five minutes!"

"I'll come down if you get Sheila to put the fire on while we get ready."

Amelia was already on the stairs with her dressing gown wrapped around her and her slippers flapping. She could already feel the warmth from the living room. Sheila was already up and warming the room for them.

"I'm glad we're friends again Amelia." She blurted the moment the door was opened.

"I'm sorry I was such a brat." Amelia replied. "It's fine. You deserve some happiness and some freedom from this mad house."

Two cups of tea were already on the mantle with plates of toast on top. Sheila always did that to keep the toast warm over the heat of the cup but it always resulted in soggy toast.

Amelia took a slice and tore a chunk off with her teeth.

"You get yourself warm love. I'll take Brenda's up. Shall we sort out the Christmas decorations tonight?"

"Great idea but I'll take this up." She smiled as she pushed the door open with her elbow and disappeared with the tea and precariously balanced toast.

"Who are you and what have you done with my moody, miserable sister?" Brenda frowned from beneath the blankets.

"I'm just being nice!" Amelia protested, noticing how Brenda's golden loose curls bounced so beautifully as she sat up.

"You're always nice Mealy. It's the smile I'm not used to. It's a bit unsettling - and so is the brushed hair!"

Amelia plonked the cup and plate on the floor beside Brenda's bed and smiled.

"You're up to something our Mealy!" Brenda grinned "and I think it has something to do with that boy with the funny accent."

Amelia simply tapped her nose to confirm the secret and went downstairs to plait her hair. Today she was going to try a more sophisticated look with a single plait laying over one shoulder. Suddenly she felt the desire to be interesting and unpredictable.

Half an hour later, plait provocatively in place, tan tights under her school socks to give the illusion of a tan, skirt rolled at the waist to shorten it a couple of inches, she was on her way.

But the new confidence which had goaded her all morning into creating the new image was now deserting her. With each step she was starting to feel more and more stupid, but it was too late now. She was at the gate and people were already whispering.

She scanned the sea of heads in the hope of spotting Franks black shiny mane but people were moving too quickly and in too many directions.

"Wow! You look great!" Came a familiar voice from behind.

"Brian! Good morning. Have you seen Frank?"

Brian lolloped over and stood above her, stooping to listen.

"Can't say that I have but we come from different directions, so I never really see him 'til maths. You've both got chemistry this morning though so I expect he's already in there."

She smiled dismissively.

"I'll see you later then?" He grinned, giving her plait a playful flick with his long bony fingers before disappearing into the crowd.

She smoothed her plait back down irritably and made her way to chemistry knowing that Frank would have taken her seat at the back again. Partly to annoy her but mainly to playfully torment her with his mind games.

It had only been a day and a half since she'd seen him, but it was the first time they had set eyes on each other as lovers, and she felt strangely nervous.

As she walked the corridors, many fearful possibilities ran through her mind. What if he'd done it as a joke? As a challenge? "Bet you can't fuck the weird bird!" she imagined hordes of boys laughing as he accepted the bet.

She stopped on the corridor for a moment. She felt sick. She imagined the whole class waiting to applaud his success as she entered looking like she did.

She closed her eyes for a moment and tried to remember his touch, his kiss. Nothing felt comforting.

"You're going to be late Miss Simpson!" Her teacher warned as he had to push by her to take the class.

Tentatively her feet crawled along that corridor to meet her fate. To take what was coming. The punishment for being so stupid and deluded as to imagine that someone like Frank would find her worth his time.

Already she could hear the babbling inside the classroom. Babbling that would fall silent the moment she entered the room.

The bell rang.

She pushed open the door, stepped inside and closed her eyes but the babbling continued. No-one had reacted to her entrance. Slowly, she opened her eyes to find that her appearance hadn't even been noticed.

She breathed a sigh of relief but the moment was to be short-lived. At the back of the room, her chair was still empty, and Frank was nowhere to be seen.

She took her place and kept her eye on the door for his appearance. She barely concentrated on the class that morning, constantly watching out of the window or back to the door but Frank didn't appear.

She tried to convince herself that he was probably just sick, but she was already sensing that he wasn't. He was avoiding her. It was obvious.

She thought back to the night before and the evidence was building. She'd felt nothing from him. She'd been tired last night and fallen asleep quickly, but Frank could always rouse her. The truth was that he hadn't tried to. He'd had second thoughts after the weight of Saturday's events. The car, the outfit, the late-night exchanges of love and devotion. Of commitment and marriage. It had all been too much and now she'd scared him off completely.

In maths, she sought out Brian.

"He's probably just sick or something. He was full of cold when I saw him yesterday morning. Probably sitting around in cold cars!" He laughed.

"You saw him yesterday morning?"

"Yeah, he came over to my house to return some LP's he'd borrowed."

"Did he say anything?"

"Only that he felt like shit."

"I mean did he say anything about me?"

"No. Why would he? He's not the kiss and tell type."

She sat down and opened her maths books, feeling a lot better. If she wasn't careful she was going to turn into one of those insecure, accusing girlfriends who cling like a leech and suspect the worst at every turn.

She completed the equation and sat for a moment to try to connect with him. She closed her eyes and allowed herself to relax into that quiet place where Frank could find her. She breathed in and out several times as she searched to feel him but there was nothing. There was worse than nothing. Today it didn't feel like she was waiting in their quiet place for him to show up. Today it felt like the quiet place was locked. She couldn't get in! A new dread emerged. If Frank was nearby, he was blocking her out.

She kicked Brian's chair to get his attention.

"Can you show me where Frank lives? You've been there?" She whispered.

"Only once. To lend him the records. I guess I could show you tonight."

"No! At lunchtime. I want to go after this lesson."

He laughed, causing the teacher to frown at them.

"He's going to think you're a nut job!" He whispered.

Brian was right. She needed to keep her paranoia in check until the end of the day.

"Ok. After school then." She whispered back before resigning herself to five more hours of torture.

Eventually the clock crawled its way to four o'clock, the bell rang, and her incarceration was over.

She raced out of the Geology room and headed straight over to the physics lab to catch Brian in case he'd forgotten their plan.

She stood at the classroom door and watched Brian talking to an equally geeky looking boy who carried a brief case and whose hair seemed to have been brill-creamed to his head.

She shuffled impatiently as Brian chatted nonchalantly with his satchel hanging from his shoulder and hands casually in pockets.

She coughed and he turned.

"Sorry mate. Looks like the wife's getting impatient." He laughed.

Amelia was even more irritated, but she needed Brian too much to risk any retribution. This lollopy, pockmarked, wiry-haired idiot was suddenly her knight in armour. She needed him to point out the damn house and quieten the noise in her over-active brain, to put her fears to rest and to deliver her back to her former state of unconditional happiness.

She simply nodded as he approached, and they walked together in silence as he guided her through the streets and finally down a small ginnel leading to a circle of houses around a small grassy roundabout.

It's that one." He pointed to a semi-detached council house on their right.

"Come on then. Let's go and see if he's in bed with the flu."

She walked through the open metal gate, up to the front door and knocked.

They stood for a while before knocking again and then Brian walked away to peer through the window.

"Bloody hell! The place is deserted!" He called.

Amelia ran to his side and peered in beside him.

The room was totally empty, only the curtains remained.

She ran from window to window and every room was as empty as the next.

"Are you sure this is the right house?"

"Yes. It's the right house. I remember those God-awful curtains and the smashed bird table. It's the right house."

"It doesn't make any sense. How was he when you saw him yesterday morning?"

"He seemed fine. I took the records and asked him in but he said he had to get back so I said I'd see him tomorrow and that was it."

"What did he say when you said that?"

"Nothing. He just raised his hand as he was walking away. Seemed like an acknowledgment but now I'm wondering."

"If it was a goodbye."

"Yep."

"I can't believe he'd leave without saying a word to me!"

Brian put his hand on her shoulder, and she immediately shrugged it off.

"You think he's played me. Don't you?"

"I really don't know but I just think that you shouldn't get your hopes up."

She glared at him accusingly.

"I'm just saying that you live literally two minutes away. He must have known he was moving out and if he intended talking to you about it, he could have. I mean, he found the time to return my records."

"But I was out most of yesterday. Maybe he called in?"

"I think he would have pushed a note through your door, don't you?"

"Are you saying that he knew about this all along? That he thought he'd just have a bit of fun with the desperate girl before he disappeared into the sunset!"

"Boys can be stupid. Stupid, selfish and careless. I've seen worse than this from lads as good-looking and sweet-talking as Frank."

She stood for a moment in the void of uncertainty. Trying desperately to reconcile the Frank who had loved her from the Frank being described by Brian. Questioning her own judgment and how clouded it might be by what she longed to be true. Then she looked at Frank and wondered if his sweet nature had suddenly been tainted by the prospect of opportunity. Frank, the boy with a face only a mother could love. It was easy to imagine how much he would relish the downfall of a boy like Frank.

Just as she felt like slapping Brian in the face, he spoke again.

"Let's not judge him too harshly Amelia. I liked Frank and he seemed genuine. Just give him a bit of time to sort himself out. I'm sure he'll be in touch soon."

She heaved a sigh of relief and put her arm through his.

"Will you walk me home? I don't want too much thinking time."

He rubbed her hand comfortingly and walked beside her.

"Of course, I will. I'm a pretty good distraction you know!" He smiled as he turned to face her."

He heard the bang before she noticed his disappearance. Brian had hit the lamppost with the side of his face and bounced backwards onto the pavement.

"You can say that again!" She shrieked. "Are you alright?"

Brian was already scrambling back to his feet reminding her of a new-born giraffe scrambling to its feet, as arms and legs writhing in all directions to restore him to the upright position.

She watched him with some concern for a few seconds as he felt at the lump on his cheekbone. She tried to hold her breath to prevent the upsurge of laughter from escaping but just couldn't hold it in.

Her boom of uncontrolled hilarity triggered an identical reaction on his swollen face and for the next half mile they squealed and crumpled along, tears streaming down faces, barely able to take a breath until, physically exhausted, there was silence.

He looked over at her and she at him.

Their faces both cracked again at the same time, so they waved their goodbye without trying to speak again.

Amelia ran straight to the toilet before finally regaining her composure. She sat on her bed and realised that she hadn't laughed like that since before her mother died and it had happened at the most unlikely moment. She thought of Brian again and smiled.

That evening, Amelia's focus returned to Frank.

She didn't mention his absence to Brenda for fear of showing too much interest in the boy that was meant to be nothing more than a fellow dabbler in the art of mind-reading.

She'd purposely kept their remarkable progress to herself. Partly because she liked the shared secret and partly because she knew Brenda would be goading her to prove it. Brenda would never grasp the quiet concentration it required and would expect a scheduled performance!

It was also a sacred connection she had no desire to share.

She lay in bed and waited for Brenda's breathing to change to the depth of a restful sleeper before she felt able to search for Frank without interruption.

She quickly detected the essence of him but trying to connect felt like hurling herself at an iron door. She recalled Frank's description of making his mind tight, like a clenched fist and that's exactly how this felt.

Frank was still within reach, but he was blocking her!

The message felt clear. She had been enjoyed once and tossed aside like a spent firework.

The anger and pain rose inside her until she felt she was about to explode. But as she swallowed those bitter tears, she could feel the blame shifting from Frank to herself. To her stupidity for ever believing a boy like Frank would want a girlfriend like her. The ugly one!

In that moment of deep despair, when most girls would turn to their mother, Amelia naturally turned to Sheila.

Adorned in her layers of cheesecloth and lace, surrounded by joss sticks, Sheila listened intently, as Amelia's tale of heartbreak and misery unfolded.

When the tears prevented Amelia from further speculation, Sheila put an arm around her and spoke quietly.

"Don't judge this boy too harshly just yet, love." She whispered. "Sometimes fate deals people a card that they didn't see coming and forces them to make decisions they didn't want to make."

"You think he's coming back?"

"I didn't say that. I'm just saying that if this love felt real to you at the time then I'm sure it was. Even if you have to let it go then don't let the circumstances degrade it. Believe me, I know exactly how this feels."

"No you don't. How could you?"

Sheila smiled. It was a melancholy smile. The kind of sad smile of a person remembering a much loved, but long passed dog. A smile full of fondness with a heavy dose of longing.

Amelia watched the smile linger for a few seconds and then dissolve.

"Were you in love once then?"

"Oh yes. I was in love. Head over heels in love."

"What happened?"

"It was all just bad timing love. He'd had a few dates with another girl from the village but one evening she stood him up and he bought me a drink."

Sheila's smile returned but this time it was a mischievous smile that lit up her eyes.

"We just chatted on those bar stools for what felt like five minutes until the landlord started to close up. To this day, I will never believe that we'd been sat there for hours. Hours with just the one drink! It still bewilders me today!"

"Did you see him again?"

"Oh yes. I saw him the next morning at seven before work! Then at lunchtime and again right after work! It was crazy. We were soaring!"

"What about his girlfriend?"

"Well, that's what you might call the curved ball. The ball I didn't see coming."

"What happened?"

"After four wonderful days of complete emersion in one another. Days of laughter and lovemaking, of plans and promises. After the best four days of my entire life, he decided that it was only fair to tie up that particular loose end and, on his return, my happiness ended."

"Oh no!" Amelia gasped with genuine horror. "He chose her?"

"It wasn't that simple. He discovered that the reason she'd stood him up was because she was throwing up. Pregnancy has a tendency to do that to a girl."

"She was pregnant?"

"Yep, and abortion was still illegal back then. There was really no decision to make."

"He married her?"

"He married her."

"She trapped him! She stole the man you loved!"

"I don't think she did it deliberately. She was a girl in a difficult situation and he had to do the right thing."

"How awful for you. So, you never fell in love again?"

"Nope. He was a tough act to follow but I've no regrets. I also did the right thing in standing aside. In letting him go without a scene. I wished him every happiness and kissed him goodbye. There's a lot of comfort in knowing that."

Amelia hugged Sheila's plum-scented neck and smiled.

"You make my problem seem small."

"Just remember it for what it was, and don't give up hope on what it might yet become. I doubt that he's got another girl pregnant, don't you?"

Amelia laughed.

"Yes. I'm sure he hasn't done that."

Sheila pushed her back by the shoulders and looked her in the eyes the way she always did to check she was alright.

"I'm glad I could help."

Amelia smiled but there was something in Sheila's eyes that caused her to feel uneasy. Something she couldn't get out of her mind as she tried to concentrate on her homework. Something that seemed to be growing stronger and stronger as she battled with it when she closed her eyes that night.

Quietly she tiptoed over the hall and tapped gently on Sheila's door before pushing it open.

Sheila sat up and squinted.

"Amelia?"

"Sheila?"

Amelia took a deep breath before speaking.

"Was the man you loved my father?"

For several seconds the world stood still.

The words that would break that silence could change everything.

Amelia waited for those words, but they never came.

The confirmation was delivered by the open arms that were now extending towards her. The arms offering her solace and comfort against the terrible truth of why Sheila had run away and stayed away for so many years, but Amelia couldn't bring herself to fall into them even though her whole body wanted nothing more.

This woman had sacrificed her own happiness to give them all a chance at finding some of their own. She'd left them a clear path to become a family, unhindered by temptation, split loyalties or guilt. Her own path, as a consequence, had been one of drowning out the screams of her heart with meditation, marijuana and casual sex. All under the sixties banner of 'free love'.

Amelia had been the cause of Sheila's loveless life. Her conception had been the accident that stole the man she loved.

She knew she owed Sheila an incredible debt. The sacrifices she'd made for their father had no bounds. Sacrifices she was still making, yet still, she couldn't bring herself to fall into the arms of her mother's rival.

She simply nodded her appreciation for the truth and gave a weak smile of alliance before leaving. This secret could not be spoken of again and, devastating as it was, she knew that Sheila was not to blame and nor was her father. They had both done the right thing. The moral thing. The result had been that somehow her father had managed to learn to love her mother and somehow both her and Brenda had never felt anything other than love in her home.

All the heartache seemed to have been borne by the woman who had selflessly stood aside and then miraculously stepped into the void when it counted. She'd given the later years of her life to bring up the children of the woman who'd stolen her former years.

There was a strange irony in it.

Amelia had no intention of letting that encounter in the car be the equivalent of Sheila's four days. She was not going to spend the rest of her life as a sad, heart-broken spinster wallowing in the dreams of what might have been.

The moment she got back into bed she tried to connect again with Frank.

Christmas was only a week away and she was tired of every Christmas being tainted with the excruciating pain and sadness associated with the absence of her mother.

This year she intended to meet it with renewed hope and happiness. Trying to locate Frank was her last-ditch effort to redeem the day.

Tonight, there was no iron door, no impenetrable clenched fist. Tonight, her mind was able to wander freely in all directions because there was nothing in the way of it.

It was a vastness of nothing – Frank was gone.

Chapter 11

That particular Christmas would be remembered as the 'Brenda's bollocking' Christmas.

As they sat silently at the dinner table after the painful morning of the dutiful unwrapping of gifts with lukewarm smiles of faked gratitude, she glowered around the table stabbing sprouts as though they were ferocious demons.

She could see that Sheila had made such an effort for her last Christmas with them but it seemed that everyone else was determined to make it a miserable affair.

Sheila sat in her usual place opposite Tom in a beautiful red and green silk blouse, her unruly hair gracefully coiled and lacquered into place over which she had playfully attached a party hat. Her eye shadow sparkled festively, and her lips shone with the apricot gloss she saved for special occasions.

In contrast, the remainder of her guests had merely swapped their pyjamas for casual everyday clothes. Brenda, at least, had combed her hair, cleaned her teeth, cleansed her face and added a spray of perfume.

Each sat quietly in their own void as they completed the task of transferring their food from plate to mouth.

Brenda was scanning the table again, feeling the rage within her again, and as soon as the last demon sprout had been assassinated, she rose from her seat with fork akimbo.

"What the fuck is wrong with you people!"

Three pairs of eyes were instantly upon her. Two pairs staring in disbelief, but Sheila's eyes danced with amusement. Brenda was the hope. The saviour this family needed.

She remained standing as she continued her onslaught.

"Are you hell-bent on making Sheila's last Christmas with us as miserable as possible! Look, I know we all have problems. Mealy's lost her study-buddy and you miss mum but look around this table for God's sake.

There are four people here who are still living, and these four people love each other. Isn't that worth celebrating?"

Amelia and Tom exchanged a glance as Brenda took a breath.

"Well, wallow in your misery if you want but Sheila deserves better than this. I don't blame you for wanting to leave Sheila. What's your boyfriend's name."

Sheila took a sip of her wine and then smiled at the grown-up face of the little girl she'd nurtured.

"It's Barry." She smiled.

"And where is he now? I mean, at this moment."

"He's at home eating a plate I took round for him while you were all getting changed."

"Did you hear that?" She asked but continued without waiting for confirmation. "Barry. The man who loves Sheila is sitting alone a couple of streets away, eating a warmed up dinner just so that we can sit here as a family one last time! It's pathetic. Sheila, go and fetch him."

Brenda watched her father physically flinch.

"Thank you Brenda." She picked up her glass for another sip to disguise the grin before turning her attention to Tom.

"Is that alright with you, Tom?"

"Of course."

Brenda nodded her approval, Amelia was still stunned by her baby sister's new found air of authority. Tom was stunned by something else – by the shame that was suddenly engulfing him.

As Sheila left to collect her boyfriend from his solitary Christmas, she was filled with pride. Who would have thought that such perception would have come from little Brenda?

Brenda, who had not yet finished her reprimand.

"And while she's gone, I suggest we all have a glass of wine, stick on the fuckin' party hats Sheila bought for us, slap on some music and show Barry that this family was worth the years his girlfriend sacrificed for it."

Amelia was sharing her father's shame.

Brenda, unlike her and their father, hadn't yet felt the pain of losing love, but that didn't detract from the point she'd made.

Wallowing in self-pity is a choice and it was time to make a new one. A different one.

She poured her father a large whisky and plonked a party hat on his head. On the head that used to sport a teddy-boy quiff but had now quietened to a plain, flat, side-fringe.

He took the glass and raised it in a silent toast in the direction of his youngest, curly blonde-haired daughter. The pretty one.

When Barry arrived, he was carrying a tin of Quality Street and a bottle of Brandy. He entered the house in a wave of wonderous energy and Brenda immediately saw why Sheila would want him in her life.

Amelia pulled up another chair and offered her hand.

"You must be Amelia?" he smiled. "I've heard so much about you. About all of you!"

As he sat down, Amelia noticed that physically he wasn't a patch on her father. He had lost most of his hair on top and he was short in stature with a rather pronounced beer-belly but he was a breath of fresh air that Christmas day.

Without consensus, he started off a game of charades, nominating himself as the first actor and within seconds everyone was laughing.

He opened and plied Tom with the brandy he'd brought after secretly slipping a glug into Sheila's Babycham. He then went on to several parlour games one after the other until everyone was exhausted.

Only then did he wish everyone a happy Christmas and wobble his way to the door, leaving Sheila to clean up after her adopted, but soon to be abandoned, family.

Tom sat in his chair with a cup of strong tea and stared into the flames of the fire. It had been years since there had been any fun on Christmas day in this house and he imagined that Brenda couldn't even remember any.

The ache for Celia had been replaced by a much bigger one. Today he was feeling the full blow of regret. The regret of the wasted years. The miserable years he'd imposed on the daughters Celia loved. The two little girls she'd tried so hard to drench in joy and happiness and he'd done the exact opposite! He'd totally missed the point and it had taken the new lover of his teenage sweetheart to point it out!

He watched Sheila clear the dishes as she sang.

Things could have been so different if he was an atheist. He could have taken Sheila back into his arms and loved her the way he always longed to. The way he secretly fantasied to.

The harsh reality was that he had fallen head over heels in love with one woman and then grown to love another and each love was of a different breed. Different in so many ways but identical in strength, intensity and greatness.

If he wasn't so damn sure that Celia was still out there somewhere he would again have the freedom of choice between love and duty.

This time, he would have chosen Sheila.

Brenda started to help with the dishes as she chatted merrily to Sheila about the many hilarious events of the day and at how much she'd enjoyed Barry's company.

Amelia noticed her father's expression and perched herself on the arm of his chair.

"Sometimes it feels mean to have a good time without mum, doesn't it?"

Tom nodded silently without looking up.

"Mum wouldn't want us to be miserable because of her though. You know that, don't you?"

He nodded again and then turned his teary eyes up to hers.

"Yes, I do know it. She was the one who taught us all to put fun and joy ahead of everything else. It felt like her life's work."

"Yes she did and whenever you told her you had nothing in the bank what did she used to say?"

Tom heaved a sigh.

"She used to say that she doesn't save money, she saves happy memories and that makes us the richest family she knew."

Tom could feel his love for Celia rising up again. The love he'd bullied his heart into feeling but a love that was nonetheless real. Feeling the guilt of allowing his ex-lover to bring up her children and the fear of allowing himself to feel any joy in this new home of betrayal.

Then came the other surge of guilt. The guilt of exploiting Sheila's love for him so selfishly.

"So why are you looking so glum dad?" Amelia asked softly as she perched on the arm of his chair.

"I guess it's because it hurts to know that she's missing out on something she'd love so much. It's felt kinder to do nothing and know she's not missing anything. Does that make sense."

"It does." Amelia smiled, "but you know it's total bollocks don't you?"

Tom grinned. He had never heard his daughter swear before.

"Seems to me dad, that there are two possibilities. Either there is no life after this one and in that case, she isn't missing out because she doesn't exist. The alternative is that she's in heaven watching us and hating what a miserable lot we've become and feeling she'd wasted her time on trying to teach us what's important."

Tom patted her hand.

"Or there's a third possibility."

"Which is?"

"That she is as trapped now, just as she was at that window. Desperately trying to get back to the family she loved. Heartbroken and alone. We were her world and I need her to know that she was mine."

Amelia had no answer to that because she knew he couldn't change how he felt any more than she could change how she felt about Frank. The heart can't be bullied so they would just have to make the most of it. Just as Sheila would make the most of a new life with Barry rather than to wallow away her days watching the man she loves, stagnate in his grief for a woman who is long gone.

That day, it seemed like Brenda was the lucky one.

The lucky one and the pretty one.

She could see how devastating Sheila's departure had been for her dad. It seemed that rejection didn't necessarily negate sorrow or jealousy and today he looked crushed.

"You won't leave us though, will you?"

"I promised you, didn't I?"

She squeezed his hand and through it she could feel his resignation to upholding that promise.

He wished he could talk to Celia for just a moment. A moment to tell her how it twisted his heart to see her face at that window. Like a caged animal clawing to be reunited with her young and with her mate. To share the anger at the doctors who refused to let him hold her in her final hours. Anger towards the God that had torn his family into two halves and left him torn between those halves and then finally anger towards the daughter who had blackmailed him into remaining in this tortuous world!

Amelia's heart skipped a beat. She could feel snippets of his thoughts. She stared at him, and he instantly looked away as though he'd sensed it. Luckily it was almost three o'clock and the Queen's speech would start soon.

"It's time for the Queen's speech." Amelia said firmly and clearly.

"I was just thinking that." He smiled. "You must have read my mind!"

"Indeed." Amelia said curtly. "Indeed."

But her sharpness wasn't aimed at her father. It was aimed at the sheer supremacy and dogged rigidity of this extreme brand of love. The brand that had infected them both and from which there seemed to be no remission.

Tom fixed his eyes on the tv screen at the courtyard of Buckingham Palace where the Queens guards stood to attention as the national anthem played. He stared blankly as the camera moved to the image of the Queen seated between a vase of flowers and a standard lamp wearing her usual pearls and broach.

His mind wandered back to Sheila and the surge of jealousy he'd felt when she appeared with Barry. He felt sickened by her disloyalty, by her abandonment and by his own arrogance in assuming he was still the centre of her universe.

Perhaps his indignation came from the knowledge that she had always remained quietly at the centre of his. Even now.

He remembered the awful day when he'd told her about Celia's pregnancy. The dread in his heart as he awaited her outburst, but there was none.

She simply hugged him gently and then brushed her lips against his.

"Well, I guess that's that then." She said with the same dignity and hidden emotions of the woman who was still delivering her Christmas message on screen.

"Is that all you have to say?" He snapped. Suddenly feeling insulted rather than relieved at her indifferent tone. "I thought you were in love with me?"

"I am." She replied. "You're the one. I know that without a shadow of doubt but love is love and duty is duty. They are not the same thing but equally important and you have a duty to do the right thing."

"The right thing for who?" He was still challenging when he knew he should have been grateful for her understanding and already be walking away.

"To that poor girl and to the innocent child that has yet to be delivered into this world. I will love you forever Tom Simpson but my misery doesn't compare to the misery that this mother and child would endure in a life of shame and loneliness without the support of a husband or the love of a father."

"You do know that I love you? That I love you just as much as you love me?"

"Of course I do. I feel it every moment we're together."

Tom remembered breaking down in Sheila's arms and crying like a baby. Sheila had been the strong one. The righteous one and he had been the guilty careless one for whose follies they must both pay.

She smiled and wiped his eyes.

"One day, Tom, you will realise that your love for that child will have grown wider and deeper than anything you feel for me."

Now, as Tom listened to the Queen speaking of resilience and how compassion is far greater than anger, he tried to compare his love for his children to that he'd felt for Sheila. It was impossible to rate one against the other because they were different beasts but what did it matter? What's done was done.

The Queen smiled back at him and suggested that perhaps we notice too much of what is wrong and too little of what is right.

He smiled back.

His life, on the whole, had been fine. His love for Celia had been a quieter love. A dutiful love but never a love of resentment or anger. She'd been a perfect wife and mother, and that had been a blessing. The memories of Sheila were safely stored in the privacy of his own mind and recalled often.

The four blissful, lustful, passionate, delicious days when two souls had fused together in a place beyond this world. Soared to heights he would never reach again. Days full of promise for a destiny that just wasn't to be.

He sighed and tried not to imagine Sheila with Barry.

Amelia understood that sigh more accurately than her father could ever imagine.

That evening, as the dusk started to fall, she put on her coat, picked up the torch, and headed for the clearing in the woods. If there were any answers to be found, that's where they would be. In the place she'd learned to connect with Frank and the place where she could see up into the vastness of whatever world lay above them.

Driven and determined, she didn't feel the cold or the thorns as they scraped her legs, nor did she feel the puddles that soaked through her coat as she lay down and stared up between the naked trees.

Desperately she searched but there was still nothing out there. Just a vast emptiness. No waves of warmth washing over her, nothing engulfing her or whispering through the trees. Frank and her mother were both out of reach now and she couldn't bear it.

She scrambled to her feet and stood tall. She opened her arms to the sky and screamed to Frank, and to her mother at the top of her voice.

"Where are you!"

After half an hour of sobbing and pleading with whatever God might be out there, she switched on the torch and drudged homeward.

The TV was blaring, and the fire was dancing merrily so she quickly discarded her muddy coat and joined Brenda and her dad in the living room.

Sheila popped her head around the door to announce that she was heading off to Barry's for the night. Tom's face instantly betrayed him as it paraded the pang of jealousy for all to see.

Then, as they settled down to watch a variety show Amelia's thoughts turned back to Sheila.

Sheila had showered and changed. Re-done her hair and drenched herself in perfume. She was on her way to spend the night with her new lover. She'd be trying to give him her heart. The heart she'd left behind in the home of the children she'd raised, and the man she loved.

As she got into bed that night, she was contemplating the fact that things couldn't really get any worse.

Brenda flounced into the bedroom, grabbed her pyjamas, and disappeared to the bathroom.

"Mealy'" she called across the hall.

"What?"

"You got any tampons or did you use them all?"

"They're here in my drawer, where they always are."

"Oh good. I thought you'd have used them all by now."

The reply caused Amelia to frown.

She frowned and then her heart missed a beat. She always had her period the week before Brenda!

She was a full week late!

Chapter 12

That night was the night Amelia would recall with sickening horror. The sleepless night of a million dreads and the loneliest hours she'd ever endured.

The arms she wanted to run into were gone now. Sheila's arms would be wrapped around Barry's ample belly and the whereabouts of Frank's arms were as lost and unreachable as those of her mother.

As Brenda snored quietly in her bed, Amelia tortured herself with images of things to come, of choices to make and of the terrible consequences of them all.

She imagined herself sitting in an abortion clinic with the death sentence of Franks baby clutched in her hand. The murder he may one day hold her accountable for when he returned. The blame he would lay at her door for failing to keep faith.

Then she imagined herself at a different clinic. The clinic where she would sit among other expectant mothers wearing a curtain ring on her finger and trying to hide her registration card with the word Miss before her name. The shame of being the only unmarried mother in the room. The dirty, promiscuous schoolgirl who had given herself so carelessly to a boy who clearly didn't care a hoot about her.

Then came the vision of her sitting alone in a single-parents council flat with a screaming infant. No qualifications, no prospects or time to ever get herself a job, let alone a career. Cutting coupons from the newspapers that others had thrown away. She imagined sitting at her window as other girls of her age laughed and jostled their way to the club with a boy on their arm. The boys that would one day become their husbands, providers and devoted fathers to their legitimate children.

By now, she was sweating again.

She wanted to wake Brenda and spill out the whole sorry tale but she knew Brenda was not a good choice. Her sister was loyal to the core but she had never been able to keep a secret. Her mouth had always been faster than her brain and something of this magnitude would be dancing constantly on her tongue until it found a careless moment to fly into the room.

In the early morning she heard Brenda get up for aspirin. Lucky Brenda. Brenda had period pain.

Within minutes Brenda was snoring again and Amelia's future started to replay again in all its magnificent horror.

Just before daybreak, sick from lack of sleep, Amelia closed her eyes and made a desperate attempt at salvation. She needed to feel Frank. At least to know he was somewhere. Somewhere within reach.

She tried to relax, just as they'd practised. She reached and reached for him and then, just for a moment, she felt as though she had felt a connection to something. The sensation that someone had, at last, answered. Someone who had picked up the imaginary phone but wasn't speaking. It was silence but not the kind of empty silence of isolation. It was the kind of silence between two people.

She was startled by it for a moment and then it was gone.

The growl of next door's motorbike starting up had swiped it away like a swatted fly.

Brenda yawned, groaned and pulled the sheet over her head.

Amelia stared silently at the ceiling.

It would be several years before she made sense of that early morning feeling of connection to something but for now, she just needed someone to talk to. Someone who would not blurt everything to the entire world or gasp in horror at her predicament. Someone who could just listen and advise. Someone she could trust.

By ten o'clock she had spent another two hours stewing in her misery while waiting for an acceptable hour to invade a household on Boxing Day morning.

She dragged her reluctant tresses into a nape ponytail, pulled on a pair of barely clean slacks and a misshapen jumper before wresting on reluctant wellies and snatching her anorak from the hook.

"I'm just nipping over to Brian's to pick up some homework notes." She called to anyone who might be listening in the living room.

She heard her father's voice saying something about dinner and Sheila as the door closed behind her.

The air outside was cold, wet and dreary. Nothing like the Christmas cards on the mantle.

Her sudden interest in fashion, hygiene and grooming had evaporated as abruptly as it arrived. As abruptly as the evaporation of Frank.

She strode purposefully through the streets and knocked firmly on Brian's front door but the moment his mother's face appeared, all her tenacity drained away.

"Happy Christmas Amelia! Brian's in his room playing his new Bowie Album, something to do with shiny dogs, it's awful. Perhaps you can get him to turn it down?"

"I'll try." She smiled meekly, remembering how much he'd been wanting Diamond Dogs all year. Brian was lucky. He was having a normal boxing day with his family. Playing his new record without a care in the world. Without a timebomb growing in his belly.

She tapped twice on his bedroom door and then opened it, being greeted by a waft of warm, sickly, sweaty-sock air. Amelia wasn't used to warm bedrooms, but Brian's family owned a business and with that came greater luxuries such as the tea maker in the corner of his room and the radiator under his window.

"Amelia!"

Brian was laying on his unmade bed, still reciting the words of the tracks when she abruptly interrupted, causing him to sit up with a mortified expression on his face.

"Sorry to interrupt." She sighed.

Brian was already gathering the strewn dirty clothes from the floor and frantically looking for somewhere to dump them out of sight. His dirty underpants seemed determined to parade themselves on the top of the pile!

"You should have called to let me know you were coming."

It wasn't a reprimand, just the resounding of a wish. Brian would have loved for Amelia to call in, if he'd had time to prepare. He would have hoovered his room, changed his sheets, wiped the dust from his record stand and sprayed the air freshener. He'd have taken a shower and used his mum's concealer to mask the herd of yellow-headed pimples that had been rapidly congregating on his chin since the lid was taken off the Quality Street tin on Christmas Eve. He would definitely have put on the new flares and fitted shirt he'd got for Christmas.

"I'm sorry. I didn't have any change." Amelia lied. The truth was that the phone box was a walk in the opposite direction and despite the fact that Brian had given her his number numerous times, she hadn't bothered to memorise it.

"Well, sit down." He smiled after dumping the clothes out onto the landing and smoothing a patch of rumpled bed for her.

"So, what brings you here. It doesn't look like a boxing day visit?"

Brian was being polite. Amelia knew how she looked and this was not the state in which a normal girl would visit a friend's house on Boxing Day.

"I'm a mess. I know. The thing is…" Her lip began to quiver in anticipation of the words that were about to released. Words that even she, didn't want to hear.

Brian instinctively put an arm around her and then scrambled under the bed and retrieved a bottle of Scotch Mac and a glass.

Amelia smiled.

"Your secret stash?"

"Yes, I keep it for all the tearful ladies who choose to visit me in the mornings on holidays." He joked.

"Oh Brian," she sighed again, "I think I'm in an awful mess."

Brian patted her hand and smiled again.

"Well, that usually means one of two things. Either you've just set your house on fire or you're pregnant."

"My house is fine." She whispered.

"Are you sure?" He asked solemnly.

"About the house?"

"You know what I meant."

"Yes, I know what you meant and, no, I'm not absolutely certain but I'm pretty certain."

"Have you told anyone?"

"Not until now."

"Well, if I were you, I'd keep it that way. No point in setting hares racing or worrying yourself sick until you know if there's anything to worry about. Then, if there is a problem. Well, I'm here. We can look at options together if you want?"

"Have you done this before? You seem well-rehearsed."

"Let's just say that I'm the kind of person people confide in when they're already in a mess. I'm not the kind of person they get in a mess with." His humble smile indicated that the statement required no appeasement.

"You're a good friend Brian."

"I know." He smiled again, this time more proudly.

Being needed and respected by a girl was a rare event.

"I think I just need a plan for either outcome." She placed her hand on his arm and he instantly allowed himself the fantasy of misreading it. "I just can't bear this uncertainty. It's killing me. I can't sleep or eat. I need to decide what I'm going to do, either way, so I can calm down a bit."

"Well, the chemist won't do a test until you're at least two weeks overdue. Are you? Do you know when it might have happened?"

"Of course I do! We only did it the once before he buggered off! It was in your dad's flipping garage!"

"Oh!" It was all Brian was capable of saying. He liked the fact that this hadn't been the torrid love affair he'd imagined, and he also liked the fact that Frank had taken to his heels right afterwards.

He took a breath.

"Well, I think we can safely say that Frank won't be coming back. He would have got in touch by now. I mean, he has your address and he has my phone number."

"I can't believe he just vanished like that." She could feel her lip trembling. "I mean, he must have known he was moving out! Why would he do that to me when he knew he was about to disappear?"

"I have no idea but you need to assume he's out of the picture so, it seems to me that, if you are pregnant, you have three options."

"I already know I'm pregnant. I can feel it and I've never been late. It would be a hell of a coincidence if the one time I'm late happens right after the one time I had sex."

"Ok. So let's assume that you are, and go through the options so you can make a plan. So," Brian took a breath to accentuate his air of logical and sensible decision making. "You have four options here. Either, you get an abortion, which should be easy considering your age and circumstances, but you will need your dad's permission. He will need to know." He watched her face drain. "Either that or you leave school, have the baby, kiss goodbye to a career, and live at home with your dad for the foreseeable future. Third option is that you go it alone. Put your name down for a council flat and resign yourself to a decade of isolation with maybe a part-time job during school hours at the local shop."

"You make them all sound so irresistible." She snapped sarcastically. She'd already gone through the options in all their miserable glory and didn't need Brian parading them before her again unless he had something constructive to add.

He looked suddenly shocked and hurt. As though she'd just pulled a gun on him!

"Sorry, I know you're trying to help but it feels like the devil or the deep blue sea to me! Either I blast my baby into oblivion with a vacuum hose or I settle for a life of solitude and drudgery."

Brian put his hand on hers and she frowned.

"What was the fourth option? You said I had four options?"

"Oh! Of course. The fourth one is very simple. You marry me."

She laughed nervously as she tried to determine if he was joking.

She looked up into his face. His eyes met hers.

He wasn't joking!

"You're serious!"

"I am."

"How exactly, do you think that would make anything any better?"

He looked hurt.

"I mean," she sighed, "that would just put the burden on you too!"

He grinned.

"Look at me Amelia! Girls don't exactly scramble over one another to get to me! It's not like I'd be throwing away my chances with Twiggy or Marie Osmond, is it?"

"But you want to go to university! You want a career! You can't do any of that with a wife and another man's kid to raise!"

"I'd be honoured." He smiled "Frank was my friend remember? And as for a career, well my dad is always pestering me to take over his garage instead of going to university so he'd be delighted if I took up the offer. A mechanic can earn good money you know."

"How can you have all this figured out when I've only just told you! It feels like you've already thought it all through!"

He shook his head slowly and smiled again.

She watched his face. He wasn't shaking his head in denial of having thought it through but in disbelief that she didn't realise she'd just handed him his dream on a silver platter.

Her heart started pounding.

She wasn't sure if it was the horror of visualising herself in bed with the gawky, gangling, buck-teethed, and incredibly spotty vision before her or if it was the sudden revelation of a fourth option to her plight.

He smiled humbly, sweetly, hopefully.

Her heart continued to thump at her chest and she knew this was fear.

"He might have wanted you to take over the family business, but I don't think he'd be happy for you to take over another boy's child!" She needed to remove option four.

"He doesn't need to know." Brian grinned.

"You mean to pretend the baby is yours!"

"You don't have to look so horrified by it!"

She was horrified by every bit of it but most of all she was horrified by the realisation that she was giving the idea genuine consideration!

"I'm sorry. I'd just not thought of it."

"And now that you have?" He asked meekly.

Amelia tried to visualise this fourth, shocking option.

She would get to keep her baby. Frank's baby. She would have a husband with a business and probably a house. She'd have doting in-laws and her self-respect but she knew she would need to put Brian's name on the birth certificate.

She also knew that she would have to share his bed.

She looked at him.

His bony, spider-like limbs protruding through his clothes, his huge feet, his jug-handle ears that had earned him the occasion nickname of 'wingnut' and then his face with the yellow crooked teeth constantly struggling to stay behind his lips. She was drawn again to the cluster of angry-looking yellow-headed volcanos on his chin and forehead. She imagined the horror of kissing him. Of pressing her lips against those jagged teeth or brushing her face against his and causing one of those huge pustules to explode onto her skin.

Brian seemed to know what was going through her mind.

"I know I'm not a pretty picture Amelia but the thing about life is that everything changes. My teenage acne will clear up eventually and my body will fill out. I won't always be the sorry mess you're looking at today."

Her heart went out to him. He was trying to sell himself the way a farmer might try to convince a market buyer that a stringy colt will bloom into a handsome stallion."

He watched her face soften and delivered his winning line. "And look on the bright side. This is likely to be a very pretty baby. Frank was quite a looker."

"It might still have my lifeless mousy hair and sharp nose though!" She smiled.

"It's probably as well that I'm not the father then." He laughed. "Who knows what we'd create between us. You'd need to be over 18 to take a peek in the damn pram!"

She suddenly burst into laughter.

He knew he'd made it to the finish line. He could sense what she was thinking now.

Brian did have a talent for lightening a situation with his inappropriate humour. It wasn't a bad gift to have. Not in a husband or in a father.

She contained her giggles and then looked at him again.

"I know what you're thinking." He sighed. "Funny but ugly as sin."

"I wasn't thinking that!" She lied. "I was thinking about the whole situation."

"I know you want a career, and I can tell you now that I'll make sure you still get the chance."

She frowned. He continued.

"I'll work in the day and I'll watch the baby in the evenings so you can go to night school. I'll do it Amelia. I promise."

She could feel that Brian was about to throw in everything to seal the deal.

She felt sorry for him. She could feel his desperation. The desperation that matched her own.

"It's a wonderful and very selfless offer Brian."

"But?"

She thought for a moment. She recalled Sheila's words – its far better to like someone who loves you than to love someone who likes you.

"But?" Brian asked again.

"But nothing. If my test is positive, let's do it!"

It was the best of a bad situation.

A favourable deal.

A bargain.

"Just one thing though." Amelia added.

Brian didn't care what the 'thing' was. He'd agree to anything.

"I want to name the baby after Frank."

He pursed his lips and nodded comically.

"Not sure about having a daughter named Frank though!"

She rolled her eyes, "Frankie."

He seemed tense at the suggestion.

"Don't you think it might raise a flag with my parents?"

"You could say it was your idea. Named after your best friend?"

He held out his hand to seal the deal.

A deal that spared the life of her child.

The deal that spared the life of Frank's child.

Chapter 13

As Amelia walked home that Boxing Day, she was trying to convince herself that this was the best possible outcome.

She visualised herself in her own house with her new baby and with the support of her dad, doting in-laws and a hard-working husband.

A future for which she ought to feel immensely grateful, and for the most part, she did but that didn't prevent her from doing what she did next.

She took a detour into the wooded area that had been her salvation so many times.

She lay down in the clearing and stared up between the trees. The winter sun streamed through the sparse trees creating a shower of tiny lights cascading down onto her. She squinted and tried to look beyond them. Far beyond the beam of the spotlight that seemed intent on exposing her. Exposing her doubt, her fear and her selfishness.

She ached.

She ached for the love she'd felt only a few weeks ago and she ached to hear his voice again. To feel his thoughts and the safety of his arms around her.

She closed her eyes, held her breath and searched for him harder than she had ever done before.

Then she gasped for breath, refilled her lungs and screamed at the top of her voice.

"Where are you, Frank? Where the hell are you!"

The tears of frustration were already stinging her eyes as she turned face down and sobbed.

Half an hour later, she was dragging her frozen body back along the path towards home.

These few minutes of silent reflection were nothing more than a short respite between the ordeal she had just left and the ordeal that awaited her at home.

As she opened the front door and stepped gratefully into the warmth of the hallway, she could smell food cooking and knew instantly that Sheila would be in the kitchen.

For the last hour, she'd been trying to decide who should know what about her situation and who she should talk to first but that waft of homeliness gave her the undisputable answer.

Sheila was the nearest thing she had to a mother and Sheila was the wisest person she knew.

The lunchtime hour dragged by with polite conversation over warmed up turkey, fried vegetables and solemn acceptance of Sheila's imminent departure from their home.

"After I've done the pots, I'll get a few more of my things together." She whispered apologetically as she started to collect the pudding dishes from her adopted family.

Tom nodded his reluctant approval while Brenda got up and gave her a hug on her way back to the living room.

Amelia simply smiled and started to clear the table. This would be her chance to speak to Sheila in private. To finally unburden herself of the questions that were spiralling out of control in her throbbing head.

Sheila would know what to do.

"Dear God, Amelia. What a mess!"

These were Sheila's first words after Amelia eventually took a breath after spilling out every detail of her dilemma.

It wasn't the reaction she'd hoped for. It was confirmation that things were every bit as dire as she'd felt them to be.

But then the salvation she'd hoped for started to trickle word by word from the motherly face of the woman she'd grown to love.

"As I see it, this Brian boy has offered you a lifeline. Question is, do you trust him? Is he a good person?"

Amelia nodded.

"Yes, I'd trust him with my life."

"Do you think his family suspect anything about you and Frank?"

"No. We never went round there and I doubt that Brian would have mentioned us."

"Well I think there are worse things you could do than to marry into this family, Amelia. I know you're not in love with the boy but love has a way of growing on people you know."

Amelia could feel her body start to relax and her breathing to quieten.

Sheila had confirmed what she'd already decided and once the decision was made, she could go forward with the determination to make this marriage work. To be a happy bride, a respectable wife and a loving mother.

"I do think though, that you should put your father in the picture about who the real father is."

"Why?"

"Well, firstly because I think he would suspect it. He knew you were spending time with Frank a few weeks ago and this boy Brian wasn't really in the picture. Also because I think you owe him the truth and it's a burden shared, for you I mean."

"You mean when you're not here?"

"No, love. I'll always be here... or here-abouts but there will be times when you feel overwhelmed by the in-laws gushing devotion to their counterfeit grandchild and your father is a strong man. A man loyal to his family and to you. You're going to need that hand to hold."

"I can't. I can't tell him that!"

Sheila smiled.

"You won't have to. I'll tell him. I'll tell him everything. I do have a way of talking to your dad you know. But first we need to get a proper test done. No point in telling anyone anything until we're sure, is there?"

Amelia hugged Sheila like her life depended on it. On this occasion, it probably did.

Sheila left that evening with several shopping bags stuffed with the next batch of her trinkets and Amelia settled down to watch TV with her family feeling that the huge burden had been lifted.

There was nothing to be done until the test in a week's time and then, whatever the outcome, she had a plan.

"Pass the mince pies then!" Brenda nudged.

She passed the tin and smiled.

Everything was going to be alright.

She took a bite of the sweet crumbly pastry and smiled. Deep inside her a new king of hope was growing, and it was a hope she had never expected to feel.

Inside her, there was the possibility that a part of Frank was resting quietly. Real evidence of the love they shared and the mere thought of it warmed her to the core.

A few hours ago, the prospect of pregnancy had filled her with dread but now, as she continued to munch on that mince pie, it filled her with joy and hope.

She needed that test to be positive.

She needed to be pregnant because she wanted Frank's baby more than anything in the world. One day, he would return.

She was sure of it and when he did he would explain exactly how he was torn away against his will. He would kiss them both and thank God that she'd had the strength and faith to give life to their child. Into this dream, she put all her trust.

The question of what would happen to Brian didn't feature in that dream at all.

In the days that followed, Sheila arranged the test for the first morning after the Christmas break for which Amelia had to skip school by faking a migraine.

She took her on the bus into town to a chemist where no-one knew them. She had no faith in the tickle-tackling women in the village chemist and one careless word could ruin Amelia's reputation for good.

They took in the sample and handed it to the Chemist who wore a white coat and a disapproving frown. The scenario was way too obvious, suddenly causing Amelia to wish she'd worn high heels and makeup. Maybe even taken a handbag and a curtain ring. Anything that might offer a hint of doubt against this being the reckoning of a promiscuous schoolgirl.

Sheila simply smiled politely and took her to the Wimpey to wait the two hours for the result. Two hours that crawled by minute by torturous minute despite Sheila's light-hearted conversation and intermittent hand-squeezing.

Reality had dawned and Amelia was no longer hoping for a positive result. Frank would not be coming back. Ever.

She watched a young man removing the Christmas decorations with a ladder. Allowing them to float to the floor just like her dreams. Soon the walls would be as bare and bland as her future and all memories of Frank would be thrown away and forgotten. Just like the torn paper lanterns that had brought fickle and temporary joy.

She put her hand on her stomach and hoped it contained nothing other than the teacake she'd just forced down.

All she wanted now was her freedom back. Freedom from motherhood, from Brian and above all, freedom from the unbearable ache in her heart where Frank's butterflies used to dance.

After a lifetime of hoping, Sheila checked her watch and nodded causing her stomach to somersault.

In less than a minute they were finally back in the chemist. The young woman behind the counter smiled at Sheila, glanced at Amelia and handed over a slip of paper without a hint of expression.

Sheila read the note, looked at Amelia with an empathetic soft smile and squeezed her hand.

Amelia felt the blood drain. Her heart stopped. She rocked unsteadily on her feet for a few seconds before Sheila caught her by the arm and helped her to the door.

She felt like she was in a dream. Voices were distorted and the objects around her were out of focus.

"Come on love." Sheila soothed. "She'll be ok." She assured the concerned assistant.

Amelia remembered being ushered down the street and back into the Wimpey bar where she stared blankly at the bare wall until a hot chocolate was raised up to her lips.

"Drink this. You're in shock, love. The sugar will help. We'll just sit here for a while until you recover your faculties."

The shock had hit her with the same sledgehammer as her mother's death. Nothing made sense and nothing mattered. Anything that ever had mattered lay behind her and in front of her was nothing other than a thick dark pathless mass through which she could never battle.

Nothing existed now other than the moment she was in.

She sipped the warm drink obediently in the hope that Sheila had all the answers, and the sweet, warm liquid would deliver the miracle she awaited.

She sipped and she waited for her faculties to return. For her substance, wisdom, and optimism to be reinstated.

In hindsight, she would often suspect that they never really did.

Her future was set on an unyielding path of its own volition. A rigid trajectory from which she could neither veer nor slacken. She was now a mother!

She sipped slowly. Savouring the last sips of her childhood.

Tomorrow she would be railroaded along the road to motherhood on the grateful, shoulders of the in-laws who would be marvelling that their unlikely son had managed to capture the heart of an intelligent, fertile girl.

This she suspected but she had no idea of the extent of the jubilation and euphoria this news would bestow on them.

Revelling in the promise of a protégé for the family business, Charlie Gilbert would deliver a manly pat onto the skinny back of his goofy son and look forward to the retirement he'd given up on. His wife would be knitting before the wool shop closed, grateful that she would live long enough to enjoy the blessing of a grandchild.

Charlie and Jean Gilbert had almost given up on being parents when remarkably, the absence of Jean's period had been mistaken for menopause. They were already in their late thirties when the miracle occurred and now, a second miracle had dropped in their laps. A miracle that snatched their son away from his own dreams and delivered him directly into theirs.

Father and son were about to embark on the life Charlie had always wanted since the day the baby had been placed into his arms. Father and son working together. Growing the legacy of his own ambition to own a business, to showcase his skill and knowledge to his marvelling offspring and then to sit proudly by the fireside as Brian stepped into his shoes.

All of this good fortune had been given to them by one person. Amelia Simpson.

Tom Simpson however, would not receive the news with any such euphoria.

As Sheila quietly held his hand and delivered the blow, his heart sunk lower than it had for many years. This was the last thing he would ever want for his daughter and as Sheila's account unfolded his despair turned to an unbearable heartache.

He knew of his daughters love for the dark-haired boy from school. He'd watched her face light up and her appearance change. He knew that feeling well. He'd spent a full week's wages on a new shirt for his second date with Sheila and those raging butterflies had never been forgotten. He'd never felt them again since his breakup with Sheila but he'd witnessed their presence on the face of his eldest daughter when she'd popped her head around the door to say goodbye, with her feet already halfway up the hall.

Sheila gently wiped the tear he hadn't been aware of shedding.

"You're not going to shout at her, are you?"

Tom looked up into the eyes of the woman who had invoked the spending of that week's wages on that shirt and shook his head.

"She needs me. She needs you too."

Sheila sighed. Tom was a good man. He wasn't trying to tie her to his own life with this remark. He was merely telling the truth.

"Yes, I know she does and I won't let her down. We... won't let her down."

"It won't be easy." Tom sniffed as he wiped his nose on his sleeve. "Keeping this secret from the Gilbert's will take it's toll on all of us. Especially on Brian."

"He won't ever spill those particular beans." Sheila assured firmly. "He's got too much to lose. The boy is as 'head over heels' in love as ......well as...."

"As we were?"

Sheila turned red.

"Yes. As we were."

Tom nodded and squeezed the hand that was still in his, before gently retracting his own. He couldn't allow his memories of those wonderful, naked, breathless, heart-entwined days to distract him from the matter in hand. He had a duty to his daughter.

The breaking of the news to Brenda was another matter entirely.

Everyone agreed that Brenda was not to be trusted with the entire truth. She was too young to measure the enormity of it and too spontaneous to keep the words inside her own head.

"You've got to be kidding!" She squealed. "You had sex with the school swamp-donkey!"

Amelia wanted to slap her and blurt out the redeeming truth. To boast about the school heartthrob who had fallen head-over-heels in love with her and then been snatched away. That it had been the ugly sister, not the pretty sister, who'd found true love. That at fourteen, the pretty sister was already getting a reputation for being an under-age tease.

A provocative flirt basking in the attention of older boys and even the occasional married man. The girl who was always standing at the bar smiling at the boys who bought her drinks and kissed her in the ginnel. The boys who went home with a lighter wallet, an empty promise and an uncomfortable bulge in their jeans.

Brenda's laughter had quickly given way to a frown as she saw the expression on her sister's face.

"I'm sorry Mealy. It was just a shock." She whispered ashamedly. "It's just that I know how you felt about Frank but I guess Brian is a good guy."

Amelia's face remained unchanged as her baby sister tried to redeem herself.

"I mean Mealy, that Brian is never going to break your heart. He'll be a really good dad to this little nephew or niece of mine. I like him. He's never gonna run off into the sunset and desert you like that bastard Frank."

Amelia gave in and smiled.

She could never be angry with Brenda for long. Her sister was thoughtless, careless and extremely frivolous but she had a good heart. A heart Amelia knew she could trust and right now, she needed that.

"Just one question then." Brenda continued with the tone of a blatantly forgiven sister. "Can I be your bridesmaid and can I wear an exceptional dress?"

Amelia laughed out loud and held her arms out to the little sister that had filled them through so many sleepless nights.

"Of course you can."

"Well I don't want any of that A line, satin crap. I want frills and flare!"

Amelia hugged her close.

"You'll be a beautiful bridesmaid Bren."

As Amelia spoke the words she was already visualising the day. The day when the bridesmaid outshone the bride a hundred-fold, but it didn't matter because this wedding was already spoiled.

This wedding had the wrong groom.

Chapter 14

As the countdown to the wedding commenced, Amelia barely had time to think.

She continued to study for her exams which would start in May, helped to plan the registry office wedding which was booked for March and juggled her pre-natal appointments.

Whole days flashed by in a blur.

Her head so crammed with 'to do' lists that she had little time to think and no time to take a step back and absorb the bigger picture.

But when night fell, and her books were put aside; when her amended 'to do' list was folded neatly, her iron-tablets taken, and her stomach checked for any dreaded signs of early swelling. When the house finally fell silent, she would lay down and face her demons.

Her demons took many forms.

Sometimes they came in the fear of a wasted life. A life that could have been so much more. A university life of adventure and knowledge, friendships and independence. Sometimes the demon was nothing other than the dread of endless sleepless nights with a screaming baby. Sometimes it was the dread of a lifetime of sex with Brian which was still an unknown experience. Always the demon she dreaded most would eventually appear. The demon that caused her stomach to tighten, the blood to drain down into her feet and her heart to pound. This was the demon that spoke to her in Franks voice as he'd held her that last time.

"No matter what happens, remember that this is real. This is it. Don't ever doubt that and don't ever, ever give up on us."

She would pull the sheet over her head to protect herself from those words; from the sincerity of his voice; from the promise she'd broken.

Sheila was one of the two remedies to thwart that particular demon.

"Men say all kinds of rubbish after sex, love. It's the hormones. They all turn into bloody Romeo and start spouting about forever. We've all been on the wrong end of that crap I can tell you."

There was something about Sheila that put everything back into perspective. Or at least, that's how it seemed at the time.

"Sometimes I feel like something is reassuring me that I'm doing the right thing though." Amelia added.

"You're delicate, emotional and hormonal. You're having one man's baby and marrying another. I'm not surprised you lie awake at night thinking you're hearing voices!"

"It's not voices I hear." Amelia corrected, suddenly wishing she hadn't told Sheila of the strange connection she sometimes feels during her frequent attempts to connect with Frank again.

"I know it's not voices." Sheila smiled apologetically for trying to add comedy value. "All the same, I'm not surprised. Imagination and hope are a powerful combination."

Amelia didn't have the energy to protest so she simply smiled and opened the door to Mothercare.

She knew what she felt in those moments, and she knew it had nothing to do with hope or imagination. Of course, she had a desperate yearning to feel the presence of Frank again but what she felt wasn't a product of that. She knew this for a fact because it wasn't Frank that she was feeling. It was something else. Someone else. And that someone seemed to be trying to calm her down and convince her that she was on the right track.

Often, she would immediately check Brenda who was always sleeping soundly beside her. Brenda had been the only other person who seemed to have this ability but it didn't feel like Brenda either.

Her real hope and imagination were quietly conspiring that it might be someone else with her best interest at heart and that someone might just be her mother. It was a comforting thought.

She watched as Sheila asked the assistant to 'lay away' a beautiful pram, paying in advance and realised that she had two mothers watching out for her and that both of them seemed to be in agreement.

She was doing the right thing. The dutiful, moral thing and there was a lot of comfort in that.

As the wedding day approached and everything had been finalised there was a sudden, unexpected lull of activity.

By Friday night there was nothing else to be done.

The flowers were keeping cool in the shed, the buffet would be delivered to the Rugby Club at twelve. The DJ had already set up his decks and the dresses hung on the picture rail in the bedroom she still shared with Brenda. The bedroom she would share for the last time before Brenda moved over the hall into the smaller room Sheila had vacated. The double bed her dad had bought as a wedding present would be in place when they returned from their very short honeymoon weekend.

"Why don't we get fish and chips for your last night as a single woman. There's a good film on tonight" Tom called around the door as Amelia and Brenda sat on the Sofa in curlers.

"Great idea!" Brenda replied excitedly. "Let's invite Sheila and Barry over and make a night of it."

"Ok, I'll call in on my way to the chippy." Tom replied cautiously. He wasn't sure it was a great idea, yet his heart had skipped a little beat.

Having the company of Sheila and Barry was a double-edged sword for Tom. It always delivered a generous portion of delight alongside a heavy dollop of jealousy. It was an unhealthy meal but one he had difficulty in resisting.

He disappeared and twenty minutes later Sheila and Barry arrived with a bottle of Champagne.

"We called in at the club and bought this." Barry beamed as he held it akimbo. "Barely half a glass each but it's good enough for a toast."

"Thank you!" Amelia gushed with genuine excitement as Tom arrived with the chips.

"What's the film?" Barry asked as he popped the cork and lined up the mishmash of glasses.

"The Graduate," Tom replied, "I always meant to go to the cinema when it came out, but I missed it."

As they sat around the TV, Amelia felt a surge of happiness. This was her family. All here together, clinking champagne glasses and gobbling chips. It was a slightly unconventional family, but it felt more complete and more bonded, than any family she knew.

They laughed as Tom squirmed at the sex scenes and they shed a tear when Dustin Hoffman was banging on the glass as the woman he loved stood at the alter with another man.

Sheila cast a glance at Amelia.

The look on the face of the girl she'd practically raised, would haunt her for the rest of her life.

Amelia was staring at the screen. Her eyes frozen and lifeless. Tears streamed down her face but she failed to acknowledge or deal with them. She was as powerless to wipe them as she was to prevent them.

Sheila had to fight the urge to go to her, but she knew exactly what the bride-to-be was thinking.

The girl at the alter was herself, the man beside her was Brian and the desperate man hammering on the window was Frank.

She glanced quickly around the room.

No-one else seemed to have noticed Amelia's reaction. Everyone was too engrossed in the plot as they stared intently at the screen.

But then, when the bride turned around and ran from the church into the arms of her true love, they all smiled. Everyone smiled. Everyone except Amelia.

Amelia simply stood up and walked from the room.

No-one seemed to notice that reaction either.

"I'll rinse these plates before we go." Sheila said cheerily.

"I'll just nip up and say goodnight to the bride."

She tapped a couple of times and then poked her head around the door.

"Are you alright love?"

Amelia was sitting on her bed with her hands wrapped around her knees which she'd pulled close to her chest.

She didn't answer.

Sheila sat down beside her and gently opened the curtain of her mousey hair with one finger.

"It's not going to happen you know?"

"I know."

"It was just a film."

"I know."

"Are you scared that it might happen?"

"No."

"What then?"

"I'm terrified that it might not."

Sheila caught her as she collapsed onto the bed.

"Oh love. I wish I could fix this. I really do but I can't."

"I know." Amelia sobbed.

"I can tell you one thing though."

"What?"

"I can tell you that I've felt exactly what you're feeling. I know the pain of not being able to have the love of your life. I've been that boy banging on the glass too. I've watched the man I love marry someone else and it's the most painful experience of my life."

"How does that help?"

"It helps because there has never been a single moment when I regretted letting your father go."

"How can you possibly say that?"

"I can say it because it's a much milder pain than I would have endured every day of my life as I watched your mother struggle to bring up the baby of the father I stole. The father I would have stolen from you!

My decision lost me the love of my life, but the alternative would have lost me the love of myself."

"I don't see the connection?"

"You are giving up on Frank to give your baby the love of a man who'll fill its life with love and happiness. Brian will count his blessings every single day. You must know that?"

At last, Sheila had raised a smile on that distraught face.

"Now dry your eyes and splash some cold water on those puffy eyes so they can recover for tomorrow."

Sheila gave her a final squeeze and headed for the door.

"Sheila?"

"Yep?"

"Thank you...... for everything. Especially for giving me my dad."

"You're so welcome, princess. So welcome."

Later that evening, Amelia made no attempt to connect to Frank. She had no reason to. No need to and no desire to. Tomorrow she was going to marry the man who truly loved her. The man she could trust to keep loving her and never to disappear without trace.

It would be a lie to say however, that she wasn't harbouring a feeling of dread about her wedding night. She'd managed to convince Brian that it was romantic to save themselves but, in truth, she'd been putting off the inevitable for two reasons.

Firstly, she knew it was going to be a very unpleasant event. She was certain that Brian had never even kissed a girl before and his clumsy attempts to kiss her had resulted in clashes of teeth and excessive amounts of saliva. The main reason, however, was that she was giving herself time to change her mind. There was no point in putting herself through that ordeal if there was a chance she would pull out before the day.

But the day was now upon her, and she had kept on course. The wedding was as certain as the dreaded consummation of it.

The morning arrived amidst a barrage of noisy hair-dryers, discarded curlers and clouds of hairspray until suddenly, she was outside the room where the guests had gathered.

Her white gown hung beautifully in cascades of delicately embroidered flowers as her sister fussed over the veil in her pretty knee-length pink and white taffeta dress.

They both peeped through the window together at the backs of the heads of people they knew. Friends and neighbours staring obediently forward in their Sunday best and tiny hats.

At the alter stood Brian with his small twelve-year-old cousin beside him as best man.

Suddenly this seemed inexplicably funny.

It might have been the size difference between the two of them or the realisation that poor Brian had no friends from which to select a best man.

Whatever the reason, Brenda was desperately trying to fight the humour of it.

She bit her lip and turned her face away. She took a deep breath and tried to think of something else.

"Little and Large!" She blurted.

Suddenly she heard a small squeak from behind her and when she turned around, Amelia's face was frozen in hysteria. She stopped breathing as she tried to contain the explosion of laughter that was bound to follow.

It was more than Brenda could cope with. Her own outburst was no longer controllable as she gasped at the words that made no sense, blurting syllables of unrecognisable origin.

Amelia tried to reply with equally incoherent garbles.

Neither knew what the other was trying to say but both of them knew that this outburst was the combined evaluation of the entire situation. The words they were desperately trying to share didn't need sharing because they both understood the hilarity of it all.

Everything that followed in that ceremony would be shamefully regretted, immeasurably enjoyed and infinitely cherished for the rest of their lives.

Eyes were wiped, composure regained, and doors opened several times as another wave of hysteria descended, crumpling them once again into a heap of uncontrollable laughter.

Eventually, they made their way down the aisle with visibly shaking shoulders.

Vows were spoken quickly in bursts punctuated by deep breaths and the blowing out of air. They did everything possible to prevent the service from disintegrating entirely and eventually spilled gratefully back into the courtyard with smudged makeup and damp armpits.

The congregation had endured the spectacle with split reaction. Many had tutted and scowled while the others had giggled and tittered.

Brian had merely smiled throughout.

Tonight, he would make love to his wife and right now she seemed to be having the time of her life. He couldn't ask for more than that.

Through to the evening Amelia and Brenda danced and laughed. They danced together, they danced with Brian and Brenda even danced with the tiny best-man.

Then, at the end of the night, Amelia danced slowly in the arms of her new husband before the taxi arrived to take them to the hotel where they would spend the next two nights before Brian moved in.

Amelia had often heard people gasp in horror when they saw an unlikely couple.

"What on earth does she see in him?" or "Is he blind?" Sometimes the joke would be along the line of "She must give a good blow job," or "He must be loaded."

She'd often concurred, equally puzzled and equivalently dumbfounded but on the night of her wedding, that veil of mystery was lifted.

The consequence of having a face and body that only a mother could love is to develop a personality and heart that everyone will love.

Affection, kindness, humility and an unassuming, humble and gracious manner can tip the scales so far the other way. The sheer gratitude Amelia sensed from Brian as they stepped into that taxi was over-whelming. His unworthiness emanated from every pore of his pitiful existence and the effect of that was incredible.

Suddenly, Amelia felt like a goddess. A goddess who was being worshipped by some unworthy earthling. It was empowering, energising, intoxicating and strangely arousing.

The less worthy he acted, the more she wanted to amaze him and the more she craved to amaze him, the less repulsion she felt.

By the time they reached the privacy of their room, she was already taking the lead. She brushed her soft face deliberately against the sharpness of his pimpled cheek and brushed her lips against the mouth that was desperately trying to conceal the huge, crooked teeth.

The gentleness of her hand in his offered a reassurance he'd not dared to expect and the more nervous he seemed, the more confident she became.

"Make love to me, Brian." She whispered.

They were the words he'd been longing to hear. Words he thought he would never hear from any woman.

He gasped a little and then folded his long, thin arms around her and pulled her into the sanctuary of his huge heart.

From that moment, she felt as honoured to be touched as he. He undressed her carefully, respectfully and adoringly and as his long fingers explored her body, she felt herself twitch with anticipation at every touch.

He stroked her thighs until she thought she might implode with frustration. This was nothing like the fumbled minutes in a freezing cold car and, although her love for Frank was still lurking deep inside her, she gasped with genuine desire as Brian eased himself on top of her and whispered so lovingly.

"I love you."

His first thrust sent a tremor through her entire body.

"Oh, God. Do I love you." He gasped.

His second thrust sent her light-headed.

She closed her eyes and allowed her hands to slide down his back and onto his buttocks, cupping them neatly into her palms as she orchestrated the rhythm that would send her into the throws of orgasm as deliciously and inevitably as the release of the pleasure that was building so intensely, and urgently, in his own body.

They shuddered in unison.

She felt his body convulse and collapse.

To have this affect on another person was beyond exhilarating and as she lay there beside that smiling spotty face, she had the warm, comforting feeling that this might just work.

Chapter 15

Frankie Celia Gilbert was born on 1st September 1975 weighing 8lbs 2oz in the maternity wing of Rochdale Infirmary, with only the doctor and a midwife in attendance.

Sheila had waited in the corridor outside after accompanying her in the taxi but neither her father nor Brian had been contacted at their places of work.

It was exactly how Amelia wanted it to be.

Just her and her new baby alone.

She had been propped on pillows when Frankie slithered into this world. Watching and treasuring every precious second of it and consciously committing it to memory. She reached down and stroked the tiny, blooded head before that first breath had even been taken. All pain was instantly forgotten as that tiny person writhed blindly until its little fist curled around her finger and seemed to give it the encouragement to fill its lungs and take that first breath.

Then the chord was cut, and her daughter was delivered into her arms in a blood-streaked towel, but Amelia could barely see for the tears. She held her baby close and watched as those huge eyes blinked open.

"Welcome to the world little one." She whispered as the frowning child tried to focus on her silhouette.

Then came the moment she hadn't been expecting. The moment that both chilled her to the core and warmed her soul simultaneously. A moment of connection. It felt like a connection from long ago. Perhaps it was just her conscience reminding her that she was living a lie but whatever it was, it took her back to those days in the clearing. Lying on their backs, hands clasped as they engaged in their own unique kind of conversation. The silent kind. In that moment between her and that tiny baby she felt the presence of the boy who'd made her feel like she finally belonged. The face of home. The boy who'd held her heart so completely and so carefully in his hands right up until the moment he dropped it.

But today, as she pulled her baby close, she wondered if he hadn't dropped it at all but taken it with him. He had never felt closer than in that moment.

"Shall I tell your mother she can come in now?" The midwife asked assumingly.

Amelia didn't correct her. It was close enough to the truth.

"Yes please." She smiled.

Sheila was in that room in an instant. Bustling and sobbing as she pulled back the towel and grinned at the nearest thing she would ever have to a granddaughter.

"She's gorgeous Amelia. Absolutely gorgeous."

Amelia took her eyes off the baby for the first time since she'd seen the head emerging and looked up at Sheila.

There smiles met. Sheila was as proud as any grandma could ever be and every bit as thrilled.

Then, barely noticeable to any onlooker, there was a moment of interruption to those beaming faces. Just a split second in which those smiles lapsed and then picked up again but they both felt it.

Nothing was ever said but Amelia knew that they had simultaneously allowed the joyous moment to be punctuated by the same flicker of dread. Frankie bore an incredible resemblance to Frank.

"I'll go and ring Brian and your dad." She said as she patted Amelia's hand comfortingly. Sheila's familiar pat that told her not to worry. That everything would be fine. And it was.

That afternoon, proud parents, Amelia and Brian cradled the dark-haired beauty between them for the hospital photographer. Additional copies were ordered for the proud grand-parents, Tom Simpson and Charlie and Jean Gilbert and of course for Sheila.

She handed the baby over to Brian.

It was a direct reaction to the treacherous notion she'd allowed to enter her head earlier.

This was Brian's daughter.

He deserved her to be his.

Soon she would give him another child, just to prove it. She kept only one secret from him. When the baby seemed low in iron, the doctor had taken a blood test and she asked for the type. Frankie was type, B.

She didn't tell anyone because she already knew Brian's.

Brian was type O.

A type O father cannot produce a type B child.

This fact was the only evidence in the world that proved Brian was not Frankie's father. It was better that he didn't know. Better that he still believed their lie couldn't be disproved.

It's often said that if a person tells a lie often enough, they start to believe it to be the truth.

That statement had never been proved as effectively as with the fabricated origin of baby Frankie.

The charade was played so devotedly and convincingly that it became effortless and with that lack of effort came a natural acceptance that fiction had turned to fact.

Throughout her pregnancy, Brian had played the part of the expectant father to perfection and his euphoria at the birth left his parents in no doubt that the child was his.

The only interruption to the fairy-tale would be an occasional moment of discomfort displayed by either Tom or Sheila before they hastily disguised it with a wide smile.

That Christmas was the happiest Christmas the Simpson's had experienced in almost a decade.

The rooms were filled with baby toys and the kitchen hot and steamy with the aroma of Turkey and sprouts.

Sheila and Amelia prepared the dinner while Tom, Brenda, Barry and Brian's parents passed Frankie around like a parcel at a children's party. Each taking a few minutes to bounce her around to a nursery rhyme before handing her to the next eager participant while Brian dozed in the chair after a sleepless night.

Between courses, Amelia took a moment to commit the scene to memory. The six people she loved the most and her new in-laws all gathered together, chatting, laughing and eating in complete harmony.

It was a perfect moment.

A moment that had been made perfect by her ferocious determination to banish the yearning for a past love.

Two other people around that table had managed to do that very same thing but Brian was probably the most vulnerable of all. His fate was not, and had never been, under his own control.

Between them, they had built an entire family on half-truths and broken hearts, but it was working. Perfection had been achieved from the most imperfect situations.

She hoped with all her heart that this happiness would last because she was in no doubt that they had built a home on a bed of shifting sand. A home that could be washed away at any second by a careless word.

They had to make this work.

She glanced from face to face.

They *would* make it work. They had to!

After dinner, they sat around the TV and tried to make sense of an over-complicated quiz game.

"I've been thinking." Brenda announced quite loudly.

Everyone looked up but no-one spoke.

"I've been thinking that it might be best if I moved out."

"What? You're fifteen. How can you move out?" Tom snapped.

"I was thinking that I might move in with Sheila and Barry."

"You can't just invite yourself to live with people!" Tom snapped again.

"I've already asked them."

Sheila turned pink.

"Oh, I see. You've been scheming behind my back. Did you know about this Amelia."

Amelia shook her head and shrugged.

"Look dad. Frankie is going to need a room of her own soon and I'm going to start my O levels next year and well…we don't always get a lot of sleep, do we?"

It was a valid statement.

Amelia suddenly felt responsible.

"It should be us who moves out Bren. You've already given up your room. I'm not going to let you give up your home as well!"

Tom suddenly realised that his choice seemed to be between losing Brenda or losing everyone else.

He frowned.

He couldn't imagine a life with just himself and Brenda in the house.

"Let's all just think about it for a while. There's no need to make any hasty decisions."

Brenda moved out on New Year's Eve and she did so with the excitement of any teenager suddenly embracing the promise of freedom.

Sheila was a responsible guardian but she was also a bit of a free spirit and she knew she could get away with things Tom would never tolerate.

On the day Brenda left, Amelia felt the wrench of it. She hated the idea of her baby sister flying the nest but she couldn't put her finger on why she felt so devastated by it.

She didn't allow herself to consider, let alone validate, the possibility that Brenda was about to spread her wings in a way that she never would.

That she would be exploring fashion and discos, boys and alcohol, under the watchful eye of a rather lenient ex-hippy who possessed a sense of fun and an open purse.

Brenda was about to do great things.

She tried to push down the resentment and jealousy by picking up Frankie.

The one great thing that the 'less pretty' sister would ever achieve was right there in her arms.

She pulled the baby close. Tenderly and apologetically.

Brenda would do fine without the strict boundaries and unyielding restrictions of the Simpson household.

How wrong could she be!

To say that everyone lost control of Brenda would be an under-statement.

She remained a devoted auntie to Frankie and she studied hard. She helped Sheila around the house and she kept her room clean and tidy, but there was another side to Brenda.

Girls who look like Brenda develop a knack of winning people over. They learn how to flash a smile and work a room. They learn how easily they can get attention, keep attention and use attention.

She was never late back from the youth club or the local disco and she was always polite but Amelia sensed that there was more going on with Brenda than they were seeing.

But the challenge of a new baby and an entire household to keep, left Amelia exhausted and often sleep deprived.

She just didn't possess the energy or willpower to address the rumours about Brenda's promiscuous lifestyle.

Brian worked long hours at the garage and saved as much as he could but they had seriously under-estimated the cost of having a baby. He was trying to study for his mechanics qualification and already working some evenings and every Saturday. Even living rent-free didn't leave a lot left over for savings and they so much wanted a house to call their own.

Amelia could see that she could never hold Brian to his promise of looking after the baby while she studied at night school. It had been a naïve idealistic and unrealistic plan but, even if he could cut down his hours, she knew that she just didn't have the mental capacity to study alongside motherhood.

In the summer holiday of that year, Amelia often took Frankie over to spend the summer days with Sheila and Brenda in the garden.

"Have you noticed anything about dad?" Brenda asked as she propped herself up on one elbow on the picnic blanket.

"Like what?" Amelia frowned.

"I know what you mean." Sheila sighed.

"Well, I don't!" Amelia snapped. Suddenly feeling inadequate.

Sheila instinctively patted her hand the way she used to when they were young.

"I think he puts on a brave face around Frankie love, but your sister's right. There's something going on with him."

"I really don't know what you're talking about!" Amelia snapped again. "Has he said something?"

"No, he hasn't. Well not to me." Brenda replied. "He just has a sort of far-away look in his eyes lately. Like he doesn't really want to be here."

The moment was interrupted by Frankie suddenly letting go of the chair she'd been clinging to and taking three whole steps before collapsing onto Brenda's lap.

"Did you see that!" Brenda gushed. "Frankie just walked!"

Everyone cheered and clapped the dark-haired, chubby infant in her white frilly dress, and the conversation about Tom was instantly extinguished by the blanket of celebration.

But later that evening Amelia watched her father intently. She shared the news about Frankie and watched a forced smile arrive on cue. She didn't mention any of her subsequent observations to anyone because she knew exactly where her father would rather be and it wasn't any place in this world. She also knew exactly what was preventing him from leaving and many times after that day, she pondered if the promise she had forced out of him had been his salvation or his condemnation.

Chapter 16

Over the next few years everything changed.

They changed so dramatically that Amelia would often recall that family Christmas as the pinnacle of her family life. The one perfect moment they'd shared.

Brenda left school with a few 'O' levels but had no desire to pursue her education any further, well not her academic education anyway.

She became a stunningly beautiful young woman. Her figure was a slim size ten but with all the curves in the right places. Her hair hung in loose waves around her waist, strands of blonde and gold catching the light, and her skin had the natural sun-kissed tone every girl tried to achieve with hours of sun-bathing or skin dyes.

Amelia couldn't count how many times people had stopped her in the street to tell her, again, that her sister looked like a movie star, a blonde Raquel Welch! She would smile and thank them before turning her face away to count to ten.

Frankie was growing into a cheeky but adorable little girl with straight, shiny black hair and the ability to roll her eyes in the way only Frank could.

Amelia was trying her best to follow her mother's example on parenting but none of it came naturally. She went through the motions of injecting fun into every day living by playing 'dress-up' or hosting mini discos in the kitchen, but something was missing. Something was always missing.

Her efforts were orchestrated. Planned. Forced.

It took her those few years to realise that her mother's spontaneity came from something deep inside. It was the priceless 'joie de vie'. That absolute joy of sharing your life with the only person you would ever truly love with every atom of your being.

The missing ingredient was Frank.

The one thing that wasn't forced was her boundless love for the little girl they'd made together.

As mother and daughter, they were inseparable and whenever they were alone and the guilt of allowing Brian to step in for Frank was removed, everything changed.

The love and joy flowed naturally and effortlessly.

At night, when Frankie wouldn't settle and felt afraid of the dark Amelia would tap her small fingers in turn as she sang 'My black cat can play piano' and instantly she could feel her relax. After a few minutes she would stop singing and simply tap her fingers in turn as though they were the piano keys and Frankie would drift off to sleep every time.

After nursery school she would sing and dance with Frankie just as Celia used to dance with her.

Her mum's favourite had been 'You are my world' by Cilla Black and Amelia would belt out the words as she twirled Frankie around.

"You are my world, you are my night and day" She sang as Frankie joined in with the random words she knew but when they got to a certain part they would grab each other's hands above their heads and sing at the top of their voices "With your hand resting in mine, I feel a power so divine!"

On one occasion, Brian arrived home from work and dropped his lunchbox on the floor to join in with that part of the song.

They all swayed back and forth to that line and Frankie committed that moment to a memory that would last a lifetime.

For years to come it would be her favourite memory of all time. The day her mummy and daddy joined hands with her and sang out their love at the top of their lungs.

It was the happiest time of her life.

Brian's business was doing well but they continued to live with Tom for many reasons. Reasons which Amelia would lay out at regular intervals to her impatient but compliant husband. Reasons that kept her close to her father and hindered further commitment. Reasons that justified her staying on the pill.

"We need to save a bit more so we can put down a big deposit and borrow less." She would remind him every time he moaned about not being the master of his own house. "As soon as we have enough, we can buy a nicer house and then we can have another baby without worrying about how we can afford the mortgage."

It seemed like a sound plan and Brian liked to hear about any plan that included the promise of a child of his own.

He loved Frankie beyond expectation but his longing for a child of his own blood ran deep and unrelenting. It was the dangling carrot that kept her husband on side. The carrot that was always in sight but never within reach. It was a situation she was managing and managing well… for now.

Often, she would sit on Frankie's bed and read her a story but there were so many times when she wanted to tell the little girl about her father – her real father – the real fairy tale. The tragic tale of the prince who had swept her off her feet, captured her heart, infiltrated her soul and then disappeared. The tale that awaited its happy ending every day of her life.

"Are you sad, mummy?" Frankie asked one night as this alternative story played behind her eyes.

Amelia smiled comfortingly.

"No, darling. I'm not sad. How could I be sad when I have such a wonderful daughter right next to me?"

It was the truth, but it wasn't the whole truth.

Often, she imagined the look in Frank's eyes as they fell on the beautiful little girl they'd made on that freezing cold afternoon in that cramped car. She lived that moment a million times in her head and never did that moment include the encumberment of a second child. A child that wasn't his own. A child that would ruin the moment, taint the fairy tale and inevitably thwart any chance of a happy ending.

Yes, Amelia was managing the situation with Brian well because she was putting off the conception of another child. It was a devious plan, but time was running out.

She didn't want Frankie to be an only child. She wanted her to have the kind of sibling bond she'd had with Brenda but there was something so final about having Brian's baby.

It was a double-edged sword. The epitome of devasting and conflicting emotions.

The trojan horse.

A beautiful gift on the surface but within it lay the destruction of her dream. The annihilation of her happy-ending and the death of the fairy tale.

She tried so hard to deny her selfish reasoning. To convince herself that it just wasn't the right time for another baby yet.

But deep inside she knew that there was another conversation she needed to have with herself.

She needed to tell herself that the life she was living was the only life she was going to have.

She needed to tell herself that Frank wasn't ever coming back. That Frank was gone.

A couple of streets away, enjoying her new freedom, Brenda was quickly becoming an independent, ambitious and calculating young woman.

Working on the front desk of the only travel agent in Rochdale, she was meeting the kind of people who had no need or desire to spend their summer holidays in dreary Blackpool.

The business of package holidays was growing fast, and she was exactly the kind of 'eye candy' needed to persuade the predominantly male clients to sign up for the numerous, lucrative extras on offer. The commissions on taxis, express check-in, priority seating, hotel excursions and room upgrades were boosting her wage considerably.

But the husbands who left the shop with a somewhat disgruntled woman on their arm were not her primary concern. Her focus was streamlined toward the aging playboys with money to burn. Or of course, the newly divorced bitter young men, hell bent on exacting revenge on their ex by lavishing their divorce settlements on a gorgeous young woman way out of their league.

Brenda was being wined and dined, clothed and bejewelled by a steady stream of unfortunate and deluded men who fell easily and willingly for her calculated seduction.

Such entanglements usually ended in tears, but the tears were never Brenda's.

The choices she was making should have invoked a fury and outrage in any normal protective father. But Tom was no longer a normal father.

"As long as she's happy." He sighed defeatedly when Sheila broke the news that she was leaving her job to sign up for a model agency.

Then, with her new career path, came a new breed of boyfriends. Boyfriends who whisked her away for romantic weekends. Boyfriends who were always at least two decades older and who could never be contacted at home but had one thing in common. Money, and lots of it!

She sailed through numerous break-ups without even breaking stride because Brenda was simply playing the game.

She was accumulating so much more than the clothes and jewellery that filled her small bedroom. She was collecting and absorbing information as she moved in these influential circles. Learning about who was who, what companies they owned and what they were worth.

Brenda was using her God-given talents to educate herself in a different way and having a fun time doing so.

Then, unexpectedly, abruptly and brutally, Amelia's family was blown apart in September of 1980 at Frankie's fifth birthday party.

When picking out her party dress, Amelia gently took out the beautiful dress her mother had bought her for that fateful Christmas. The dress that had never been worn but the one she'd been saving.

She showed it to the little girl regularly and every time she would say the same thing.

"Oh mummy. It's so so pretty. Can I try it?"

Amelia would always reply in the same way.

"Let's just hold it up against you so you can see how it will look when you are big enough."

She would hold the dress up to her daughter and let her look through the mirror.

Her mother had been right that it would have looked beautiful on that eight-year-old version of herself, even with the mousey lank hair. The moment always ended with a pang of regret as Amelia hung it back in the wardrobe.

"Come on. Let's get this party going!"

Frankie clenched her fists excitedly, just as she always did. She loved her mother's zest for fun, forced or not, just as Amelia had loved it in Celia.

She draped her arms around her little daughter and pulled her close. She was determined to emulate her mother in every way possible. To honour her, to keep her legacy alive and to try to earn the same respect, trust and adoration from Frankie that her mother had earned from her. All the things she had so shamefully hidden until it was too late.

This was the one person in the world that Amelia would lay down her life for and to feel that phenomenon of a mother's love was both terrifying and exhilarating. It explained the devastation her mother had felt in that shoe shop, her relentless quest to negate it and finally, it explained the expression on that desperate face banging on the hospital window.

Amelia shuddered against Frankie's tiny form and hid her sorrow with a huge grin.

"Come on then. Your friends will be here soon."

She kissed Frankie's head and took her downstairs.

Everyone had gathered at Tom's house for the event, and it turned out to be a reasonably amicable affair.

Sheila and Barry had turned up with the cake and Brenda had turned up with several expensive outfits that Amelia would be terrified of ever letting her wear.

Eventually parents collected their exhausted, over-sugared children and the family sat around the streamer-ridden table for a glass of wine.

"Well, that was fun!" Sheila beamed as she removed her shoe and rubbed her aching foot.

"Yes, it was." Brenda replied. "Well done Mealy!"

"Oh, it was a joint effort." She smiled. "Brian came up with all the games."

"That used to be dad's job." Brenda laughed. "Must be good to be relinquished of that responsibility eh dad?"

Tom didn't respond.

All eyes immediately turned in his direction.

"I'm sorry." He said as he fought the tears that were clearly about to burst onto his face.

Tom pushed his chair back. Stood up and left the room while everyone exchanged bewildered looks.

Amelia was the only person at the table who didn't display that look of disbelief.

"Bren. Play with Frankie for a minute, will you?"

Brenda nodded and picked up an un-opened board game.

"Let's see what this does Frankie."

Frankie stared at the open door through which her grandad had disappeared and walked uneasily towards her aunt.

By the time Amelia had reached his room, he was sitting on the bed with his head in his hands.

She sat down beside him and rested her hand on his back.

"What is it dad?" It was a rhetorical question.

He didn't answer.

She noticed the grey flecks of hair against his temples and the deep lines beside his eye that resembled the legs of a spider protruding from the socket. She'd never noticed these things before. Time had moved on and suddenly she missed her old dad. The Teddy-boy dad. The cheeky happy dad. The version that had somehow left without a goodbye. She wondered if he too missed the version of her from those days. The scrawny little girl who would throw herself into his arms every single day as though she hadn't seen him for years.

He suddenly looked in her direction and she was in no doubt that he grieved those two people just as she did.

She averted her eyes and saw the packed cases in the corner of the room.

"What's going on dad? Are you leaving?"

Tom raised his red, tearstained face up to meet his daughter's.

"Oh love. I can't do this anymore."

"Do what?"

"This! All of it!"

"But you have a family here. Me and Bren, Brian and Frankie. We're all here."

"I know." He sighed. "I know this won't make any sense to you but I feel like I'm drowning, and Brian agrees that a change of scenery would do me good."

She pulled him close.

"I don't understand."

"Every day. Every bloody day that I'm here watching you all grow. Watching, and being a part of this lovely family, I feel like I've gone to the cinema to watch a film without your mum. Like she's running late or something and the later she is, the more she's missing. Do you get that?"

"Yes I do, but you've always told us that she's watching over us. That one day we'll all be together again so how can she be missing it?"

"Because sometimes I doubt all of that. Sometimes I think that she's not anywhere and if she's not anywhere then why am I torturing myself?"

"Torturing yourself?"

"I'm putting myself through the agony of seeing Sheila with another man every fucking day! Why am I doing that if your mum isn't anywhere?"

Amelia was stunned.

He held her at arm's length and took a breath.

"Look. I promised you that I'd be here if you need me and I will but I can't do this day in and day out. Aching as I watch all the wonderful things your mum is missing, aching for the love that I'm missing. Feeling guilty if I so much as laugh or feel some joy for a moment then wishing I could share it all with someone. With your mum or with Sheila. I don't know. I just think I need to get away from this for a bit."

"But where will you go?"

He smiled.

"You're going to say I'm mad."

"Go on?"

"I've got a mate at work whose father passed away a couple of months ago. His mum is up in Scotland trying to run a sheep farm on her own. He's packed up his family and moved in to run it and he's asked if I want to do the same."

"A sheep farmer!" She almost laughed.

"There are worse things to do to clear your head." He smiled, "and I think it will give my bloody lungs a clearing out at well."

Amelia frowned.

"Come on, you must have heard me coughing whenever I lay down. I'm sure it's working in all that asbestos dust. I've already heard rumours that it's not good for the lungs. The Scottish air is bound to do me good."

"I guess so and if you think it will help."

He nodded.

"It won't be forever and I think I need to take stock, if you'll pardon the pun. Will you deal with the others?"

She nodded as she rose from his bed.

"Oh, and Amelia?"

"Yes?"

He caught her hand and pulled it to his mouth.

"Don't make the same mistake."

"What mistake?"

"The mistake of drowning in discontentment."

"I don't know what you mean?"

"Yes you do. I can feel your unsettled discontentment and it's going to steal every single moment of a happiness that's right in front of you. I know you're not fully invested with Brian. I know you have one leg in and one leg out!"

She smiled uncomfortably at the metaphor.

"I'm right, aren't I? You're still living in hope that Frank is going to walk through that door and whisk you both away for a new life."

"I…" She couldn't think of anything to say.

"Just think on this for a moment." He continued. "Maybe we are both just hankering after a person just because we can't have them? Have you considered that?"

She shook her head.

"It's human nature to want the things we can't have." He continued. "We do that from being infants. Snatching toys from another child that we don't even want."

"What's your point?"

"My point is that we should both consider the possibility that the things we are yearning for might have turned out to be a huge disappointment. If I had your mum back, maybe we would have drifted apart by now and if I had Sheila then maybe it would never have been how I remembered it. Time changes us all."

Amelia could feel her heart sinking at the possibility that he might be right. That Frank might have turned out to be a huge disappointment. That Brian might be twice the man Frank was and she'd wasted so many years aching for the one that got away when the one she really loved was right here with her.

"Are you going to be alright love?" He kissed her hand.

"Oh dad," she hugged his neck, "I wish we'd talked more. I wish we'd shared more. We've been in this house together for years, but it's taken until now to realise we could have been such a comfort to each other. I wish you didn't have to leave."

He smiled warmly.

"I'm glad we had this chat, Amelia. I love Brenda too but well, you and I, we have always had something a bit special."

"Don't go."

He smiled again.

"I promise I'll be back as soon as my mate gets some help. Just give me a few months to clear my head, my heart and my lungs eh? I'll stay for a day or so more if you want."

She nodded and returned downstairs.

Later that evening she challenged Brian.

"Dad said you agreed with him about going away! Why would you do that?"

Brian felt his face go red.

"He'll come back and when he does, he'll be a much happier person, you'll see."

She didn't reply. She just sighed and got into bed.

Brian turned away onto his side, feeling the guilt. He really didn't have an opinion on how much good or harm it might do to Tom but he did have an opinion on the good it would do for Barry.

It had been a throwaway comment that started the whole thing, but it had struck a chord with them both.

A few weeks earlier they'd called in for a pint at the club while Amelia and Sheila were out shopping for Frankie's birthday dress.

"Cheers!" Brian smiled as Barry handed him a pint.

"Yep, here's to the second-placers." Barry toasted.

"What?" Brian frowned.

"I mean to me and you. The second-placers. The men who are keeping the bed warm for the first place men."

Brian took a sip of his pint and frowned at the short, pot-bellied man before him.

"Come on, Brian," he said curtly, "we both know that we are here but for the grace of God."

"I don't know what you mean?"

"Well, I know that with just one nod from Tom, my Sheila would jump ship before his head had stopped, and you, well you must know that Amelia would do the same thing if Saint Frank ever made a comeback?"

"Do you really think that?"

"I know it, and you do too. We second-placers need to stick together."

He clinked his glass again with Brian's.

"I guess we do then."

"Yep. We need to watch each other's back mate. Keep the wolf from the door so to speak."

Barry took a gulp and then licked the foam from his upper lip.

"I guess there's not much you can do to keep Frank at bay but maybe I could do a bit more for myself... with your help."

It had been a short but rather strange exchange, but it had planted a seed of unrest in Brian. Perhaps one day he might also find himself in need of an ally?

The conversation resulted in Brian's enthusiastic encouragement when he told Tom he'd heard from Barry about the idea of moving away for a while. He assured him that he'd take care of the girls and then he reinforced the rumours about the asbestos plant. It all made perfect sense, to take a break. To get out of Rochdale, out of Yorkshire and, more importantly, out of Sheila's reach.

Two days later Tom left.

Amelia remembered the day for many reasons.

It was the day she felt the full extent of her guilt for forcing a promise from a man who was clearly living in misery.

It was the day Brenda became distant and disengaged.

It was the day she walked in on Sheila to find her sobbing inconsolably at the kitchen table.

There's a saying that you don't appreciate something until it's gone and that had never been proved more emphatically than the departure of Tom from the lives of everyone around him.

The independence they had longed for failed to deliver the rewards they'd imagined and, in its place sat a huge void of emptiness in the Gilbert house. The father that had so often felt like an intruder was missed beyond all expectation.

Brenda became irritable and anxious.

The father she had strived to impress had suddenly turned his back and left without ever realising what he meant to her.

He'd cast her aside as compliantly and easily as he'd agreed for her to move out without ever fighting for her to stay.

He'd simply shrugged and watched her leave with the same indifference as he'd simply waved his goodbye as he left for a new life in Scotland. No hug. No tears. No heartfelt words.

She was hurt but not surprised. She'd never been close to their father like Amelia was. She'd been closer to mum, but mum was gone, and dad never tried to make amends for it.

Her quest for his attention had failed repeatedly. He'd failed to voice his disapproval of her erratic lifestyle, failed to rage at her loose moral standards and failed to save her from herself. She concluded that he didn't really care. It was that simple.

Brenda was the pretty one, but Amelia was clearly the worthy one.

Chapter 17

In the spring of 1981 Brenda met, seduced, and ran away with, a forty-five-year-old divorcee called Lawrence who owned a luxury apartment in Knightsbridge.

This devastating revelation had been revealed to Amelia in the form of a tatty hand-written note pushed through the letter box early one morning.

'Sorry I didn't say a proper goodbye Mealy but I'm in a rush. New boyfriend, Lawrence is picking me up in half an hour. What a hoot eh? I'll send my address. Love to Frankie and love to you too xx'

"She'll be back." Brian soothed. "You know Brenda and men!"

"I'm sure you're right." She agreed as Brian put on his coat for work. But Amelia wasn't sure. She had a bad feeling about it. She read the note over and over again and in those few words she could feel Brenda's pain. The veneer of indifference through which her disappointment, heartbreak, and tears blatantly seeped.

An overwhelming feeling of abandonment descended. Abandonment and loneliness.

They were once a family. A family of four living in this house and one by one they had left. She was the only remaining survivor. Or perhaps the only remaining prisoner still stuck here in these same rooms as the day she'd been born.

She then saw Frankie appear in the hallway in her pyjamas.

"Hey princess. Didn't know you were up yet!" Brian called with outstretched arms.

Frankie ran to him, and he scooped her up and buried his face in her tummy, causing her to laugh.

"Are you going to work daddy?" She asked as he plonked her back on her bare feet.

He knelt down and swept her dark floppy hair from her eyes.

"Yes, sweetheart but I'll be back right after school."

"Can we play horses?"

"You bet we can."

He kissed her and then he kissed Amelia.

"Don't worry about Bren love. We'll drive down to London and visit her as soon as you get the address."

Amelia tried to smile.

"She can always phone us at the garage if she's in trouble." He seemed to know what she was thinking. "Tell you what. Why don't you get onto the phone company and get one installed at the house? Then you can call her instead of waiting for her to make the effort."

"Really?"

"Really. Anything for my girls." He grinned. "It's good for emergencies as well. It's not like we can't afford it."

Two weeks later, without a word from Brenda, the telephone was installed amidst a flurry of excitement. Frankie couldn't leave it alone.

"I wish I'd never told her about ringing 160 for Dial a Disc!" Amelia blurted as she padded down the stairs in her dressing gown.

"She's having fun." Brian laughed.

"Yes, but it's seven thirty in the morning and she's dancing to that God awful song again in the freezing hallway in bare feet!"

"She'll get bored with it."

"Hopefully before we go bankrupt or before I end up at the funny farm. Honestly, if I hear that 'Baggy Trousers' song one more time I'm going to implode!"

"Look at you," he laughed as he pulled her in by the waist and started to tickle her, "you need to get with the times woman!"

He let go of her and grabbed a handful of his trousers above those knobbly knees and started to sway. "Baggy trousers, baggy trousers." He sang as Frankie turned the receiver into the room so they could hear it.

"Oh, get off to work!" She laughed. "Honestly, sometimes I think I'm the only adult in this house."

As she closed the door and took Frankie into the living room, she was already counting her blessings. Brian was everything a woman could want in a husband, and he was no longer the spotty teenager she'd once ridiculed.

His words had struck a nerve though. She hoped she wasn't getting old before her time. She looked in the mirror and captured her hair up into a high ponytail. That looked much younger, much more fun. She sponged on some base make-up and framed her eyes with painted brown liner and instantly, she looked more like the girl she remembered.

She didn't want to be the only adult in the house. The stuffy party-pooper.

After dropping Frankie at school, she called in on Sheila out of sheer loneliness.

Within seconds of taking her first sip of herbal tea, she'd poured her heart out while Sheila sat silently and soaked up her sorrow like a cloth cleans up a spillage.

"Do you still try to make that strange connection to Frankie's father?" She asked.

Sheila could always join the dots and instantly see the full picture.

"Not really." Amelia sighed. "I mean, yes, I've tried from time to time. Sometimes I've even taken Frankie to our special place in the hope that he would somehow sense it, but there's nothing there."

Neither spoke for a few seconds and then Amelia continued.

"I have tried again when I've been lying in bed though and I've sensed something else."

"Like what?"

"I really don't know. It's not Frank. I do know that, but I feel something that's so hard to describe. I don't like it."

She frowned for a few more seconds as though trying to put a name to it.

"If feels very close, and it feels like the sensation of being watched but through your mind. I know it sounds ridiculous."

This time, Sheila frowned.

"It's like the silence of someone hiding close by."

Sheila shuddered.

"I'm sure it's just your imagination, love" She comforted. "Hadn't you better be making your way into town if you've got to get all your shopping and get back in time for Frankie?"

Amelia looked at her watch and instantly jumped to her feet.

"It's almost twelve! I totally lost track of time. Now I'll need to catch the half past bus."

By 12.45 she was trundling along on the rickety double-decker. The view looked different from the bottom deck, but she had never climbed the steps to the upper deck since that last trip into town with her mum.

Trying to keep balanced on a moving bus while climbing that spiral of steps used to be so much fun. Then being thrown from side to side as they staggered like drunks to the front seat used to make them all laugh so hard. She'd just never been able to face the re-enactment without that lacquered head bobbing up those stairs behind them.

That last bus ride of hilarity to buy new shoes seemed like the pinnacle of happiness. A memory now frozen in time to be enjoyed and wept over without any dilution, blurring or tainting.

She sat quietly and contemplated her lot. She had a good life. A safe life. A life that might be a little lacking in excitement, but which was more than compensated for, by the peace of mind she should treasure.

They had a happy marriage. A respectful relationship between husband and wife. Respectful, considerate, affectionate, and loving. She sometimes noticed the lack of passion. The absence of sweating, breathless nights of wild abandon. Of spontaneous, impulsive, experimental sex but she'd never experienced that with Frank either.

She appeased herself with that but deep inside there was always the voice shouting to be heard. The voice from her heart arguing against her placation. The only reason she hadn't experienced the passion she craved was because he'd vanished before they'd had the chance. She didn't want to hear it. She didn't want to imagine it. It was defiling her contentment and she needed to be content. She needed to feel complete, and the memory of Frank's kiss served only to reinforce the certainty of a kind of love she would never feel again.

The bus stopped at the lights and her mind stopped with it. Holding that thought.

There was a stark difference between her relationships with Frank and Brian and she'd settled for the lesser of the two. For a life far removed from the one she'd felt destined to lead.

The bus jolted forward, and her thoughts did the same. This was no time for brooding.

Her life was better than most and perhaps it was now time to lay her painful memories to rest.

She would stop hankering after the puppy love she'd stupidly held on a pedestal for so many years. A love that would most likely have come to nothing anyway. She would lay the memory of her mother to rest along with her shame and regrets and on Saturday she would take Frankie into town on the bus. They would sway their way up those steps and bounce left and right between those chairs as they hurtled to the front. She would then sit on the front seat with her daughter and sing at the top of her voice. The way she had with Brenda. The way she should have done with Frankie years ago!

Her newfound optimism resulted in her decision to treat herself to a milk shake from the Wimpey bar before ladening herself with bags of vegetables from which she would make a special dinner tonight.

She sat silently stirring the thick banana sludge with her straw and smiled at the image of Frankie sitting at her school desk and of Brian, covered in grease, cursing under the bonnet of some cantankerous car.

Her moment of reflection was suddenly interrupted by a nudge in the back.

"Amelia?"

"Frank?"

"Frank!"

Chapter 18

The world stopped turning.

Amelia's heart stopped beating.

Her expressionless face frozen in time.

She tried to take in her surroundings. Noises echoed all around her. Jabbering conversations that made no sense.

"Are you alright?" There was no mistaking the voice.

He moved around the table and sat down opposite.

And there it was. The face she'd imagined a million times. The face that was meant to be in class on that terrible morning a lifetime ago. The face that she'd hoped to see every day on every street for the last six years. The face that was supposed to rescue her by shouting through the glass at her wedding.

Now there it was.

Directly in front of her, and there were no words to be said.

He reached for her hand, and she snatched it away.

He put out his hand again and turned her face towards him. This time she allowed it. She allowed it because she wanted him to see it. All the anguish and despair, the tears and the devastation. The toll of his six years of abandonment. The impact of his broken promises.

She wanted him to witness the wreckage of her broken heart and the human shell she'd become.

She could feel him reading her thoughts, her emotions and her anger. He hadn't lost the ability to connect with her at all. He was sucking it all out of her against her will.

She tightened herself against him.

"I know I hurt you." He said firmly.

Her eyes widened in disbelief at the understatement.

"Hurt me?"

"Amelia, please let me explain."

She stood up.

She could feel herself shaking with anger. After so many wasted days and nights yearning for this boy, he was now the last person on earth she wanted to be around.

He caught her by the arm.

"Please Amelia. Please!"

She sat back down.

"How did you even find me here?"

"I don't know." He said genuinely. "I was just suddenly drawn to this place, but I was already on my way to find you. I was going to start with your old house this evening."

She gave a little laugh suddenly imagining his shock at coming face to face with Brian.

"You said you wanted to explain."

"I do." He looked around the café but there was no-one within earshot. No-one worth worrying about anyway. "I don't know where to start."

She remained silent.

"Perhaps the best place to start is to tell you that my real name isn't Frank Gilbert. Well, it is now but that wasn't always my name."

"Go on."

"When I came to your school we'd moved here from London, as you know but it wasn't for health reasons like I'd said. Well, I suppose you could say that staying alive is a health reason." He smiled.

She was in no mood for jokes and remained solemnly silent.

"Ok. We came here on a witness protection programme."

He could see he'd finally got her attention.

"My previous name was Grahame Palmer."

He obviously expected a reaction, but the name Palmer meant nothing to her.

"Amelia, my dad's family were a well-known family in London. A family of crime. A family of gangsters."

She vaguely remembered something in the news about a gold thief of that name.

She frowned.

Frank checked the room again and then continued.

"My dad wanted out. He really did and the year before we came to Yorkshire, he did the one thing that a member of a family of crime should never do!"

"What's that?"

"He agreed to give evidence against his father, my grandfather, in return for amnesty but it all went so terribly wrong."

She kept her eyes on his.

"The police promised witness protection, but the word was already out before the creaking wheels of the Metropolitan Police had managed to start turning".

"What happened?"

It was Frank's turn to swallow the inevitable tears.

"His father. My own grandad ordered a hit on us. Well, not on all of us but on the one thing that would hurt him the most. His children. He ordered a hit on me and my sister!"

"Oh my God." Amelia could feel the emotion flooding over her from across the table.

"It hadn't even been one day since his conversation with the police when a motorcyclist shot at us as we walked home from school."

Amelia knew where this was going. This was the sister who he'd had a connection with. The sister who'd died.

"Your sister was shot?"

He nodded as his hand tried to cover the emotion on his face.

"She died in my arms within minutes. I still can't believe it happened. It's still like a terrible nightmare."

"You were lucky not to be hit too!"

"No, I wasn't. There was only one shot. Tamsin was just the warning. He was keeping me as leverage. In his world a son is worth far more than a daughter."

"That's terrible."

"Yes, it is, but that's the kind of people we were dealing with. My grandad killed his own granddaughter to send a message to my dad to back off, and the worst thing of all is that Tamsin was worth a thousand of me."

"I'm sure that's not true." She whispered as she put her hand over his.

"Oh yes. It is. She was perceptive and kind, witty and hilariously funny. She could always put a smile on my face instantly and she was also a straight A student. She was younger than me but, in many ways, she was much wiser, braver and sweeter."

Amelia was relating his description to herself and Brenda when they were younger. Brenda was always the sweeter one.

"So, they moved you here?" She asked. Quickly changing the subject.

"Yes, they did but on the Sunday morning. The morning after our…"

"Yes, I know what you mean."

"Well, a car arrived with two plain clothed officers. They gave us two hours to pack up and leave but we couldn't talk to anyone. I sneaked out to see you but decided to drop off some records at Brian's. You remember Brian? His dad owned that garage."

Amelia tried not to react.

"I dropped them off and then went to your house, but no-one was in, and I hadn't brought a note as there wasn't anything I dare write down. It was awful."

Amelia smiled but inside she was seething that she had missed out on that explanation from Frank by watching the Planet of the Apes!

"So, they thought the family had found you?" She asked.

"Yep, and Grandad was in custody, but his trial was a long way off, so they had to get us out of here, not just until the trial but for good. This family have a way of orchestrating events from within the prison walls. We had to disappear."

"I couldn't seem to connect with you. Were you blocking me out or were you too far away?"

"I'm not sure. Probably a bit of both. It was safer for everyone that you didn't know any of it. Where we moved to isn't really important now but what *is* important is why I'm back here. I want to know if there's still a chance for us?"

Amelia released a huge huff of air at the enormity of the question. Frank had no idea what he was asking of her.

"I know what you're probably thinking. I've got a cheek for just turning up and expecting you to fall back into my arms. I've also lost my mind if I'm thinking you'd want to run off with me but it's not as dangerous as it sounds."

Amelia wasn't thinking either of those things.

Frank was back and he had a cast iron reason for everything that had happened.

It was everything she'd ever wished for. Everything she'd hoped for. The miracle had finally happened but the reality of it felt nothing like the fantasy. She felt nauseous. In her fanciful dream of this moment, she simply fell into his arms with Frankie, and he carried them away to the life they were always meant to lead, but today her stomach was pulsating at the enormity of the decision which lay before her. Her fantasy spared no room for empathy towards those whose life she would destroy. Her father, Brenda and Sheila as she tore both herself and Frankie from their lives. Brian. Poor Brian who had stepped in and saved her in her darkest hour and managed to mould himself into the perfect husband and father without a single second of complaint. Then there was Frankie. She had never considered the effect on Frankie!

She tried to push her despair back down inside as she tried to focus again on Frank's story.

"We moved abroad. You don't need to know where but I'm only here for a week and then I have to get back. It's too risky to stay any longer but over there we are completely safe. I promise you that. My Grandad got a twenty-year stretch and that's a sobering situation for his minions. He'll probably die inside and that's going to limit the risks any of them will be prepared to take on his behalf."

Amelia was reeling.

Her nausea was starting to subside. She was allowing herself to consider that the situation was not as bad as it would have been a year ago.

Brenda was living the high life in London; her father was enjoying the Scottish countryside and Sheila had Barry.

She could prove easily that Brian had no claim over their daughter.

Perhaps this was it. Perhaps the stars had finally aligned.

She felt the mercenary in her rising. Smothering any compassion for the survival of her established little family with its sweet smiles and mediocre lovemaking.

She recognised this side of herself. It was the side of her that had caused her to cast aside that beautiful dress and storm out of the house without a second thought for her mother's feelings. The selfish, ruthlessness that Brenda didn't possess.

She shook it off.

This moment had been handed to her for a reason. It was her time to do whatever she wanted and right now, what she wanted was to wrap her arms around the boy she'd be longing for, for so many years.

"There are a few things you should know."

Her words may have sounded like a threat, but Frank recognised them instantly as a tentative acceptance of his offer. She was merely laying out the caveats.

He sat silently and listened to Amelia's own story.

Sometimes he gasped and sometimes his eyes widened. On occasion he stiffened or shook but always, he reverted back to the boy with the same love and compassion in his eyes that she so vividly remembered.

Yet, as she watched his reactions, her resolve had waivered and as she sat there in silence to await his response, her heart had never been so divided.

Part of her was hoping he would just get up and walk away, allowing her to go home to Frankie and Brian. To rent a video and get fish and chips. To feel the comfort of knowing the truth without destroying everything because of it.

But the other part of her was hoping that he would silence her fears by scooping her up and carrying her away. Taking his rightful family off to a new life. Just like he was meant to on her wedding day.

The remainder of her was sitting firmly on the fence between head and heart. Between peace of mind and passion. Between the known and the unknown and she no longer knew which path would deliver the future she wanted.

After a very long silence he finally spoke.

"We have a child?.... A daughter?"

She nodded.

"I need to see her. Amelia, I need to see her!"

She felt his desperation and desolation but there was no time to discuss something so complicated.

She looked at her watch. She hadn't even managed to get to the market stall yet and soon she would need to collect Frankie from school.

He saw her unrest.

"Look. This is a hell of a lot to take in. For both of us. Could you meet me tomorrow morning for an hour?" He asked as he tried to wipe away the tears from his face.

She nodded.

"Somewhere more private?"

Her heart skipped a beat.

"The hotel over the road? I'll go book a room."

Her stomach turned a somersault.

She nodded again and left.

The fruit in her bag bore no resemblance to the fruit she'd intended to buy. She didn't even remember buying any.

She sat on the bus and, of all the shocking information she'd just absorbed, the only question in her mind was which underwear was good enough to wear tomorrow!

Frank crossed the road to the hotel, but he didn't need to book in because he was already staying there. He'd been there since yesterday. Planning to contact her again and evaluating the risks. Lies had become part of his everyday conversation. Every word he uttered was filtered, double checked and re-filtered. Pure habit had caused him to lie about the hotel but now he realised that it had been a somewhat trivial detail to withhold in the light of everything he'd just blurted out.

As he pushed the door of his room all the way open and waited a moment, just as he'd been taught, he was already starting to panic about telling his secrets.

Six years had gone by, and everyone had moved on. The woman in the café was no longer the girl he used to lay down with between those trees. He poured himself a beer and started to sweat. She might have retold his story to Brian and her blabbermouth sister before he even had chance to drink it! Perhaps he should change hotels, just in case?

He closed his eyes to assess his situation. The last few years had changed him. He trusted no-one.

He tried to recall her demeanour. To understand why the very sight of her had caused him to spill everything out so freely. Then he felt it. He felt her. He was sure she was on a bus. On a bus and thinking of him!

He put his tea down and lay down on the bed.

He smiled. They still had it! This was the same girl he once knew and the girl he could trust with his life.

The girl he had already trusted with his life.

He hoped his instincts were still intact.

Chapter 19

The next day was Friday and Amelia had been awake for hours before Brian's alarm went off. She'd sneaked out of bed to flick on the emersion heater so she could take a shower after he left. She intended to go directly into town after dropping Frankie at school, which meant she needed to take her shower and sort out her hair and makeup as soon as Brian left.

But today Brian seemed to be taking forever to get out of bed.

"You're going to be late!" She reminded him for the second time.

"Well, I do own the place!" he joked, "and it's not like I've got any urgent jobs this morning."

She huffed, threw back the covers and got up.

She clicked off the water heater before Brian could notice it and roused Frankie before making the tea and putting toast on the table.

"I don't feel well today mummy." Frankie groaned as she pushed her toast fingers around the plate.

"You look fine to me." She replied curtly. "Do you want something different?"

Frankie shook her head and continued to squish the toast into the plate.

"She does look a bit peaky love." Brian butted in as he ambled into the kitchen with a wink in Frankie's direction. "Maybe it wouldn't hurt for you girls to have a lazy day together? It's Friday after all."

"She's fine." Amelia snapped. "You shouldn't encourage her to shirk off Brian!"

"She's five years old. What's she going to miss? Algebra?"

"I'll see how she is in half an hour." Amelia relented as she handed him his lunchbox.

"Ok. I can take a hint! Jeez!"

Brian left and immediately she ran upstairs to take her shower, curl her hair and do her makeup.

When she came back down Frankie was curled up on the sofa in her school clothes.

"I really don't feel well." She groaned again.

"Well, I've got to go into town this morning so I don't think a trip on the bus will help." She replied more compassionately. She'd made the effort to get dressed and that suddenly filled Amelia with guilt, but this was about their future. Both of them.

"Tell you what! I'll drop you at school and then call back in at lunchtime and if you're still not well, I'll bring you home for the afternoon."

Frankie dragged herself from the sofa and slid her arms into her coat.

On the way, she seemed to perk up a bit so Amelia dropped her at the gate and headed for the bus stop.

Half an hour later she was standing in the foyer of the hotel waiting for Frank.

She smiled at the receptionist several times and fidgeted constantly until Frank arrived and escorted her upstairs.

Over her shoulder she saw the raised eyebrows flash between the girl behind the desk and a bellboy.

"I feel like a prostitute." She complained as soon as they were in the privacy of his room.

"Well, you look nothing like a prostitute…. For once!" He grinned at the reminder of their one and only sexual encounter.

Her involuntary smile melted away as she glanced around the room. It was clear that Frank was not short of money. The room was huge with furniture of traditional oak and in the centre stood the biggest bed she'd ever seen.

She walked over to the dresser and pulled out a chair but before she could sit down, he caught her by the hand.

"Amelia. I have no idea what we're about to decide but I do know that this is the moment I've imagined a million times and no matter what happens after today I just want to hold you again."

She turned to face him.

"You've no idea how many times I've imagined this moment myself." She whispered. "What I would have given for just a few seconds back in your arms. For a few moments of feeling your heartbeat and now that moment is here, I hardly know how to deal with it."

He put his finger under her chin and turned her face upwards. His eyes locked on hers and she could feel her whole body relax as the years fell away like crusty bark from a weathered tree and all that remained were the teenagers of long ago. The saplings they had once been. Two innocent souls full of hope, buzzing with expectation of the life to come and drunk on the sheer thrill of it. Debilitated by love and allowing themselves to be swept along into a wonderful future that they could already taste.

She raised a hand to touch his face.

The face now tarnished with the lines of life's worries and those gentle eyes now uneasy, anxious and a little saddened.

As she stroked his cheek, she felt him relax a little.

Suddenly he pulled her in so tightly that she could barely breathe. Clinging to her like an infant might cling to its mother.

She didn't move. She could feel the need in him, and she allowed the moment to run its course.

He relaxed.

She held his face between her hands and gently kissed the lips she'd ached to kiss for the longest time. Her lips brushed his and his hands fell around her waist.

For a split second she thought of Brian, but this was not about Brian. This was not about anything other than the two people in that room.

The image of Brian dissolved as easily and completely as the years.

Nothing had changed.

She could feel every atom of the boy who'd consumed her so completely in those hazy days of childhood. Those youthful days when the promises made would last a lifetime. A time long before promises lost their meaning. Long before promises were made and broken as frivolously as Lego houses.

Tentatively he unbuttoned her blouse. She could feel his hands trembling on her flesh and a surge of arousal shot through her like a thunderbolt.

She knew that already they were past the point of no return. Her wedding vows had been obliterated by the touch of a hand.

As she undressed him she realised that she had never before seen Frank's naked body. Never touched him intimately at all.

Their passionate, yet fumbled encounter had been a blur of frantic fumbles, tugged clothing, and gasp-punctuated kissing.

She unbuttoned the remainder of the blouse he was struggling with, and then she unbuttoned his freshly pressed trousers and slowly allowed them to fall, before kneeling to slide them from under his feet.

Frank caught her immediately by the arms and tried to pull her back up.

"What's wrong?" She whispered.

He didn't reply. He simply pulled her back up and silenced her with another kiss.

For him, everything was wrong.

He'd been beyond uncomfortable to have her kneeling before him with her face only inches from the most intimate part of his body.

He tried to recover, but the chasm between them had opened up like a huge gorge. Like the abyss itself.

Frank had never been in a situation like this before and he could see, very clearly, that she had.

Frank had kept his promise.

He bit his lip and tried to recover.

It wasn't her fault. She was a wife and mother now and with that came the indisputable fact that she had experience and knowledge far beyond his.

How could he have ever hoped that she would wait for him in the way he'd waited for her? It was ridiculous even to have considered it when he'd simply vanished without a word. More so now, in learning that he'd left her alone and pregnant.

He kissed her forehead and tried to smile.

"There's nothing wrong." He lied. "I guess it's just been a long time. A lot of water under many bridges for both of us."

She could feel his insecurity.

"Well for me," she smiled, "there's been only one bridge, but I expect there have been a few sexy bridges crossed by you!"

She was fishing and he knew it.

For a moment he couldn't decide which way to play it. He could confess that there had been no-one else since her, and only one similar encounter before her, or he could puff out his chest, jiggle his eyebrows and wink before throwing her onto the bed in the hope of bluffing his way through.

The very thought of it caused him to smile. This wasn't some random girl he'd picked up in a bar. This was Amelia. The girl who always knew what he was thinking and feeling.

"Not seen a single bridge." He sighed.

The enormity of his confession caused her stomach to tighten. She took his hand and kissed the back of it.

"None of that matters." She whispered. "We both did what we had to, to survive. To survive so we could get right back here in this moment. This is just us. Amelia and Frank. Nothing else matters."

He slowly stepped out of the trousers that were still around his ankles and pulled her close and as her contours melted into his own he could feel his body starting to relax. The arousal that had previously eluded him, the arousal that had scurried away in fear and hidden, was now timidly yet clearly re-emerging. It crept over his body like the warmth of the sun emerging from the cover of a cloud.

He felt the blood pumping through his loins and finally engorging his penis with a need he'd been longing to fulfil for so many years.

Amelia's hand snaked down his stomach and gently she curled her fingers around the part of him she'd never touched before and the thrill of it caused her to shudder. She tried not to compare his body to Brian's, but it was impossible not to acknowledge that this intimate part of his body was as incomparable as their faces.

She marvelled at the smooth softness of the skin that was so perfectly containing the straining muscle within it. That softness was simply begging to be caressed and to be kissed.

She felt his whole body stiffen with pleasure as she planted tiny kisses along the shaft before gently guiding him into her mouth.

From that moment, it seemed that nature took over.

Frank could feel himself touching her in a way that his conscious mind had never envisaged. His instincts were being guided by hers and he didn't care anymore if she'd had a hundred lovers because he could feel that this was something new, something deliciously unique for both of them and he allowed himself to be carried along on its crest without protest.

Then, in the sweaty, breathless aftermath of orgasm. As they lay side by side with hands clasped between threaded fingers, something remarkable happened.

"Can you feel that?" She gasped quickly, as though trying not to disturb it.

"Yep." His reply was equally hurried.

They had made a connection far greater than any that had flowed between them beneath those trees.

Thoughts, memories, and fears were flowing from mind to mind as vividly as if they were talking.

She sat up suddenly.

He was already propped on his elbow.

It was un-nerving and frighteningly revealing. This thing between them had taken on a life of its own. Taken control and they needed it to stop.

They pulled away their hands.

"I always said you talk to much!" He laughed as he tried to make light of it.

"That was awful, I could see …"

"Shush. Let's distract ourselves."

"But what do you think happened?" She asked anxiously.

"I don't know."

He walked naked to the tea stand and flicked on the kettle.

"I think, " he said finally, "that the other connection we just made."

"You're talking about sex?"

"I was going to put it a bit more delicately and say emotional but yes, the sexual one! I think it might have created some sort of new ingress. Like a new door opening."

"Do you think that, whatever it was, it's going to stay that way?"

"I bloody hope not. I'm slamming that door shut right now!" He grinned.

"Have you ever felt a connection since you left?" She asked hopefully.

"No. Have you?"

She nodded.

"A few times I have felt like someone was listening to my thoughts but I couldn't hear theirs. I thought that it might be you?"

"Not me. You must have been tuning in to someone else. Maybe you have a stalker!" He laughed.

She smiled but the words he'd spoken had already gone through her own mind several times. That there was someone else out there who had the ability to infiltrate her thoughts without giving her access to theirs.

She shook the notion away and looked back at him.

As he stood naked beside that tray, ruffled and glowing, with a couple of teabags in his hand, smiling like the cat who'd just got the cream she realised that this was probably the best moment of her life.

In less than an hour her world had been blown apart and the fragments of that explosion were still in the air. Soon they would start to settle all around her, and that perfect moment would be buried beneath the debris.

Decisions needed to be made and with each of them came a huge price tag.

Her life with Brian and her hour with Frank were already in fierce competition and she was already assessing her options.

Making love with Brian was cordial and tender. But reaching a climax was always a very 'hit and miss' affair. He relied heavily on following a recipe. A routine. On logical, tried and tested, sequences. Just like starting a stubborn car. But with Frank there had been no recipe. That excruciating, delicious climax was as inevitable as the strike of a fired bullet. A bullet that was on its own trajectory from the pull of the trigger. They had been locked on target with that very first meeting of eyes.

Her body had trembled at the kind of touches that would normally cause her to roll her eyes. It seemed that every inch of Frank's skin was charged with electricity and every touch, clumsy or misdirected, ripped through her. Awakening every nerve. Her entire body anticipating the next thrill. Aching unbearably for more.

It had been a moment of startling enlightenment.

That sexual response had nothing to do with how a person is touched and everything to do with who is doing the touching. Sheila had once tried to tell her that ninety percent of arousal happens not in the body but in the mind and as she watched Frank pour the water into those cups, she would confidently challenge Sheila and argue that the number was nearer ninety-nine per cent!

Surely this was nature telling her exactly who she was meant to be with and although she reminded herself that there would be consequences. Terrible consequences. She had experienced this side of herself before. She was pretending to think it all through, but the decision had already been made.

"Can you tell me more about your sister." She asked softly.

He walked over with the tea and sat down beside her.

She watched his eyes soften.

"Tamsin was a couple of years younger than me. Cute but with a sort of comical face. Cheeky as a monkey but she had the biggest heart I've ever known."

He took a breath, and she took his hand.

"We were walking home from school, hardly talking as it happens, as we'd had some sort of a spat over me having to wait for her all the time."

He took another breath.

"I heard a crack behind me. That's how I'd describe it. A crack, and I turned round. It was no more than a second, but she wasn't behind me anymore, she was up against the wall crouching with her hand on her chest. I still didn't realise what had happened. I didn't hear the motorbike or see it. I just…." His voice gave way. "I'm sorry."

"It's alright." She said shamefully. "I shouldn't have asked."

"No. I've said this a hundred times already. I should be used to my own words by now. I ran over to her and she tried to speak but when I looked down I could see so much blood oozing through her fingers. I think I shouted. Someone did, and

I think it was me. I can't remember but I put my face down to hers and she tried to say something again. Then that was it. Her eyes froze. They just froze. Like glass eyes. I knew she'd gone."

Amelia stroked his face which looks as glazed and lifeless as the face he'd just described.

"I'll never know, you see." He continued. "I'll never know what she wanted to say."

"Oh Frank. I'm so sorry."

"My mother used to say that only the good die young. That they are meant for a kinder place than earth and I tried to take comfort in that."

"You believe in heaven?"

"I don't know. Maybe. I like the idea of it. The notion that God took her away to rescue her from that shitty life we were living. To a place where only the sweet and gentle people are allowed."

"It's a lovely thought."

"Yep. I doubt that I'll ever get to see her there then."

Amelia tried to make light of it.

"Don't be ridiculous! You're exactly like her!"

"No. I'm not." Frank sighed. "I was an asshole to her." He sighed again. "I have so many regrets. Regrets at the fun I poked at her, the times I refused to let her join in, the times I told her she was an ugly little goblin and she wasn't. I never told her that she wasn't."

"She would have known all of that. You don't have to hear love or to see it. You can just feel it and know that it's there."

"I don't think I can bear any more regrets Amelia and right now I'm thinking of that other little girl I've let down. Our little girl. I need some water."

He pulled himself away to regain some composure by filling a glass at the basin and gulping it down in one go.

"I brought you something." She announced as she reached down for her bag to retrieve the school photograph of Frankie.

Frank peered over at the piece of card she was holding and put down the glass. He walked back to the bed without taking his eyes from the image of the smiling little girl.

Slowly he lowered himself onto the bed and reached for it. Taking it so delicately in his hand as though afraid he might break it or break her.

"It's.."

"I know." Amelia soothed.

"She's….she's…"

He covered his face with one hand and continued to hold the photograph in the other. She heard him take a breath and blow out the air.. She heard him swallow hard and then he removed his hand and looked at the little girl again.

"She's me!"

Amelia felt shocked at his reaction. She'd always acknowledged a resemblance but never to this extent. She looked at his face and then back at the photo again.

He was right. They had identical features.

"Has no-one ever said it!" He blurted.

She shook her head and as she shook, she wondered if Frankie's face had been the elephant in everyone's room.

"I suppose you were lucky that I wasn't really around for long, and that Brian's family only saw me a couple of times."

Amelia felt the relief instantly.

Of course, that would be why they'd never mentioned the uncanny resemblance to a boy she'd known for just a few months. Dad and Sheila were already in on her secret but what about Brenda! Surely, she'd noticed? Perhaps faithful little Brenda had chosen not to upset the applecart. Perhaps Brenda thought that she, herself believed that Frankie was Brian's!

"Can I keep this?" He asked as he pulled it close to his heart as though challenging her decision.

"Yes, of course. She's your daughter after all."

He flopped onto his back and held the photo up above him.

"I can't believe we created something so wonderful. Look at her! I've missed so much of her life already."

He turned over and caught her by the hand.

"I have a photograph for you too."

He reached for his coat pocket and handed her a picture of a huge bungalow surrounded by a sunny, flower-filled garden.

"Is this yours?"

"It's ours!" He corrected.

She stared again at this little piece of paradise.

"It's beautiful."

"Can you see that other house just along the road? That's my parents' house. Frankie could walk there whenever she likes."

Amelia was picturing the life he was dangling before her eyes. The open space, the sunny days and clean air. She pictured Frankie on a swing in that front garden and Frank standing over a bar-b-que with all Frank's family gathered. No mother in her right mind would deny her child a life like this.

"I can't miss any more of Frankie's life." he pleaded, "not one second of it. I came here to take you back with me and now I just have to make that happen. Do you have passports?"

"Passports!"

"Yes, do you have them? Both of you?"

"She's on my passport from a week in Majorca last year but I can't just leave!"

"Why not?"

She thought for a moment. The only person to consider, was Brian.

"Where to?"

"I can fix everything. My home is in Australia. I know it's a long way but Frankie would love it."

"Australia!"

"Yes. It was the best place to relocate us. No language barrier and so many Brits going over there for a new life right now that no-one asked any questions. We didn't stand out at all."

"Frank, I really don't think this is a good idea."

"Are you afraid Brian would challenge you for custody? I assume he's named on the birth certificate?"

"Yes, he is but he can't stake any claim over her?"

"Why not?"

"Because her blood group obviously doesn't prove that you're her father but it proves that he isn't."

Frank smiled widely as though fate had just flicked the traffic light from amber to green.

"You have to say yes. You just have to. Isn't it what we always wanted? Isn't it?"

She couldn't argue.

"Australia is just such a shock. Such a long way. Why didn't you tell me that in the café?"

"The same reason I didn't contact you after I left."

"You didn't trust me!"

"I did trust you. I've always trusted you, but you have this thing don't you? This ability. Like I do. Like my sister did and maybe Brenda did too, to some extent."

"What difference does that make?"

He took her hand and sighed.

"I'm just saying that you have this ability to communicate but you never managed to block me out. You never managed to learn how to block anyone out. You just said yourself that sometimes it felt like someone was listening so how could I be sure that you would be able to keep a secret as huge as this one?"

She couldn't argue with that either.

"It's all such a mess." She huffed.

"No, it isn't. It used to be a mess and now it's very simple. We are two people in love with a daughter of our own and a new life waiting for us. What could be simpler than that?"

She remembered again the advice from Sheila. Always say yes to a proposal just to keep your options open until you decide.

"Ok then."

"Ok then?"

"Ok then!" She gasped again as he knocked the breath out of her with a colossal hug.

"Do you have a phone and a safe time to call?"

She scribbled it on the back of the photograph.

"Tomorrow morning is safe. Brian works in the garage until two. Sunday I have no space but weekdays I'm alone from half nine until three.

"I know this is a rush Amelia but it's not safe for me to hang around. If we are going to do this, we need to leave soon. I'll call you in the morning after you've had time to think."

"In the morning it is then." She could hardly believe the words that were falling from her own mouth.

His heart was pounding out of his chest with joy.

Her heart was pounding with fear and with dread.

Chapter 20

She arrived back in the village just after twelve and called in to the school to check on Frankie.

The receptionist peered over her spectacles.

"Franke is at home Mrs Gilbert. Your husband collected her just after ten. She was running a fever and we couldn't get hold of you at home so we rang the garage. He said he was going to call the doctor."

Amelia's heart fell to her feet.

"Thank you. Thank you" She garbled as she crashed back through the door leaving behind the judgemental woman who seemed to be accusing her of everything that she was already accusing herself of. Hoping Frankie was alright, hoping she could come up with an alibi before she reached her own door. Hoping this wasn't a warning from the universe.

As she stumbled along in her high heels, she was already visualising the terrible confrontation ahead......

-Where the hell have you been? Why are you dressed like that? Why did you leave her when you knew she wasn't well? What was so important? What have you been up to!

She strode as fast as she could, talking aloud to herself.

"Think. Think. Think!"

But she couldn't think.

She opened the door and she saw Brian warming milk on the stove.

"Oh. Thank God you're back."

"How is she? What happened?"

"Don't worry." He replied reassuringly. "She's fine. It's just a septic throat and she's got some penicillin."

"I called in at the school and they told me you came out of work!"

"Of course I came out of work. She's my daughter and you're not the only one capable of being a parent you know!" He smiled. "Stop worrying. She's fine. Everything's fine. You weren't to know."

She walked over to Frankie and put a hand on her forehead.

"I should have known." She confessed as she smiled at her daughter in acknowledgment. "She told me this morning that she didn't feel well."

"Kid's say that all the time love. Stop punishing yourself."

The guilt descended on her like a suffocating smog.

She almost wished Brian had waged the attack she'd imagined. That Frankie had sulked for not being believed. At least then, she could have justified a counterattack. She could have justified packing up herself and her daughter and storming out of there.

She sat on the sofa after pushing Frankie's blanket-covered feet gently aside.

"I'm sorry darling." She stroked that warm forehead again and Frankie smiled back.

"There you go." Brian said proudly as he handed over the cup of milk. "Looks like you didn't get much shopping done?"

"No." She lied. "I was looking for a new swimsuit for Frankie but not one shop had a suitable one in her size."

"Oh what a day you've had." He said comfortingly. "Good thing you've got a husband who quite likes an excuse for an afternoon off. I'll make you some cheese on toast."

As she sat on the couch with Frankie's hand in hers watching Brian at the grille, her heart started to ache again.

"There you go!" Brian smiled as he handed her the plate.

She tore off a mouthful of the cheesy toast and concluded that it was quite good. Just like her life here.

The rest of the day would have been an unplanned yet rather wonderful, lazy family day. A day of colouring books, magazines and chocolate biscuits but to Amelia it was beyond any pleasurable reach. She watched it happen but held herself back from it all. It felt too cruel to contribute to the making of any new cosy memories in a life she might be about to destroy.

Eventually, after Frankie had managed some jelly and custard for supper and taken her last dose of penicillin, she found herself alone with Brian.

He sat beside her on the sofa and held her hand. There was nothing unusual about it but on that night her hand didn't reply to his little squeezes. That too, felt cruel, so she simply allowed her uncommitted hand to rest loosely in his.

Eventually the clock managed to drag itself to ten o'clock and the TV was turned off, the doors locked, and the stairs climbed.

She turned on her side in bed and tried to lay perfectly still. Tried to act like she was already asleep, but that didn't stop Brian's hands from circling her waist and pulling her back towards him. She felt his groin against her buttocks, his chest against her back and his breath on her neck as he settled for sleep. She both loved and hated it simultaneously. She loved and hated the comfort of it. Loved and hated the contentment of it. Loved and hated the wretched betrayal in her heart and the wretched excitement in her stomach.

She lay awake most of the night. Sometimes she thought she'd dozed off for a while, but it was difficult to know for sure without putting the light on to check the time.

She stared in the direction of the window, waiting for the first glimmer of daylight to frame the curtains.

Sometimes her eyes adjusted to the darkness, telling her that she'd had them open for some time.

She remained still. Still and silent.

The choices before her, teased and tormented. Choices equal in joy and misery. Equal in righteousness and wickedness. There was no favourable choice here.

She gazed around the shadowy room and blinked several times. Directly in front of her she could make out a shape. The shape of a small table with the silhouette of a kettle! The room seemed larger. The room looked exactly like the room of Frank's hotel!

She held her eyes tightly closed and then opened them.

The table was no longer in view. The room had shrunk back to the size of her bedroom and she could hear Brian's familiar breathing.

She needed sleep!

She lay quietly again, praying for sleep to take pity on her and fold her into its restful arms but it wasn't sleep that she could feel approaching. It was something far more tangible. She could feel Frank. She felt his presence as clearly and as powerfully as she had many years before. She'd forgotten the fear and comfort of it, but tonight it felt different. Stronger and sharper. She wondered if this connection had evolved into something else. If she had connected in such a way that she'd shared his senses and seen what he'd seen. That fleetingly she had shared the image of his hotel room.

She panicked. She didn't like whatever it was. It felt too weird and too dangerous. She instantly tried to block him out by making her mind as tight as a fist, just like he'd taught her, but she could still feel him. He was right. She was incapable of closing the door to her mind, leaving it as exposed as a public library for anyone with this capability to wander in whenever they liked.

She sang songs in her head to keep her private thoughts out of reach and she felt Frank melt away.

Finally, the welcome ribbon of light appeared around the curtain. The alarm blurted rudely, and Brian moaned, smacked his lips and rubbed his eyes.

She needed to make the impossible decision, and soon.

Sheila always said that once a decision has been made, the anxiety of making it will disappear no matter what you choose. From that point on, you will just get on with it.

She wished that she dared to confide in Sheila right now. If anyone could guide her, it was Sheila. That bundle of sweet-smelling, pastel-coloured layers of cheesecloth and tassels, who had so easily filled the void her mother left. The voice of reason, and indisputably, the perpetual voice of her moral compass. Perhaps, she considered, that this unshakable morality was the very reason that she did not.

As Brian swung his legs onto the floor and stretched up his arms to start his own day, she pulled the sheet over her head.

She considered her options again, but this was a decision that could not be made.

It was an impossible choice because both of her options were the wrong thing to do and the right thing to do.

Soon spring would give way to summer, and she wished she could see the path her life was about to follow. She tried to imagine those different roads and what each month might hold. She then thought about Christmas and tried to visualise what it might look like this year.

First she imagined the warmth of her father's return. She imagined Brenda coming home in her fancy outfits with her devoted 'sugar daddy' on her arm. Of Sheila and Barry walking down the street carrying the Turkey again. She imagined the aroma of mince pies and the comforting warmth of a glass of sherry.

She then tried to imagine a Christmas in Australia on the beach with Frankie playing in the sea and an exotic barbeque or picnic. Of Brenda calling long distance from some high-class London event and her father enjoying a farmhouse Christmas with his friend and their family as he looked out over the beautiful Scottish mountains. Sheila and Barry would finally manage to have a private celebration without all the cooking and washing up of a large gathering.

She heard the door close quietly as Brian left for work as usual, without disturbing the whole household.

She pulled the sheet back over her face again but this time she imagined different scenarios.

She imagined Christmas day sitting opposite Brian and trying to hide the tears. A day spent wondering how Frank was coping back in Australia without his beloved daughter. Of the guilt in her heavy heart and the yearning for his touch. Of the desolation of knowing that she was in the wrong place with the wrong person. The torture of knowing that her real life was happening without her, thousands of miles away.

Then she imagined yet another scenario. She imagined trying to console Frankie on that warm beach. Of her broken-hearted little girl who had been torn from the only father she'd ever known. Of the hatred in her eyes for her own mother. Of her hatred towards the man who was pretending to be her new father. Of the desperate calls from Brian, begging to see his little girl again. Begging to hold her and comfort her.

She pulled the sheet down again to give herself some air. She was sweating. She felt sick. Her stomach felt tight and her whole body started to shake.

She wished she'd never found Frank again. She wished she'd never married Brian. She wished so many wishes as she sat shaking on that bed.

She wanted Brian, she wanted Frank, she wanted happiness for her daughter.

She wanted the impossible.

At ten o'clock the telephone rang.

Chapter 21

Franks tone was both gentle and unassuming.

"You must be in absolute turmoil darling,"

Immediately she warmed to him. He wasn't taking any of this lightly. He knew what he was asking of her and that fact in itself put him firmly on her side.

"Thank you for understanding. This isn't easy."

"My God. I know it isn't. You're totally between a rock and a hard place and the last thing I want is for you to feel pressured. To make the wrong decision."

"What do *you* think I should do?"

He gave a tiny false laugh.

"I'm in no position to say because I don't know anything. I don't know anything about your marriage, your family life or your daughter, I mean *our* daughter."

She smiled as she held the receiver against her cheek. This was Frank. Frank at his best. Selfless and understanding. For the first time in days, she had someone to talk to. Someone who was on her side.

"I love you." The words fell effortlessly from her mouth.

"I love you too. I love you enough to know that you're in an impossible position here. I love you enough to want to take that burden away but I want you so badly. You and our little girl. Amelia?"

"Yes."

"If it's what you want…..I do love you enough to let you go."

"You could handle that?"

"It would break my heart all over again, but I would do it for you. You know that."

She remained silent.

Eventually he was the one to break that silence.

"Look, I've spent the last six years preparing for this moment and part of that preparation was accepting the reality that it might be for nothing. That I might return home alone but at least I would have been able to get on with my life then instead of clinging to a dream."

He stopped for a moment and then added something in a whisper.

"That was before I knew I had a daughter though."

Amelia felt his pain, but she also felt the pain Brian would feel at having that same daughter torn from his life.

To Frank, she was just a face on a photograph but to Brian she was the living, breathing daughter who jumped on him as he lay in bed, sat on his back as they watched TV and ran to him with every picture she painted.

Amelia was firmly back on the fence again and she could hear the clock ticking.

"How long do I have to make this decision?"

She felt his disappointment in the silence that followed. He'd realised the deal was not yet done. That the goofy beanstalk of a boy who used to tend the petrol pump had somehow become a worthy opponent!

"Not long. I could maybe stretch my visit here to next Saturday at the latest but before that I need to sort out the tickets and other documents."

Amelia felt a touch of irritation. It seemed he'd waited six whole years before sharing any of his plan with her and now she had only a few days to decide.

"Why now? Why couldn't you let me know what you had in mind a few years ago?"

He sighed audible down his nose.

"I had to wait until my Grandad was sentenced before I dare risk putting my dad back in danger. He was the key witness and if he'd been found before the trial ended it would have been 'game over' for all of us."

Instantly she felt like a traitor for challenging him.

"It must have been terrible for you, keeping your silence all these years and just hoping. I'm sorry for asking."

"I kept myself busy." He replied humbly. "Sorting things out. Getting a job and putting a deposit down on the house. Talking to the witness protection board, stuff like that."

She felt that familiar knot in her stomach.

The next moment of silence held no disappointment for Frank. He could feel the scales shifting but it was not the time to relax. He needed to tip them all the way in his favour.

"There's been a lot to sort out. Getting permission to bring you over for a start. Waiting until the end of the trial to get this tiny window of opportunity before my grandad's shock at being incarcered turns to rage. Rage and revenge. He had to be careful before the trial but now he has nothing to lose. The longer I'm here the greater the chance of his cronies finding me."

The enormity of his commitment and loyalty took her breath for a moment. He'd spent six long years in working up to this moment while she'd been playing happy families with his geeky friend!

"So, what's the plan now?"

It wasn't so much a question but a promise.

The scales had tipped. Tipped and landed firmly in his favour.

"Are you saying what I think you're saying?"

"I am."

She was sure she could hear his heart leap for joy.

"Can you pack a small case? Just a change of clothes, any medications and your passport and get it to me before Saturday?"

Amelia could hear the words, but she was reeling.

"I could take it on the bus to town and meet you at the hotel?"

"No. I'll pick it up a few streets away from your house. I hired a car from the airport."

She heard the door from the lounge open.

"Yes, that's fine. I have to go. Frankie's here."

"Tuesday at ten. Back of the co-op. Oh and Amelia?"

"Yes."

"Give my little girl a hug from me."

"I will."

The decision had been made.

The relief Sheila spoke of had, at last, descended.

She could already feel herself taking a step back from her life here. Already distancing herself emotionally from Brian.

She couldn't understand what had taken her so long to commit. This was everything she's ever wanted and if she let it go it would never come around again. She would have spent the rest of her life in unbearable regret. Laying between those trees through every season begging into the sky for him to come back.

On Monday morning, after taking Frankie to school, she climbed into the loft and took down her small red Avon case.

She packed a couple of changes of underwear and trousers for each of them, a nice dress each and a jumper. In the zipped lid, she carefully placed the passport. She then returned it to the loft and closed the hatch.

On Tuesday morning, after taking Frankie to school, she retrieved the case and made her way to the back of the co-op. A red car was already parked and the door opened as she approached.

Frank smiled and took the case.

"Would you like to come back to the hotel for an hour?"

It was exactly what she'd been hoping he'd ask.

She would remember that day as the day her marriage to Brian ended.

They spent the entire day in bed.

Making tea and making love.

Devouring sandwiches and each other.

Reminiscing and planning a future as they gradually reopened the doors that had been so slammed shut so abruptly years ago. Holding hands and letting their dreams flow effortlessly between them.

"Where can I pick you up on Saturday?"

"I'm going to say we are going to the community centre at ten thirty for a Tupperware party but it's probably best if you're not hanging around there for too long."

"I'll park up somewhere close and wait until I see you walk by then shall I?"

"Yes, there's a very secluded lane about fifty yards down the road. We have to pass it, so I'll make sure you've seen us. You can follow us in and pretend to be an old friend. I'll come up with some reason for getting a lift to somewhere else.

Franke won't take much persuading if I mention shopping. God knows what I'll tell her at the airport though."

Her stomach turned a somersault at the thought of it. Now, she was imagining a scene at the airport as she tried to drag a screaming child through the departure gate.

"Stop visualising the worst. We'll work it out."

She'd forgotten how easily he could read her, and she was grateful for it.

Finally, they had nothing to hide from each other.

They were Amelia and Frank again. The lovers lying in that clearing between the trees, dreaming of a life yet to be lived.

They parted with a silent promise. This time she knew they would keep it.

That evening, back at home, she felt irritated by Brian's welcoming kiss. Even more irritated when he held his arms out to Frankie, picked her up and swung her around.

She didn't want to witness it. Any of it!

By Thursday, she was getting her ducks in a row. She couldn't risk anything interfering with her plan to meet Frank at the back of the community centre at ten thirty.

"What time will you be finishing work on Saturday."

"Not sure. I've got two MOT's booked in so it depends on how they go. Why?"

"Oh. It's just that one of the kid's mums from school is having a Tupperware party in the community centre."

"You want me to watch Frankie then?"

"Oh no! Kids can go along. I was just letting you know that I probably won't be in when you get home."

"Ok."

On Friday morning an unexpected debate about the fictitious Tupperware party started at breakfast.

"I don't want to go mum. Can I go to work with dad instead?"

"You can't come with me." Brian replied sympathetically. "It's not safe for you to be in the garage".

"Why not?"

"Because we'll be lifting cars up in the air, that's why."

"Well, I can just sit in the office and colour."

Amelia interjected.

"Your father said no, Frankie and that's the end of it!"

She swished her thick black hair over her shoulder angrily and scowled. "Whose party, is it?"

"I told you. It's the mum of one of your classmates."

"Who?"

"I can't remember. Does it matter?"

"I want to know who will be there to play with."

Amelia could feel the prickles of sweat on her neck. She couldn't believe the grilling she was getting.

"Frankie. Please stop being difficult and finish your breakfast."

Franke was now sulking. That was the last thing she needed. It was going to be difficult enough to pull this off without a reluctant child in the mix.

"We can just spend an hour at the party and then maybe we can go into town and take a look around Tammy Girl?"

Frankie smiled and nodded. She loved that shop. It was the only shop in town that stocked real fashion clothes for children.

"Sounds like a fun day to me." Brian said as he rose from the table, "then tonight we could get a fish supper and watch Gladiators."

Amelia simply nodded.

She didn't have it in her heart to verbally acknowledge the evening that was never going to happen. The last family night with chips and Gladiators, had already passed.

As he left the table and ambled his lanky physique towards the door, she felt a surge of pity for him.

She quickly intercepted the danger of indecision.

This was no time for wavering. It was pity, not love. She needed to repeat the fact in her head several times.

Her resolve was reinforced by an afternoon call from Frank.

"Are we all set for tomorrow."

Amelia felt her stomach turn.

"Yes, but I feel sick thinking about it."

"I know this is hard Amelia. Hard and awful but we have to keep our eyes on the prize. Frankie is still young. She'll adapt and in time, if it feels right, and it's safe, maybe Brian could visit us."

It was a sweetener. A totally unrealistic, impossible suggestion designed to alleviate some of the guilt and self-reproach they were both feeling. They grasped it with both hands. It was a tiny glimmer of salvation among this heap of selfish treachery.

On Friday night Amelia put Frankie to bed and then slid in beside her for a moment.

"Are you sleeping with me tonight?" Frankie beamed.

"No, love. I just fancied a cuddle."

From tomorrow onwards it would be just the two of them. They would be making a new life together with the father Frankie had yet to meet. She desperately needed a moment of bonding. To forge an alliance that would sustain them through the challenge ahead.

She wrapped her arms around Frankie's dainty frame and watched her own mousey hair drop over the silky raven mane beneath her. The hair gifted to her by her father. By Frank.

"Are you sad mummy?"

"No. Why would you think that?"

"Dunno. You feel sad."

"Well, I'm not sad. I'm happy. I just needed a hug."

Frankie frowned.

"You are not leaving us, are you?"

"Of course not!" Amelia laughed and broke the hug. If she wasn't careful, she was going to arouse suspicion. She smiled again. "I will never leave you... not ever!

She kissed her goodnight and closed the door feeling nervous at the way Frankie seemed to have tuned into her. Just like Brenda could!

That night she didn't sleep.

Her mind was crammed full of contradictions.

Anticipation, dread, excitement, self-loathing and fear.

Sometimes she sensed Frank. She knew he was waking regularly, and tuning in. He'd know exactly how she felt. There would be no need to explain anything tomorrow. There was an undeniable comfort in that.

At times, half asleep, the conversations in her mind became muddled and indecipherable. Other voices. Other thoughts. Voices echoing the wickedness of her treachery and betrayal. Voices imploring her to reconsider until eventually the arrival of Saturday morning was announced by Brian's alarm clock.

Their last morning together.

He rose from the marital bed for the last time. Brought her a cup of tea for the last time.

Kissed her a final goodbye and closed the door.

Chapter 22

As she drew back the curtains to the familiar scene of that well-loved street, she had no idea that this day would deliver something far beyond the reach of her own imagination.

Those pavement slabs stained with the memories of hopscotch and skipping lay abandoned and silent in the early morning mist. The bluebells along the narrow verge would soon be replaced by dandelions as spring gave way to summer. For the return of chalk and ropes, roller skates and pogo sticks and the tears and laughter of the next generation.

She tipped the last dregs of her lukewarm tea into her mouth and swilled it around before swallowing. As usual, all the sugar had sunk to the bottom. Brian always forgot to stir her tea.

She pulled up a chair and stayed at the window for a few more minutes. Torturing herself with that last morning view and trying to commit it to memory. Every weathered gate, broken fencepost, carelessly abandoned bicycle and deliberately abandoned pile of dog dirt. The imperfect sight of a wonderfully perfect life.

She soaked it up, filed it away and took a deep breath. The hands on the clock had barely moved.

Today, timing was of the essence. There was little room for error if they were going to make the flight from Manchester without allowing too much slack for Brian to join the dots and intercept them, For that reason, she decided not to leave a note.

She peeped in on Frankie who was sleeping soundly. It was better that way. Perhaps she would sleep late today and relieve them both of the difficult conversations that might otherwise ensue.

She checked the clock again. It wasn't even seven yet! This was going to be the longest few hours of her existence,

She applied and re-applied make-up, styled and re-styled her hair. It was almost seven thirty. She made more tea being careful to close the kitchen door to quieten the kettle. She made toast which she chewed but seemed unable to swallow then she sat by the kitchen window and stared out at the street again.

Her thoughts turned to Brenda and with it came a surge of guilt. She couldn't leave without checking on her baby sister.

She dialled the number.

"What's up Mealy? Do you know what time it is?"

"Yes, sorry Bren. I just wanted to check you were alright."

"It's not even eight yet. Have you been doing that weird stuff again?"

Amelia grabbed at the excuse.

"Yeah. Just had a feeling and needed to hear your voice."

"Well, you've heard it now," she giggled, "can I go back to sleep before you wake Lawrence?"

Amelia sighed. She hadn't even remembered the name of Brenda's latest sugar-daddy.

"Yes, you can go back to sleep. Take care of yourself Bren."

"I will and thanks for the reminder of how weird and spooky my sister is."

She could picture Brenda's grin. She was probably still lying in bed with her head propped on one hand and her silky blonde curls cascading down her naked shoulders. Brenda was living a life so different from her own. A life where telephones sat within reach of the bed and bedrooms that were warm enough to sleep naked in. She imagined a huge bed in the centre of an equally huge bedroom with floor-to-ceiling windows and a view of the city. A clutter-free, laundry-free, toy-free, pyjama-free life.

"Goodbye then Bren."

"Goodbye? Who the fuck says a word like goodbye! Go back to bed you weirdo!" Brenda was still chuckling as she put down the phone.

Amelia held her own receiver in her hand for quite a while as she battled the tears. Holding the receiver close so she felt like she was still holding Brenda to her body.

Just before eight she heard Frankie's footsteps on the stairs, so she lit the gas fire.

"Can we go into town this morning mummy?"

Amelia felt irritated by the child's persistence.

"What did I tell you yesterday! We are going to the party first and then we can go into town."

Frankie looked shocked at her mother's outburst.

"Oh yes. I forgot about the Avon party."

She immediately mellowed in realising Frankie had merely forgotten and then she panicked. Frankie said Avon but she was sure she'd told her it was Tupperware! She couldn't remember!

"I'll make some Weetabix." She said softly as she ruffled the uncombed tangle of her daughters hair. Perhaps the nature of the party wouldn't come up again.

The rest of the morning was spent in the purgatory of re-wiping surfaces that had already been wiped, checking and re-checking the readiness of coats and shoes and watching the hands of that hideous clock creep and crawl around its never-ending face.

Finally, the watershed of ten fifteen arrived and she ushered Frankie into the hallway to put on her shoes.

She went back through the house to check the backdoor when Frankie called out.

"Dad's home!"

She felt a surge of adrenalin rise through her body!

"Amelia?"

"What are you doing home!"

"Well, that's the thanks I get for offering to run my girls to the party!"

"Run us to the party? It's less than three hundred yards up the road!"

"I know but I'm heading that way and there's roadworks and traffic lights outside the community hall. The pavement's blocked so it's safer to drive through than walk."

"I promised to call in at the co-op on the way to get Frankie a Mars bar." She lied as Frankie frowned.

"I've got a KitKat in the car she can have."

Amelia was trying to contain the anger inside. The anger and frustration of her husbands over-protective, ill-timed interference. He was spoiling everything. Making it all so much harder with his annoying consideration and blatant unwelcomed adoration!

Her guilt had just grown by tenfold.

"I'm sure we'll be fine." She forced a smile.

"Well, there was another reason actually."

Her heart skipped a beat.

"I've got to pick up an exhaust pipe across town so I'll be passing through the town centre, and I thought that maybe if you'd decided to give the boring party a miss, I could drop you girls off for a bit of shopping instead?"

"We can't give the party a miss Brian, I already told you that!" Anger had just knocked guilt right out of the park.

"Well, come on. You can decide on the way." He winked at Frankie as she slipped on her shoes.

Amelia was seething. Why did he have to keep saying that? Why, of all days, was he taking so much interest in a flipping Tupperware party or Avon party or whatever it was meant to be!

As they got into the car, it started to rain.

"See? Good thing you've got a lift."

Amelia didn't reply.

They drove along the road into the queue of traffic crawling towards the roadworks. Brian had been right that it would have been dangerous to walk. The pavement was totally blocked off and visibility was poor. Walking between traffic and cones in the lashing rain and dark skies would have been pretty scary.

Amelia could see the lights of the community hall up ahead and her stomach started to churn. As they crept towards the entrance of the hidden lane on her left she knew she would probably get no more than a second to glance down it as they passed.

Frank would be looking for pedestrians. He wouldn't know she'd arrived. Now she was going to have to think of a reason to drag Frankie back to the lane after Brian left!

Suddenly the lane was upon them and the traffic stopped again. They were directly upon it. She wiped the steam from her window and peered out. She could see the bonnet of a red car! She wound the window down to try to attract his attention, but he'd parked a long way down, almost on the bend where it disappeared into the countryside.

"What are you doing? The rain's coming in!" Brian shouted.

"Sorry, just needed some air."

She could just make out the silhouette of Frank in the driving seat. Just as he'd promised, he was waiting with her ticket to the utopia she'd imagined since the day they'd giggled their way out of that dirty garage.

This was it!

This was the moment she'd waited for.

She pictured the beautiful, tree-lined street again. The huge garden and the sun shining on the roses. This was the life she'd dreamed of and it was just a few steps away. She pictured the moment Frankie would meet Frank. It was a moment she'd played out in her head a million times, and she knew that, despite her self-denial, she had never given up on the boy who'd held her hand in that clearing on those cold dark nights.

"I don't want to go!" Frankie screamed suddenly.

"What are you talking about?" Amelia snapped. "It's a Tupperware party! We'll only stay an hour then we'll head into town.

"I don't like it!" Frankie's voice held a disturbing note of panic. Amelia turned to look at her. She was staring right at her with wide eyes staring from a face that had suddenly lost all its colour. Frankie was sensing something, and she was sensing it from Amelia.

Amelia tried to block her out. Close her mind as tight as a fist but Frankie was still staring right at her.

The cars crept forward as the lights turned to green and then they slowed again right opposite the community hall as the lights turned back to red.

The traffic was stood now. This was the time.

Her heart was pumping, her hands were shaking. She was about to open the door when Brian's voice made her jump.

"Well, this is the moment of decision."

"What!"

"Are you going to go and look at Tupperware or are you going to stay in the car and hit the delights of Tammy Girl?"

"Tammy Girl!" Frankie squealed.

"We are going in here first Frankie. I've already told you."

"Just an hour? You promise mummy?"

"One hour." She lied.

"Well, you better jump out quick before the lights change!" he hassled, as he peered ahead between the wiper blade stokes.

As she reached for the handle, Brian put his hand on hers.

"Have a great time love. You know that I love you?"

"Of course."

"We love you too daddy, don't we?"

"Of course."

Brian then leaned over and gave her the gentlest of kisses. It was a kiss unlike any she'd felt before, from anyone. Brian had been her salvation and every bit of that salvation, that feeling of undeniable safety, was embodied in that single kiss. The kiss of home.

For a moment she was derailed by it. The choices rose up before her again, like monsters from the deep. Raging choices battling to be heard, to be acknowledged, to emerge victorious. To be chosen. To win.

In the dark distortion of the blurry windscreen, she saw the hazy red light turn to amber and then to green.

Her mind was numb. Her voice frozen in time.

She felt the car start to move and she heard Brian's voice but it was just a sound. Undecipherable words droning beside her.

She blinked hard.

The lights came closer until they were in front of her, beside her and then out of view.

"Amelia?"

"What."

"I said…to Tammy Girl it is then?"

"What?"

"You didn't get out!"

"Didn't I?" She said blankly.

She stared at the road ahead, but nothing was being absorbed. Her mind was a frozen lump of nothingness. A mass of overcrowded stagnant notions with no space to think or to function.

Her next memory was of Frankie tugging at her sleeve.

They were in the warmth of the shopping centre. Brian had driven away, and Frank was four miles back, up a hidden lane, still waiting.

She drew in a huge breath and tried to stifle a scream.

She felt her legs shaking as she tried to act normally but disparity of her situation was totally debilitating.

She'd been confronted with a decision, and she'd failed to make it. The consequence had been that the decision had made itself.

"Frankie. We need to go home."

"We've only just got here!"

"Yes, but mummy doesn't feel very well so we need to go home."

She wondered how long Frank would wait for them. Surely, he wouldn't just leave without them. She checked her watch. They'd missed the eleven o'clock bus back already.

"Ok. Perhaps just a quick look for a new dress and then we'll get the next bus."

For the next half hour she followed Frankie around the shop like a lapdog. She acknowledged every dress her daughter picked out with an approving smile regardless of its suitability.

She paid for a dress without commenting on the awful rainbow taffeta and persuaded her beaming daughter to return to the bus station with the bribe of a hot chocolate from the kiosk.

The station was overcrowded, and the buses were all running late due to road congestion after several small collisions in the rain.

Amelia's panic had long-since turned to desolation. She tried to make some sort of connection to Frank but it was impossible to concentrate in the hustle of the bus station and the constant interruptions from Frankie.

She tried to convince herself that it wasn't too late. The situation was still redeemable. Frank had waited six years and she was sure he would wait a few more hours if there was still a chance of making the flight.

It was past twelve thirty when they finally managed to get on a bus with standing room only.

The bus trundled along at snail's pace. Pulling in at every stop and taking forever to get back into the stream of traffic again. Then came the roadworks. She checked her watch. It was almost one o'clock and they were stood.

The driver had to get out to retrieve a wheelchair from the hold and very kindly helped the old man from the bus and settled him into it.

Eventually they got back into the queue for the roadworks when a lorry driver reluctantly allowed them in.

Her heartbeat quickened as they approached the community centre which was now on their right and more difficult to see across the opposite stream of traffic heading for town. Soon they would pass the entrance, but it was impossible to see anything. The windows were steamed up and seated passengers blocked her view in every direction.

A few minutes later they were at the bus stop from where she could see the street that had tugged at her heart strings only a few hours ago. The street that now felt dreary and dull with the pools of water standing over the blocked drains and filling the air with their rancid stench.

The fond memories were washed away in its inky sludge and dog-fouled verges.

She knew, without doubt, that this was not the place she wanted to be and a few hundred yards away, her ticket out of here might still be in the hand of the man she loved. The impulse to grab Frankie by the hand and hurtle back to the lane was raging inside but she knew it would result in disaster.

She frantically redirected her mental energy from frustration to damage limitation.

There was a good chance that Frank was still close by.

The ten thirty rendezvous had included quite a bit of margin for the unexpected and for toilet stops and even if they missed the flight, she was sure Frank would telephone from the hotel and book a later one. All she had to do was to get in touch with him as soon as possible and make a new plan.

There were only two places he would expect her to contact him. The hotel or the rendezvous point. The latter was still within reach and the hotel was just a phone call away.

Her plan was sound. Sound and logical and her heart lightened.

As she took Frankie's hand to cross the road, the rain stopped, and the sun was peeped out from behind the clouds. It felt symbolic.

Brian's van was in front of the house and that meant she might be able to come up with an excuse to leave Frankie with him and nip out again.

"Did you buy anything?" Brian asked as they shook the rain from their coats.

"I got a dress daddy. It's like a rainbow!"

"Sounds wonderful." He frowned as she dashed into the living room with the wet paper bag.

"I'll make some tea." Amelia smiled as she pushed by him towards the kitchen.

She opened the fridge door to see the milk bottle with only an inch left in it. It was the perfect excuse. She poured most of it into the sink.

"I'm just nipping out for a bottle of milk."

"I'll go. You're wet through." Brian replied from the living room.

"It's fine, she wants to show you her dress." She called back with her hand already on her coat again.

The door clicked shut and she was once again in control of her own destiny.

Chapter 23

Her steps were hurried. She had to do whatever it is she was going to do in the time it would take to get a pint of milk from the Co-op.

She needed to make a decision at the gate. Left to the phone box or right to the lane?

She processed the options in seconds. If she called the hotel it would take time to put her through to his room and then they would need to have the conversation and she'd still have to go for milk. If she opted for the lane, it was a longer walk but she would pass the Co-op on the way. She turned right and started to run.

By the time she'd reached the shop door she was wired with dogged determination.

She pushed her way to the fridge, secured a pint and marched to the counter.

"Excuse me, I'm in a hurry." She blurted at two women who were chatting at the counter with none of their purchases yet unloaded.

She thrust the money on the counter and fled with a trailing, "Keep the change."

"Just a minute!" The assistant called after her.

She turned back.

"Don't forget your receipt!" She smiled sarcastically.

Amelia snatched it harshly, stuffed it in her pocket, flung open the door and was back out on the road running in the direction of the lane.

Breathless and sweating in her huge coat she slowed to a walk to take the muddy corner onto the lane.

As her eyes rose up from the negotiation of potholes and puddles, she came to a halt and stared.

The red car was still parked.

With sodden shoes and glugging milk she hurtled towards it but it was blurring. She needed to calm down and let the blood supply return before she fainted.

She returned to a brisk walk and approached the driver's side.

Frank looked up, frowned, smiled and then wound down the window, and the moment that barrier between them disappeared she could feel him, the very essence of him, more powerfully than in the café or even the hotel. Today she could feel him again, just like the old days. Just like the times she would close her eyes in her lonely bed and feel him all around her.

"You waited." She gasped between badly needed breaths.

"Of course, I waited, get in."

She walked to the passenger side and reached for the door. Her hand missed the handle several times until he eventually opened it from the inside.

"I don't know what's wrong with me. I need to calm down."

"Where's Frankie?" He frowned.

"It's a long story but I don't have time to tell it. Can I have another hour or so?"

He looked pale.

"Are you alright?"

He blinked a couple of times and then spoke.

"Sorry, think it's this weather. I had a blinding headache earlier but yes, I'm alright."

"So?"

He seemed to be trying to gather his thoughts. He counted under his breath as he looked at his watch.

"If you can get back here by four, we could still make it but without any stops or airport meals."

He seemed remarkably calm about it. Calm and unconcerned. He smiled so serenely that her own anxiety started to ebb away.

He was staring out of the windscreen but she had to keep blinking to keep him in focus.

"I think I need some air."

She looked at him again and he turned to face her but the image of him was wavering, and the edges looked blurred. This was no time to pass out. She had to keep focussed.

She nodded.

"I'll be back by four then."

"By four." He repeated.

Suddenly she was back on the lane with no recollection of getting back out of the car, but she had no time to ponder her own state of mind. If this was going to work, she now had to put some trust in her five-year-old child. To persuade her to keep a secret from the father she doted on. To follow her blindly and without a fuss. To put her trust in the mother that didn't deserve any trust at all.

"I need to go."

"Just a minute," he grinned through the open door "aren't you forgetting something?"

He leaned in for a kiss.

She put her lips against his and seemed to melt into him for several seconds causing her whole body to sigh. She never felt the pressure of his lips, but she felt the merging of something far more compelling.

She gave him a reassuring smile and strode away feeling the pull of it. It wasn't just a longing from inside but a physical pull like that of a huge magnet.

"Don't forget your milk!" He called as he thrust it through the open door at her.

She raised her eyebrows and took it gratefully. That would have been a disaster.

She checked her watch. She can usually make it to the Co-Op and back in five minutes, but this would be more like ten. She would have to say there was a queue or the till wasn't working.

As she neared the house she dropped back into a walk. Partly to recover her breath and partly to appear to be dawdling in case anyone was watching from the window.

She noticed a couple of things as she walked those last few yards but nothing unusual enough to raise any alarm.

Next door's gate was hanging of the hinges, Frankie's bike was no longer leaning against the house wall and the bird table had disappeared from the house opposite.

She looked at the windows of her own house.

No-one was looking out for her.

She hadn't bothered to take her keys so she just tapped her usual tap on the front door.

She saw a figure approaching through the frosted glass but it didn't look like either Brian or Frankie. It looked like the silhouette of a woman. A young woman with long blonde hair.

The door clicked open.

"Mealy!"

"Brenda? What are you doing here?"

The two women starred at one another in silence for several seconds.

Amelia was the first to regain her faculties.

"Why are you here, Bren?"

Brenda was still staring.

Without taking her eyes off of her sister she called behind her.

"Brian! Brian! Get out here. It's your wife!"

Brian knocked Brenda aside and grabbed Amelia by the shoulders.

"Oh my God! Oh my God!"

Amelia could feel the dread rising.

"What is it? What's happened? Where's Frankie!"

Brian and Brenda exchanged another look but neither spoke. Brenda caught Brian's attention and nodded towards the milk bottle in her hand. Brian's eyes widened.

"Tell me! Tell me what's happened!" Amelia begged.

She felt Brenda's arm around her shoulder as Brian relinquished his grasp on her.

"I think you should come and sit down, Amelia."

"I don't want to sit down! I want to know what the hell is going on here!"

Amelia started to shake as Brenda lowered her into a chair. She knew that something terrible had happened. She knew that her world was about to implode and for that reason she allowed herself a few more moments of ignorance before she faced it.

Brenda was now kneeling before her with both of her hands on her own. She could feel all four hands shaking, but she didn't know who was causing it.

Eventually she took a deep breath and stole herself to face the terrible news.

"Has she gone? Frankie, has she gone."

Brenda gently brushed back the strands of damp hair from her face.

"No, Mealy. Frankie is fine. She's gone to her friend's for a sleepover."

The relief hit Amelia as forcefully as the dread had. It took her breath, her ability to speak and her capacity to move.

Brian was standing over them with the same bewildered expression he'd had since he came to the door.

"Is it dad?"

"Dad's fine too." Brenda continued to stroke the same strands of hair.

"Then what?"

Brian's face changed.

"Amelia, where the hell have you been?"

Brenda shot him a reprimanding glance.

"What do you mean?" Amelia frowned.

"Where have you been?"

For a moment she thought Brian had followed her. Perhaps he'd seen her kissing Frank in the car. This was a disaster but why was Brenda suddenly here. She put her hands to her head and tried to come up with an alibi.

"Brian just wants to know what happened Bren and where you've been."

"I've been to the Co-op. He knows that. I told him that. I've been for milk. Look!"

She held up the milk angrily.

"This is ridiculous!" Brian snapped.

"Mealy?" Brenda said softly. "Look at me Mealy."

Amelia recognised her sister's tone. She trusted Brenda implicitly so she gazed compliantly into those huge familiar eyes.

"We know you went out for milk. But where did you go after that?

Amelia's expression froze on her face.

She glanced from Brenda to Brian and back again. Waiting for something. Anything. Some hint of how much they knew. They watched her and they exchanged knowing looks but neither spoke.

Gently, Brenda removed the bottle of milk form her hand and placed it on the floor.

"You must have just bought this Mealy but on your way back from wherever you've been. Can you remember where you've been?

It sounded like a trick question. Of course, she remembered. She'd been in a car with the man she was planning to run away with. Were they waiting for a full confession? They seemed to be treating her as though she wasn't in control of her faculties!

Amelia shook her head frantically. She decided to call their bluff and force them to reveal how much they knew.

"I haven't been anywhere else. I went straight to the Co-op and came right back!" She said harshly.

"You must have been Mealy. Can you remember where?"

She shook her head again as she tried to make some sense of this nonsense.

"I went for milk. I went to the Co-op and I brought back the milk!"

She could feel her face turning red.

Brian gave Brenda a nudge.

"She's wearing the same clothes."

He looked concerned. Brenda frowned.

"Is she? Are you sure?"

Amelia was still trying desperately to read the situation and the matter of her clothes was a curved ball.

Brian and Brenda remained silent for a moment and then Brenda slid an arm around her shoulders.

"We reported you missing Mealy."

Amelia laughed.

"After ten minutes? It usually takes me five minutes at best, and you reported me missing after ten fucking minutes!"

"You were gone longer than that." Brian said calmly.

Amelia laughed again. She knew they were lying but she didn't know why.

"I checked my watch. It was ten minutes. Have you both gone mad?"

"I can't believe this!" Brian seemed close to tears. "Just tell her!"

Brenda scowled at being handed the responsibility of it.

"Mealy, you went out for milk on the Saturday. On 19th April 1980.

"So?"

"So, today is the 19th April 1981."

Chapter 24

Amelia looked from one to the other. Waiting for one of them to burst out laughing and pat each other on the back for playing out the hoax so convincingly.

Neither laughed.

This was all ludicrous. It had to be some sick joke, but her heart was already pounding.

She went out of this house for ten minutes.

Just ten minutes.

The words in her head suddenly escaped again.

"I checked my watch, and it was ten minutes. Do you hear me? I was gone ten fucking minutes! Do you think I've been in these same clothes for a year? You're mad. Both of you. The world's gone mad!"

Had she not been so stunned and disorientated she might have noticed a different kind of concerned glance pass between Brian and Brenda.

"I think she needs to lay down for a while. Can you take her into the living room Brenda, while I turn back the bed sheets for her?"

Amelia didn't react.

Brenda nodded to Brian and then guided her into the living room and sat down beside her on the sofa.

"We are going to sort this out." Brenda whispered. "I'm sure everything will come back to you after a good sleep."

Amelia's brain was whirling again. She knew she'd bought the milk right after leaving the house. Before she's met or spoken to anyone. Before she'd had time to be knocked unconscious or abducted by bloody aliens!

Brian returned and nodded again to Brenda but she didn't notice because she was retracing her steps.

Then she remembered the rude shop assistant.

 "I got a receipt. I know I did!"

She fumbled in her pocked and produced a slip of paper which looked brand new and thrust it at Brenda.

Brian watched Brenda unfold it.

"What does it say?"

Brenda's voice was hardly a voice at all.

She stuttered and shook as she read aloud.

"It says 19th April 1980!"

This time the stunned expressions passed between all three faces without prejudice.

Amelia put her head back in her hands.

"I was only gone for ten minutes." She sobbed. "It was just ten minutes!"

"You take her up to bed." Brenda said firmly. "I'm going to fetch Sheila."

Brian was kneeling beside the bed holding Amelia's hand when Sheila arrived outside the bedroom door.

Amelia was staring at the ceiling. She hadn't uttered a word since Brian guided her upstairs and into bed.

She didn't question the hurriedly changed sheets or the absence of her perfumes that had stood on the bedside table. She didn't notice the unfamiliar blouse spilling from the wash basket or the blonde hairs wrapped around her hairbrush on the dresser. Her conscience was too full of her own guilt to suspect anything of the people she had wronged. Her only thoughts were to wonder how Brian had managed, if she really had been gone for a year. How he'd coped and how Frankie had got through an entire year without her. She couldn't bear to think of it.

She smelled Sheila seconds before she felt the familiar chubby hand on her arm.

"Amelia love, we've been so worried but you're safe now. You're home."

Amelia slowly turned her eyes from the ceiling to Sheila's smiling face.

"Do you remember anything? Anything at all?"

She shook her head and returned to staring at the ceiling.

"I've made you some sweet tea, Mealy." Brenda interjected as she arrived at the side of the bed with a mug.

Gently Sheila eased her up into a sitting position and placed the mug in her hands.

Amelia sighed deeply and took a sip.

She saw Brian give Sheila a nudge. She continued.

"We reported you missing at first but then the Police asked us to check if anything was missing, like your passport or clothes."

Amelia flinched.

"We couldn't find your passport love or that little red case of yours. Do you know anything about it?"

She shook her head again without speaking.

"Brian was worried that you'd left him. He even thought that your old boyfriend might have turned up but we told him you would never leave without Frankie. You wouldn't, would you?"

"I would never leave without my daughter!! She hissed. "I went out for milk. It was ten minutes ago!"

"Alright love. Alright. You try to get some rest. I'll stay right here."

"Me too." Brenda echoed.

Brian stood up and stroked her forehead before whispering.

"I'll give you ladies some space. Maybe there's something you want to share, but not with me love?"

She closed her eyes to shut out his unfaltering compassion. His humble humility. His undying support for her.

Brian left and the two guardian angels kept their vigil over her.

A few minutes later they heard her sigh again.

"I did take my passport." She confessed shamefully. "I took it a week ago and put it in Frank's car. Well, a year and a week ago according to you!"

"Frank came back?" Brenda shrieked.

"Where were you going, love?" Sheila frowned.

Amelia looked at Sheila and then to Brenda.

"It's alright," Sheila continued, "Brenda knows that Frank is Frankie's father. She's always known it, but she thought maybe you didn't. Or that you weren't sure."

"You didn't say anything."

"I didn't want to upset you." Brenda smiled, causing her sister to feel even more guilty, if that was possible. The person she'd decided not to trust had been protecting her for years!

"So, where were you going?" Sheila repeated.

"I was going to take Frankie and run away to start a new life. I know it was selfish and cowardly and heartless but I just wanted that life so badly."

"So, tell me about getting the milk. Did you really go straight there and back, or did you go somewhere else?"

There was no point in lying anymore. She felt exhausted and lying took up so much energy.

"I was supposed to take Frankie and meet him this afternoon but everything went wrong and we ended up back here so I nipped out to explain it to him. I'm supposed to be meeting him again later but now I can't because Frankie isn't here and its not even the same year anymore."

"I was actually asking if you'd been with him for a year and made up this story to avoid the confession of it." Sheila smiled.

"I'm not making anything up. I went out and came back and I did those things today."

Sheila thought for a while before asking another question.

"Did you meet up with him?"

"Yes, but only for about ten minutes! I went for the milk, sat in the car for a few minutes and then ran back. That was it."

"You don't remember having an accident? Being hit on the head or anything?" Brenda asked.

"You think I had an accident. Lost my memory and lived somewhere else for an entire year and then suddenly put my old clothes on, picked up a pint of milk and returned?"

"It's possible." Sheila said gently. "But it's also possible that someone drugged you and kept you somewhere sedated and then, when they were done with you, dressed you back in the same clothes and sent you home."

It sounded ludicrous but it was the most logical of the two explanations Sheila could think of and the other one? Well, the other one was putting the fear of God into her.

"How did he seem?" Sheila was trying to remain composed.

"How did he seem?"

"He seemed fine. Why?"

"He didn't seem different in any way?"

"No. Why are you asking me that?"

"It doesn't matter love. We'll sort this out. Try to get some rest and tomorrow you can give Frankie the biggest hug in the world.

It was with that image that Amelia started to close her eyes. She heard the door close and assumed she was alone but when she opened them again Sheila was still beside her.

"What is it?" She knew when Sheila was holding something back.

"I don't want to frighten you, love but I need to just tell you something so you can tell me different."

Amelia sat up again.

Her tiredness had disappeared, and Sheila had her full attention.

"A long time ago I knew a woman who claimed to have experienced something similar."

Amelia could feel the fear rising inside her.

"How similar?"

"She said she was planting vegetables in her allotment one day when her husband turned up in his car at lunchtime to help her. After he left, she said she walked straight home but when she got there…."

"What? What happened when she got there?"

"The same thing that happened when you got home. A whole year had gone by."

Amelia could feel the prickles of her pores secreting moisture.

"Where was her husband then?"

"That's just the thing love. Her husband had been killed at work on the morning she disappeared, and everyone assumed she'd run away because she couldn't deal with the grief."

"I don't understand what you're saying. He was with her at lunchtime?"

"He can't have been, can he? His car was still parked up at work where he'd left it that morning."

Amelia gave a little laugh.

"You're telling me she spent her lunchtime with a ghost? That's ridiculous."

Sheila shrugged.

"Sometimes I think that people don't always realise they died, and their spirit gets left behind for a while."

Amelia was reeling. She'd had enough shocks without Sheila's mumbo jumbo stories.

"But she saw his car as well? How could she see a car that wasn't even there?

"I think she might have been seeing what he saw. A bit like you used to see things Brenda saw when you did that connection thing."

Amelia started to shake. She was suddenly ice cold.

"I think that maybe she'd joined him for a few moments in another place." Sheila continued. "A place in between lives"

"And you think that whenever this happens a year goes by? I can't take any more! Please leave me alone! Leave me alone. You're all in it together! You're trying to drive me insane!"

She felt Sheila's arms around her and gave in. Sheila would never conspire against her, but she was sure that Frank was very much alive.

"So, that's why you asked me how he was?"

"Yes. But you said he was fine so perhaps none of this is even relevant. Forget I said it."

She wanted to agree and tell Sheila that none of this bore any resemblance to this afternoon, but this was Sheila and she had to tell her everything.

"He said he'd had a blinding headache but it had gone by the time I got there."

She felt Sheila tense.

"Also," she said, as she closed her eyes tightly, "he was so, so, just so peaceful and calm. I've never seen him like that before."

"Well, I'm going to stay in Frankie's room tonight. I want you to try to get some rest and call me if you need anything. Anything at all. We'll get to the bottom of this. I promise."

She heard Sheila's heavy footsteps on the stairs and then she heard whispering. She wondered how much they were sharing with one another and how much they were really sharing with her.

She walked quietly across the hall into Frankie's room and looked around.

New pictures were on her wall. A poster sized print of the Care-bears. She felt the tears building at the bridge of her nose.

She opened the wardrobe and there was no sign of the hideous rainbow dress. She wondered if it had been worn so often that it had fallen apart or if it had been instantly discarded for the waste of money it had been.

She rifled though her daughters clothes and right at the back she spotted the pink satin bow. She followed it with her fingers and slid her hand upwards to feel that soft cream velvet again.

She imagined that Frankie would be bigger now but still not big enough to wear that beautiful dress even though she'd always been tall for her age. She had been eight and Frankie would be six by now. She sighed.

A feeling of dread rose suddenly from her feet, through her body and jammed itself in her chest. She recalled the moment she'd spent with Frankie on that last night and the fearful little voice she'd had to console. "You're not leaving us are you mummy?" Her heart ached and her mind raced. Perhaps Frankie had tuned into her just like her father could! Perhaps she'd sensed the conspiracy. The wicked plot to run away!

But now a whole year had gone by, and Frankie would probably not even remember the conversation or the trip into town for the terrible rainbow dress.

She sighed again, closed the wardrobe quietly and went to the top of the stairs.

Downstairs three people were sat around the kitchen table and Amelia sat on the top step to eavesdrop just as she had as a child.

"We need to get Frankie back here!" It was Brian's voice.

"I'd leave her be for a while," Sheila replied. "Let's try and make some sense of it all first. I'll give them a call later, when Frankie's in bed and ask them to break the news to her in the morning and then bring her round. The journey will give her chance to process it, and the night will give us all the chance to recover a bit, from whatever this is."

Brenda was the next to speak.

"Sheila's right Brian. This is no time to expose Frankie to this mayhem."

"You need to ring your father though, Brenda." Sheila said firmly. "Get him back here."

"I know. I'll call him in the morning."

"The phone is right there. You need to call him now. He could be here by tomorrow night. He'd want to be here."

"Will you call him instead?" Brenda asked.

Amelia didn't witness Sheila's sigh or the sympathetic nod of her head. She knew that Brenda was dreading any communication with Tom.

Brian remained silent. Silent and stunned.

"I know it's hard but he's still your dad Brenda. He won't stay angry forever."

Brenda knew she was right, but forgiveness was a long way off and there was now the chance that Amelia would turn on her, with the same fury her father had once rained down upon her.

Amelia heard this last exchange and wondered how Brenda had managed to anger her father. He'd probably attacked her over her immoral lifestyle and the shame she'd brought on the family.

She heard someone approaching the bottom of the stairs and picking up the phone, causing her to step out of view.

She listened to Sheila's side of the conversation.

"I know, Tom I know, but that's what she's telling us!"

Silence

"Yes, she could have lost her memory."

Silence.

"Ok, I hear you. I'll get her checked out in the morning but right now she needs some rest."

Silence.

"Yes, Brenda knows. She's right here. Do you want to speak to her?"

Silence

"I'm not going to argue with you Tom. She's back and Brenda is right here so if you want an argument, you'd better get your arse down here!"

Amelia shuddered and went back to her bed wondering why on earth her father would be as cold as this towards Brenda. It seemed disproportionate.

But Amelia didn't know the terrible truth. The sequence of events that had taken place since her disappearance.

Brenda had been living in her bubble of fantasy in Knightsbridge when Amelia disappeared. Her life had been easy. Easy and luxurious. Her latest lover was attentive, generous, and extremely rich. Her days consisted of long mornings in bed, extravagant lunches and lazy afternoons of shopping.

She owned more clothes and jewellery than she could ever wear and her birthday present that year, had been a huge diamond ring which she interpreted as a commitment.

Her modelling career earned her some pocket money, but she didn't really commit to it with any degree of ambition. She had officially become 'eye candy'.

When Amelia disappeared, she rushed back to Rochdale by train on the Sunday and told Brian about the strange phone call.

"She actually said goodbye Brian! Mealy never says goodbye, she says tara."

After two days of trying to console and reassure Frankie, she made a call to Lawrence in Knightsbridge.

"I need to stay a few more days lover. Just until I find my sister and make sure she's alright."

"Whatever you need darling. Do you have money?"

"I brought a few pounds, but I could really do with some more. I also need clothes so I wondered if you could bring some up here?"

"I can, but not until next weekend. Can you manage until then?"

"Yes. I'll ring you later in the week with the address."

She put the receiver down and smiled to Brian.

"I can take you, if you want."

"To London?"

"Yes, I've got the van. If Sheila comes over to take care of Frankie, we could be in London by eight tonight and back by midnight."

"I guess you're not getting any sleep either then?"

"Nope, and I'd rather be doing something than staring at the ceiling in the dark, worrying. It's not like the police are doing anything. As far as they're concerned, she's not missing. She's run away with another man."

Brenda felt instantly sorry for him. She wasn't going to say it, but she also thought that was the most likely scenario.

"Ok let's go on a road trip." She smiled.

The trip to Knightsbridge turned out to be the cliché of all clichés.

Brian waited in the beautiful, well-lit underground parking area while Brenda disappeared into the lift.

He turned on the radio and waited.

After half an hour the lift door opened again and Brenda struggled out with two large suitcases, a tearstained face and a bruised cheek.

"What the hell happened!"

She slid him the cases and plonked herself into the passenger seat before slamming the door.

Brian loaded the luggage and slid back in beside her.
"Brenda?"

"Can we just go?"

He drove for almost an hour before Brenda started to talk.

"I caught him in bed with someone. Not just someone but
the daughter of his best friend. She's barely fifteen Brian. I've
only been gone two days. The bastard!"

Brian was shocked but he wasn't surprised.

"Men like him, Bren. They're used to having whatever they
want, whenever they want it. It's how they live."

"I know. Everyone warned me. Even Mealy warned me.
It's the kind of man a girl like me tends to attract."

During the remainder of that silent car journey, both Brian
and Brenda were making a personal journey of their own.

Brian warmed to Brenda in a way he never had before. He
saw her for the vulnerable, insecure, and beautiful person she
really was.

Brenda saw the richness of Amelia's life with Brian and
Frankie. Her sister had something priceless in the love of a
good man. A man who loved her illegitimate daughter
unconditionally. Her sister had experienced the love, of not
just one, but two, good men and Brenda was now suspecting
that she might have left one for the other.

She looked back on her own relationships of which there
had been quite a few. Rich middle-aged men or young spoiled
playboys, every one of them. It had taken her far too long to
see the pattern. Shallow, arrogant, and egotistical.
Frequenters for lap clubs, casinos, and other misogynistic
establishments. These were not men who loved women but
who loved to exploit them, and she had fallen for it more times
than was credible.

She looked over at Brian and wondered why God chose to hide that goodness behind a body of virtual repulsion. Probably to protect them from the pretty, materialistic girls. Girls like her.

When they arrived back and opened the door, Tom was sitting at the kitchen table with Sheila.

"Dad!" Brenda ran into his arms and suddenly all thoughts of Lawrence evaporated. It was a shocking but welcome relief at how quickly he was ejected from her life. The realisation that he was nothing to her and never had been. The only people who mattered were the people in this house. Her father, Frankie, Sheila, Brian, and of course her missing sister.

The sobbing started instantly on her father's touch.

"We'll find her love. Don't worry. We'll find her."

Brenda nodded!

And for the first few weeks they'd believed it.

The physical searches, the constant, heart-breaking attempts to console the little girl who asked for her mummy a hundred times a day. The disinterested policemen who listened and scribbled but raised their eyebrows at one another and nudged each other before leaving again. Officers who were tired of being dragged back to the same house time and again and listening to the rantings and hopes of a family who refused to accept that Amelia Gilbert had run away without her daughter.

The whole family were unconsciously starting a process. The process of grieving and this was the first stage. But this first torturous phase, like all the phases, would pass.

The phase of denial.

.

Chapter 25

The phase of anger passed more quickly but with terrible force.

Anger born of the eventual realisation that they could no longer continue to deny what had happened here. That Amelia was truly missing.

Frankie was no longer indulged but reprimanded for her constant whining for her mother. Tom accused Brian frequently of failing to protect Amelia. Of causing her to become unhappy and even of making her life so miserable that she would leave behind her own daughter.

These allegations were made in haste and retracted just as quickly but they had left their mark as firmly as a boot print in soft soil.

Brian tried to take it. To make allowances for a distraught father but the injustice hit hard and resulted in him frequently returning home to his parents. Sometimes with Frankie and sometimes without.

Sheila also sought refuge away from that house and her visits became less frequent.

The family was broken. Fractured and fragmented and the only relationship to survive seemed to be the one between Frankie and Brenda who clung together like limpets. They comforted and supported one another unreservedly and morphed quickly into the new relationship of mother and daughter.

Then something suddenly and unexpectedly changed again.

Anger was inevitably replaced by the phase of bargaining. A desperate attempt to reverse the irreversible. Prayers and resolutions. Self-made vows to live a better life, to give to charity, to be kind, honest and truthful. Anything at all that might convince a higher power to reward the sacrifices with Amelia's return.

Eventually depression descended as the realisation that God was not listening to anyone or, if he was, he was not in the mood for negotiation.

Weeks had gone by, and depression settled like a dark cloud on a hillside. Quietly and invisibly. This was the phase of nothingness. Of solitude and quiet existence interrupted occasionally by the concerns for a little girl who had become withdrawn and strangely dispassionate. It was the month of contemplation. Of not knowing or understanding how to feel. Of going through the motions of existing in an emotional vacuum and it descended on every member of the family at the same time.

Tom returned to Scotland without a reaction from anyone, including himself. He simply floated out of their lives without leaving so much as a noticeable void.

Brenda was the first to disrupt the nothingness.

Perhaps she was healing faster or perhaps she was just stronger, but she suddenly and abruptly announced the end of stage four with the announcement of a family party.

"We need to get everyone together and have a family party. The way we used to!"

Brian frowned his disapproval and Frankie simply smiled mildly at the thought of cake and games.

Nothing more was said until Frankie was in bed.

"How can you even think of throwing a party Brenda?" Brian snapped as he cleared the table.

"Oh Brian," she sighed, "I miss Mealy more than you will ever know but look at us! Mourning a person who is probably not even dead. Missing a person who is probably not missing us, at all. Isn't it time we accepted that there's a possibility that she's started a new life without us?"

"You really think that?"

"Don't you?"

"I'm not stupid and I know that she would probably be capable of leaving me but I know she is not capable of leaving Frankie! She would never leave Frankie behind!"

Brenda sighed again.

"Well doesn't that lead us to the other possibility?"

"You think she's dead?"

Brenda shrugged her shoulders.

"I just can't help making the comparison to the sudden disappearance of that Frank boy she fell for. You must have considered the connection yourself?"

It was Brian's turn to shrug.

"You think she went looking for him? After 6 years!"

"We don't know, do we? Maybe he turned up and she just left. We may never know so we have to make a decision because we can't go on like this."

"What decision?"

"We have to decide if we should all go our separate ways again or if we want to try to make a go of this as a family. To make some new memories and to give Frankie a life worth living."

He put his hand on her shoulder and nodded.

"I vote that we stick together and try to build this family all over again." He smiled. "We can do it can't we?"

The phase of acceptance had arrived!

In later years, neither Brian nor Brenda would understand the inference, the acceptance, or the possible misinterpretation of this conversation but they would forever understand the result of it.

That evening Brenda and Brian climbed the stairs hand in hand and lay down together in the marital bed.

The family had re-aligned, re-adjusted and regrouped. The huge hole Amelia had left, had been filled and the family was once again complete.

Brenda would sneak out in the morning and sneak in at night and although there was a huge serving of guilt attached, they could not deny the positive impact this arrangement was making on Frankie.

She seemed to sense a new commitment in the house and to feel the security of two parents again.

Things started to look up and as the summer ebbed away, the first peals of laughter returned to the house. A joviality that might have continued unabated had certain unfortunate circumstances not come together in the perfect storm.

It was in the last days of the school summer holiday and the day before the planned family party. Brenda and Brian had consumed a couple of bottles of wine the previous night and consequently slept in.

Tom had been up until two tending a sheep and decided to set off back home instead of going to bed and risking the holiday traffic.

Frankie was already awake when the knock came on the door.

"Gramps!" She squealed as he scooped her up.

"I brought you a present." He grinned as she tugged the toy lamb from his rucksack. It felt good to be home.

"Where's auntie Brenda?"

"Still in bed."

Tom made his way up and knocked on Brenda's door.

The door behind him opened and Brian's face appeared.

"Tom! You're early."

"I set off in the early hours to miss the traffic. Where's Bren?"

Brian didn't answer.

Tom recognised that look.

He pushed past Brian and entered the bedroom where Brenda was holding the sheet over her naked breasts.

"Dad I…"

"Save your breath."

Tom turned around and walked back down the stairs, kissed Frankie and left.

There had been no contact from that day.

But now, with the return of the prodigal daughter reinstated in the marital bed, Tom had to be told.

Brenda watched Sheila go out into the hallway to make the call Amelia had overheard.

Tomorrow, her estranged father would return and blow her world apart. He would remove the lid from her box of secrets and shake out her deceit, betrayal and lies for all to see.

Tomorrow the sister she loved, the niece she adored and the man she'd grown to love would desert her as completely as the father who already despised her would devote every bit of his love on Amelia. The worthy one.

Chapter 26

Amelia had been laying in the darkness trying to make out the odd word from the covert discussion downstairs.

Waves of uncertainty washed over her. Each, taking their turn to change her mindset.

Whispers of conspiracy? Of concern for her sanity? Of disparity to help? Of desperation to do the right thing? Of disbelief in her story? Of accusations she truly deserved!

She took a deep breath and tried to put herself in their shoes. She wouldn't believe her either and she was wasting her time and energy on second-guessing the verdict of the kangaroo court beneath her.

He mind turned to Frankie and the big reunion in the morning with the little girl who'd spent a year without her mummy. The little girl who she'd brought back from town only a few hours ago! She stifled a scream. A scream that was raging to be released and was aimed at everyone and everything. At herself and at the universe at large.

The next half hour was spent in the tortuous effort of retracing every second of today's trip to the co-op. If she really had lost her memory and been somewhere for twelve whole months then there had to be some remnants of it somewhere inside her head.

She closed her eyes and tried to remember every detail. She knew that it was still the same day when she was in the car. She'd asked for more time to prepare Frankie. She'd agreed to get back there by four o'clock. She concentrated on the journey back from the lane. She had the milk she'd bought, in her hand. It was still the same day as she got out of the car. She remembered starting to walk away and then she remembered something else.

As the door to the car closed, she'd felt something. She'd felt the tug of leaving him behind. A physical tug that she'd fought for several seconds before she felt the release of it.

It felt like the phone receiver being put down!

Like the slamming of a door.

Like barging through a barrier.

Sheila's fanciful story about a man who hadn't realised he was dead, now had her full attention and the terror of it had her firmly in its fist.

It was all starting to make sense.

His face seemed strange. Almost out of focus but perhaps it wasn't her vision to blame at all.

He'd known how dangerous it was to come back here. She remembered the anxiety on his face in the café, in the hotel and when he'd collected her case in the street. He wasn't just nervous, he was terrified.

Whatever threat he'd been living under for the last six years had been powerful enough to keep him away and she was only just beginning to realise how devoted he'd been to revive their love. The love she'd once cast aside in the belief that he'd deserted her.

She sat up in bed.

This new theory, unbelievable and incredible as it was, suddenly seemed plausible.

She recalled the headache he described. The sudden headache that had disappeared as quickly as it came. Perhaps he'd been injured. She turned cold … or killed!

She felt like she was about to throw up.

She banged her head several times with the heel of her hand to bully her brain into finding the answer.

She needed to force herself to believe that it might be true. Just for a moment, but every atom of her existence was warning her off. It felt like the road to insanity. To a place from which she may never return. To certain incarceration.

She lay back down and pulled the pillow over her head to suffocate the thoughts within it.

Silently she lay. Hiding from the hunter of her sanity.

But slowly and surely, she felt the ambience of her theory seeping through the feathers of that pillow, through her fingers and back into her mind. It was the only explanation.

She removed the pillow, propped herself up on it and tried to remain calm.

She checked her watch. It was still only 3.40 pm.

Was it possible that to Frank, this was still 1980? That he was still in that car waiting for her, unaware of his own plight?

If she sat there any longer, she would never know. If Sheila was right, then the last remnants of her first and last love would melt away and he would never know how hard she'd tried. She owed him this even if it was just a final goodbye.

Quietly she placed her feet on the floor and moved onto the landing. From there she could see the front door and her coat and shoes beside it.

Step by careful step she crept towards them.

The voices in the kitchen continued to babble on and the clattering of teacups masked the occasional creaking of a stair board.

A small part of her hoped she would not have to face that final goodbye. That the receiver had been replaced as she'd stepped out of that car and would remain on the hook. |That her final attempt to contact him would be too late, and tomorrow, she would hold Frankie in her arms again, kiss her husband again and regain the calmness of a satisfactory family life. Yet deep inside, behind those comforting hopes, burned an urgent and insatiable desire to find Frank.

Sheila's words echoed once again. Her belief of a place in between life and death. A transient place of uncertainty and confusion and she suspected that Frank might be hovering there. Anchored by his desperation for the life he'd planned, and by his unyielding love for her and his desire to hold his daughter in his arms.

She reached for her coat and placed it silently over her arm before gently picking up her shoes. She knew that just one small sound was likely to result in her being tackled to the ground and brought to task for the cheating, two-timing slut she really was, but if she made it from the house and re-entered his world again there was a chance that another year might disappear.

That Frankie would arrive home in the morning to find her gone again.

The impact of her absence on her little daughter might have resonated more compellingly if she'd had any experience of the sorrow of separation, but it had no impact. How could it when she'd brought Frankie home on the bus that very afternoon! Missing Frankie was not something she'd ever endured.

For the second time in the same day, she found herself facing an impossible decision.

A decision as urgent and perplexing as those awful moments at the traffic lights.

Both options were again equally compelling but equally devastating. Equally right and wrong!

If she went to Frank and the worst was to happen, could she live with the fact that she'd denied Frankie and Brian another year?

If she didn't go to Frank, could she live with the guilt that she'd failed to choose the man she loved for a second time that day? The boy who had been forced to leave her six years ago and returned as a man without ever giving up on their love. The boy who had kept his promise and risked his life to come back to her.

The man who had, very probably, already given that life in his efforts to rekindle their love.

Frank deserved to know the truth. He deserved a final goodbye and to be held by her one last time.

Then she imagined Frankie hurtling through the door in the morning calling for her mummy. Elated that the miracle had happened and she could bury her face in her mummy's arms again.

She felt physically sick. What if her mummy wasn't there in the morning! What if her moments with Frank stole yet another year of her life. What if Frankie rushed in to find her gone again?

She tried to reason with herself. It was an unlikely scenario. She would keep her wits about her. But if, by some unlikely chance, she did lose another year, then at least she would be believed and she would have a lifetime to make amends.

There would be nothing pulling her away because Frank would be gone and out of reach. Just like her mother.

She stepped out of the door and quietly clicked it shut.

This time she chose Frank!

Chapter 27

Three hundred miles away, Tom was sitting on the rickety wooden bench, behind the cottage in Scotland chewing a large stalk of grass.

The huge rolling hills stretching out into the distance like a child's drawing. Overlapping humps in slightly different shades of green.

The hills he used to climb with the large staff for support only a year ago.

He chewed the sweetness out of the stalk until it became stringy and tasteless on his tongue when he cast it to the breeze and snapped off a new one.

Tom had been hoping that he could remain here is Scotland and never have to see his daughters again but now everything had changed.

Each, in turn, had presented him with the perfect excuse to stay away. Amelia had obviously run off with the boy from school and Brenda had jumped into her husband's bed the moment she left. He could have lived out the rest of his days here without ever having to inflict more heartache on his loved and cherished girls.

He'd hoped they would never have to set eyes on the pathetic person he'd become. Never know that he had dropped to half his original weight and had to fight for every breath he took.

The staff that once propelled him up the hillside before him was now nothing other than the crutch that enabled him to totter from bed to bench and bench back to bed.

He hadn't sheered a sheep or filled a bucket for over six months and now paid for his keep by simply handing over his social security cheque to the family who now cared for him and had been forced to take on a new farmhand in his place.

"You'll get my room soon enough." He would jest to the young man who was cycling from the village to complete his chores.

"Don't ye be goin' anywhere." The young father would reply. "The exercise does me good, so it does."

Until today's phone call Tom had been content with his choice. His girls both seemed content with their lives and he couldn't bear to add further loss to the losses they'd already suffered. He'd managed to alienate himself from both of them so they would never feel the sorrow or emptiness of his passing.

But now everything had changed.

It seemed that Amelia had left the arrogant boy who deserted her all those years ago. Probably seen his true colours. And now she was back to reclaim her place. Her daughter and her crown.

He sighed at her selfishness.

Then there was Brenda.

How he had despised himself for alienating Brenda. Accusing her of stealing her sister's life when all she'd ever done was to step in and try to fix the mess Amelia left behind. Brenda was never cut out to be a dowdy housewife with a mop in her hand, but she'd stepped up. She'd held that family together.

He sighed again. This time at his own cruelty.

He'd pushed Brenda away for her own good. Forced her to find the support and love she needed elsewhere but now he could see how wrong that had been.

Brenda needed him now. More than ever because she was about to lose everything else.

He threw the soggy remnants of the second stalk away and reached for his staff.

He was going to have to make the journey home.

He suspected that another month or so would see him through the pearly gates, but he could no longer sit peacefully in God's waiting room for his ticket to be called.

He needed to steal himself for one last battle.

His daughters needed him. They both did and it was his duty to sort out this mess.

It would be his swan song.

He smiled at the thought of it, and he could feel Celia smiling back.

By three thirty he was in the car with an overnight bag. Luckily, driving was still something he could do. In fact, being behind the wheel was the only time he felt like an able-bodied man.

He placed the bottles of cola on the passenger seat beside the sandwiches he'd wrapped in brown paper. Then he carefully arranged his three inhalers within arm's reach and started the engine.

If the traffic wasn't too bad, he could be back with his daughters by ten o'clock.

Suddenly, the idea of it filled him with unexpected delight. He hadn't planned to set eyes on either of them again but now, the mere thought of it felt desperately overwhelming.

How could he have considered spending his last few weeks away from the daughters that had always been, and still were, the loves of his life.

As he took the first turning towards the south. The reunion was taking on a new urgency. An urgency born of the realisation that mostly, it had been nothing other than his own selfish ego keeping him away.

Whilst it was true that he dreaded having to witness yet another round of unbearable heartache on his children's faces, there was also the dread of allowing Sheila to take this image of his frail, breathless, skinny body to her grave.

He wanted her to remember him as the agile young man who once rocked her around the clock on their very first date. He wanted her to continue to yearn for him and to ache for him just as she had for the last two decades.

Such had been his selfishness, and such had been her unfaltering devotion.

He took a swig of cola to flush away the lump in his throat, wiped the tears from his eyes and drove more purposefully towards the people who meant everything to him.

As he drove, his years of stubborn stupidity resounded in his mind like a tragic play.

So much wasted time. So many wasted years. A wasted life!

He raged at his inability to cherish the joys of parenting. His stubborn determination to become the grieving, miserable widower despite the affect on everyone around him. His rigid sense of duty to be faithful to his deceased wife. To Celia, who probably didn't even exist anywhere anymore.

He flicked on the wipers, as the rain started to fall, causing him to squint closely at the rickety sign ahead.

It was a welcome but temporary distraction from the awful truth. From his colossal regret.

As his own illness progressed, he'd felt the realisation of his impending demise and with that realisation came the demise of his faith.

Suddenly he was facing the magnitude of his incredible stupidity. Of the life he could have lived. Of the happiness that had been only an invitation away.

He's spent many hours of late punishing himself with the images of what could have been. The images of his daughters continuing to thrive in a vibrant and joyous home with a real mum and dad. A mum and dad who were every bit, if not more than, in love as their first parents.

He had undoubtedly wasted his own life along with the lives of so many others and now it was all too late.

Until today he had wanted nothing more than to fade away. To hope that Amelia was now happy even without Frankie. To hope that Brenda would react to his death with nothing more than a shrug and get on with her new life. Amelia's old life.

But today his foot leaned heavily on the accelerator because the need to put it all right, had become insufferably urgent.

He needed to hold both of his daughters close and try to sort out this mess before he had to desert them again. He needed to whisper a thousand apologies for all the laughter he never made, all the parties he never gave, all the music he never played and all the joy they were denied.

He ached to hold Sheila close again. To admit at last that she had been his one true love. His first love. The love that never needed to be nurtured or coaxed and had never lost a molecule of its purity.

He removed his foot from the peddle and pulled over. What he was about to do suddenly filled him with incredible pain, excruciating guilt and pain.

Perhaps it would be better for everyone if he didn't go? Surely, they were better off in not knowing that they had been denied so much. To hear his infuriating confession and then to learn that he would be gone from this world before any amends could ever be made.

He banged the steering wheel several times and stared out into the rain.

In Rochdale Amelia was approaching the turning into that muddy lane again. She had been marching purposefully until the turning came into view and suddenly, she stopped.

If she turned that corner and the lane was empty, she could go home and sneak back into bed before she'd been missed but if that red car was still there, the consequences could be catastrophic.

How could she begin to tell Frank about the year that had somehow passed since she left him a few hours ago?

She wrapped her coat around her rain-beaten legs and tried to think.

Things could be even worse.

She could lose another year in the time it took to convince him that escaping together was no longer possible because ….

She sighed as she anticipated the ludicrous words …..because she believed that he was no longer a living person but just a lingering remnant of the man who'd fought so bravely for her. It sounded insane, even to her! Perhaps there was a chance he was still alive and a future was still within reach?

It was a gamble.

Leigh Oakley

She remembered her father's words when they used to play with the toy roulette wheel.

"Never place a bet unless you can afford to lose your stake!"

Today the stake was high but so was the prize.

She could lose another whole year of Frankie's life or she could gain a whole lifetime with Frank.

She felt the surge from her stomach and watched the vomit spew from her mouth onto the sodden grass verge. She wretched again and then again.

Her bet had not yet been placed and the wheel was quiet and still but as she hovered between black and red, dullness or danger, she almost heard it spin into action.

In Scotland, Tom turned the key in the ignition and slammed the car into gear.

He'd been a coward far too long. It was time to face the consequences of his unbelievable stupidity. His many victims deserved to witness the extent of his remorse.

His decision had been made!

Amelia wiped her mouth and edged towards the opening. She held onto a tree and slowly peeped around it.

At first the lane seemed empty, and she felt momentary relief but even before that relief had been felt, she saw the outline of a shape slowly emerging against the background of the bushes. The familiar shape of that red car was slowly but surely coming into view. Almost as if it was manifesting itself purely for her!

She watched the image become clearer until she could make out the shape of Frank still sitting at the wheel and she felt no fear.

It didn't matter if that image of Frank was real or imaginary. Alive or dead.

All that mattered was that Frank was within reach and no matter what happened next, he would always know that she hadn't let him down again.

She was no longer in doubt. The recklessness of love had taken control at the mere sight of him, and she slammed everything she had on red!

She walked calmly and gratefully towards that car as the virtual wheel continued to spin in her mind.

Her decision had been made despite the risk, the terrible consequences. She had heeded her father's words and on that she had based her decision.

A year of missed memories with her little girl for what might be either a whole lifetime or just one more moment with Frank?

Her decision had been made.

She chose Frank.

Leigh Oakley

Printed in Great Britain
by Amazon

60829355R00161